Enchantment

His
Enchantment

DIANA COSBY

KENSINGTON

Kensington Publishing Corp.

www.kensingtonbooks.com

KENSINGTON BOOKS are published by

Kensington Publishing Corp.
119 West 40th Street
New York, NY 10018

All Kensington titles, imprints, and distributed lines are available at special quantity discounts for bulk purchases for sales promotions, premiums, fund-raising, educational, or institutional use. Special book excerpts or customized printings can also be created to fit specific needs. For details, write or phone the office of the Kensington special sales manager: Kensington Publishing Corp., 119 West 40th Street, New York, NY 10018, attn: Special Sales Department; phone 1-800-221-2647.

First electronic edition: December 2013

ISBN-13: 978-1-60183-169-9
ISBN-10: 1-60183-169-2

First print edition: December 2013

ISBN-13: 978-1-60183-218-4
ISBN-10: 1-60183-218-4

This book is dedicated to those who have served and are serving in the armed forces.

God bless our troops and their families.

ACKNOWLEDGMENTS

I would like to thank Matthew Newsome for his historical insight into medieval Scotland over the years, and the members of The Society for Creative Anachronism (SCA) in the Richmond, Virginia, area, who during my research for the series, graciously allowed me to attend a coronation of their king dressed in my heroine's garb. The SCA is an amazing organization where reenactors help to keep our history alive. In addition, I am thankful for the immense support from my husband, parents, family, and friends. My deepest wish is that everyone is as blessed when pursuing their dreams.

My sincere thanks and humble gratitude to my editors, Esi Sogah and Alicia Condon, my agent, Holly Root, and my critique partners, Shirley Rogerson, Michelle Hancock, and Mary Forbes. Your hard work has helped make the magic of Griffin and Rois's story come true. A huge thanks as well to Joe Hasson, for brainstorming *His Enchantment* with me and allowing the magic of this story to breathe life. A special thanks to Sulay Hernandez for believing in me from the start.

And, thanks to my mom and dad, my children Eric, Stephanie, and Chris, the Roving Lunatics (Mary Beth Shortt and Sandra Hughes), Kathy Geiger—president of my fan club, Nancy Bessler, my family and friends in Texas, and the Wild Writers for their friendship and continued amazing support!

Chapter One

Scotland, 1257

Beneath the October dawn, Princess Catarine MacLaren scoured the sheer face of the ben, then the roll of field that fell away to the magnificent loch shrouded by a thin veil of fog. "I see naught."

"Nor I."

Catarine glanced at Atair, her senior fey warrior, his fierce scowl framed by coal-black hair secured by a leather strip behind his head. "We saw the English knights moments ago. Their trail shouldna just disappear."

"Indeed," Atair replied, his deep voice rich with concern. He scanned where the remainder of the fey warriors moved through the knee-deep grass, searching for any indication of a small band of men having passed through. "The English knights are human. We trailed them with ease through the Otherworld. Yet, with each step away from the magical portal, any sign of their presence is fading."

"Aye, something is greatly amiss." She frowned at the ring of stones enfolded within the blanket of fog, the daunting presence of the strategic pillars majestic against the bands of dawn severing the azure sky. "How did the Englishmen know to use the stone circle to travel to the Otherworld? More troubling, how were they able to pass through? Only the fey can use it to travel to Scotland."

Atair rubbed his brow. "I am unsure." He glanced toward her. "Mayhap our losing track of them is for the best."

Anger slammed her. "The best? How can you say that when the royal palace was attacked and my uncle murdered?"

His mouth tightened. "Exactly the reason your father requested that you and your sisters separate and go into hiding. Until he confirms that whoever murdered Prince Johan was indeed a threat to the entire royal family, King Leod wished nae to expose you or anyone else to danger."

Catarine angled her jaw. "Nor would my father expect me to ignore that en route to our designated location, we caught a glimpse of the English knights fleeing the Otherworld."

"'Twas nae King Leod's request that his daughter endanger her life," Atair stated, his words tight.

"Nay, the decision to follow the English knights in hopes they will lead us to whoever planned the attack was mine." Catarine understood Atair's frustration, but being of age and with a small contingent of the fey guard beneath her command, 'twas her choice to make.

He crossed his arms, frowned. "It does nae mean I have to like it."

Far from intimidated by the gruffness in his voice—that of a man who was more a friend than a guard—she arched a brow. "And when was the last time I made a decision you approved of?"

Atair dropped his arms at his side. "'Tis naught to joke of. I fear for your safety."

The last of her anger faded. "I know, but 'tis nae as if I am either naive or helpless. Once my sisters and I turned five summers, we were trained with a blade by the finest tutors."

"Your Royal Highness—"

"Catarine," she interrupted. "We have known each other since our youth."

Somber eyes held hers. "And we are nay longer children."

"That we are nae." Exhaustion weighed on her as she noted the roll of clouds moving in. "And I worry that my father will indeed confirm that the attack was but the first toward the royal family."

"Why do you say that?"

With a sigh, she brushed back several strands of hair from her braid, loosened from the last several hours of hard travel. "Early this morning my uncle sent runners beseeching the royal family to meet him in the royal garden posthaste. In his missive he stated the reason 'twas of the greatest urgency that concerned us all. Before I or anyone else arrived, English knights attacked, and their arrows found their mark."

"Prince Johan's warrior instinct saved your family." Atair's frown deepened to a hard edge. "Still, human arrows killing one of the fey should be impossible."

"It should be," Catarine agreed, "leaving one terrifying explanation—the arrows were spell-tipped."

"'Tis the only explanation," Atair agreed with disgust. "But who would cast a spell upon a human's weapon to enable them to kill the fey?"

Fear rippled through her. "Someone who dared allow humans access into the Otherworld for such a nefarious deed. It could be any of the fey nobility who have challenged the royal family's claim to the throne over the years. Or"—she mulled the terrifying possibilities—"if 'twas due to the lust for power, the traitor could be anyone. Discovering the reason is why we must trail the English knights."

"Do you know if your father found any written notes stating Prince Johan's concerns?" Atair asked.

The gruesome image of her uncle sprawled on the pathway in the royal garden, the stench of blood, and the arrows embedded in his chest clawed through her mind.

"Catarine?"

She swallowed hard. "When my father arrived moments after me, he searched the area, then his brother's chamber, in hopes of finding a clue. Whatever the threat to our family, my uncle refused to share it except to our face."

"Thank the heavens a royal guard caught sight of the men as they escaped and was able to give a description."

"Aye. I still canna believe humans were brought into the Otherworld for such evil intent." Catarine glanced to the field where the fey warriors continued their search, then shook her head with an exasperated sigh. "There is little reason for us to continue. The trail of the English knights is lost. We must return to the stone circle and try to track them from there again. There must be some sign of their passing that we missed."

Embraced by the mist of dawn, Atair gave a soft whistle.

The fey warriors looked over, then hurried toward them through the thin veil of fog.

Once everyone had returned, Catarine nodded to each man. "We are——"

A man's shout echoed in the distance.

"Get down!" Atair warned.

Catarine dropped to the ground, flattened herself alongside the fey warriors. The rich scent of earth mixed with the weathered grass as a steady breeze rustled through the thick blades, shielding them from view.

"Look. Near the water's edge," Sionn, one of the fey warriors she'd known since her childhood, said in a low voice.

Catarine peered between the dew-laden blades of grass. In the distance, through the smear of thinning fog, she made out a fairly large group of warriors.

"I count over twenty men," Sionn said.

"Look behind them," Atair whispered. "Several more knights are leading two people from the water's edge. From their garb, they are nobility."

Nobility? Catarine frowned as she noted a man and a woman walking with the group, the luxuriousness of their garb indeed confirming Atair's claim of their royalty.

"Halt!" Another shout, distinctly male, echoed from a distance behind them.

Stunned, Catarine met her senior fey warrior's worried gaze. "We are caught between the two groups!"

"The tall grass and brush should keep us hidden," Atair replied.

She prayed so.

Heavy footsteps pounded nearby.

As the men ran closer, Catarine withdrew her dagger.

"Halt in the name of King Alexander III!" a deep male voice ordered from the group closing in on the knights leading the noble couple.

Stunned, she glanced toward the knights hurrying away with the royal pair. *King Alexander III—could that be Scotland's king and his queen?*

Orders rang out from the knights near the water. Several men broke from their ranks and rushed up the hill toward the attackers while the remainder hurried the couple away.

Atair glanced over. "If they come closer, we will have to fight."

Her body taut, ready to jump to her feet, Catarine nodded.

Several feet away, blades scraped.

A cry of pain echoed.

Outlined by the fog, an armed man staggered toward them, crumpling to the earth but paces away.

"The battle 'tis nae yours, Lord Grey," a Scot warned the towering man with rust-colored hair and a beard as he struggled to his feet. "Go back."

"Like bloody hell," the rust-haired man boomed. "'Tis my king you are abducting!" Arms trembling, Lord Grey raised his blade, swung.

The men clashed. Amidst the fray, grunts and curses filled the air, the slide of steel as common as the fall of men and the gasps of their last breaths.

Horrified, Catarine watched as the life-and-death battle played out before her. Without warning, an urge swept over her to jump into the fight and aid Lord Grey in protecting Scotland's king. Dagger clenched in her fist, she started to rise.

Atair caught her wrist. "What are you doing?"

Heat warming her cheeks, she flattened herself against the ground. "I . . ." She wasna sure, which made nae a bit of sense. She was fey, nae human. Scotland's king and his people were nae her concern. Still, the need to help the man fighting to save his king remained. Uneasy, she studied the mix of men engaged in battle, her gaze returning to one—the rust-haired Scot.

Like a defiant god, Lord Grey forged ahead, his each slash at the man before him making Catarine hold a nervous breath. Why? 'Twas nae as if she knew him. Never had she seen the man in her life.

Muscles bulged as Lord Grey lifted his blade, swung.

The Scottish knight before him screamed, then fell.

Another Scot charged the rust-haired Scot from behind.

Catarine stifled a gasp. Heart pounding, she watched as the man swung; his blade angled up, stained with a slash of red.

With a cry of pain, Lord Grey crumpled to the ground.

Nay! She must help him!

Atair's hand on her wrist tightened. He gave a hard shake of his head.

What was she thinking? She couldna expose their presence. But for an unexplainable reason, urgency to reach Lord Grey swept over her.

Long moments passed, and Atair released his hold on her wrist.

The cacophony of blades slowed to an errant shudder.

Then silence.

Their movements weighed by fatigue, several warriors from those who'd kidnapped the king and queen backed away from the litter of bodies.

"What of the dead?" a man with a deep Scottish burr nearby asked.

"Leave them," a gruff voice farther away ordered. "We must reach Stirling Castle."

"And what if the king doesna comply with our lord's request?" the Scot with the deep burr asked.

"Then he will die," the gruff voice replied. "Let us go." The slide of metal against leather hissed as knights shoved swords into their sheaths and started west.

Sunlight pierced the wisps of fog as Catarine watched them catch up with the distant group leading the royal couple. "King Alexander and his queen are in danger."

Atair eyed her, perplexed. "Their fate is nae our concern. We must find the trail of the English knights who entered the Otherworld and give chase."

So caught up was she in the battle, in her concern for Lord Grey, that for a moment she'd forgotten her purpose. Chagrined, she focused on the stone circle in the distance, then back toward the departing men.

"If the English knights we are trailing passed this way"—Sionn paused with upset—"after that battle, I fear any trace is destroyed."

A sinking feeling in her gut, Catarine nodded. "We will soon see." She pushed herself into a kneeling position, keeping her body below the tips of the tall grass.

"The Scots should be far enough away," Atair said as he crouched beside her, "but I want to take nay chance of us being seen." He faced

the other fey warriors. "Go toward the stone circle, but keep low."
He started back.

Sionn moved beside Catarine. "I will keep close by."

Tenderness touched her. Her friend worried about her. She gave
him a warm smile. "I believe I am able to defend myself."

"Aye," Sionn replied, "but I am staying still the same."

"Let us go then." Catarine started through the thick, dew-laden
grass.

A man's pain-filled moan echoed from behind.

She whirled.

Between the blades of sturdy grass, shafts of fragile sunlight
illuminated a lone rust-haired man staggering to his feet.

Lord Grey!

Waves of emotion swamped her, that of pain, of anger so deep
'twas as if it lived. Catarine dug her fingers deep into her palms as
she fought to steady herself against the onslaught.

"What is wrong?" Sionn asked.

"I . . ." How did one explain these raw emotions? In disbelief,
Catarine stared at Lord Grey, then understood. Somehow, incredibly,
she was sensing what this Scot was feeling. She stepped toward him.

Sionn moved to her side. "Catarine, what are you doing?"

"I must help him."

At her voice, the rust-haired Scot's head snapped toward her.

The impact of his green eyes held hers, pinned her as if a sword
to flesh. Sensation roared through her.

"Who are you?" Lord Grey's deep burr demanded.

Sword raised, Atair ran back and moved beside her as the other
fey warriors formed a protective circle. "Dinna answer."

Catarine shook her head. "He is nae a threat."

"You know naught of him," Sionn warned, his voice rich with
suspicion.

Atair nodded to the daunting man. "Who are you?"

The Scot straightened. "Trálin MacGruder, Earl of Grey, personal
guard to King Alexander," he replied, his each breath rattling with
agony. His body began to waver. "Who be—" On a muttered curse,
he collapsed.

"Nay!" She broke through her guard's protective circle and rushed toward Lord Grey.

"Catarine!" Atair called.

Panic slid through her as she faced her senior fey warrior. "I . . . I must help him."

Atair shook his head. "We must go. Now."

She should agree. 'Twas imperative to find where they'd lost the trail of the English knights—if it still existed. More, to remain here with a stranger, a human, went against everything she had been taught.

Aching inside, she shook her head. "I canna leave him."

"Canna?" Atair strode to her. "What are you talking about?"

Unsure looks passed between the fey warriors.

Emotion swamped Catarine, and urged her to where Trálin MacGruder lay moaning in pain. "I canna explain more." She ran toward the noble.

The soft thud of Atair's steps echoed behind her. "Catarine!"

Sunlight broke through the clouds as she knelt beside the injured earl.

Atair caught her forearm, drew her to her feet. "What do you think you are doing? Do you want to get yourself killed?"

Lord Grey moaned.

Stiffening at the pain he was enduring, at his each labored breath, she shook her head. "The Scot is far from a threat."

Atair's gaze narrowed. "He is human."

"I know," she replied, her words somber. "But here"—she touched her finger against her brow—"I know I must help him."

"To aid a human is forbidden," Sionn argued as he and the other warriors halted nearby. "We are granted the ability to leave a thought in their mind, naught more."

"I know," she replied.

Atair's mouth tightened. "What of the trail of your uncle's murderers? Is it now unimportant?"

Guilt swept her. Her fey warriors were right. To help this Scot in any mortal manner went against the laws of the Otherworld. She started to turn away.

"D-do nae go," Lord Grey whispered as he lay upon the ground.

He coughed, and his entire body rattled. "I must save my king and queen."

Rays of sunlight illuminated Trálin MacGruder's hard-boned face; that of a warrior, of a man determined. But it also highlighted a firm mouth that would make a woman dream, and his green eyes, which behind his pain, shone kindness.

"You speak of King Alexander and Queen Margaret," she stated, pulling herself from her wanton thoughts.

Shrewd, pain-filed eyes studied her. "Aye," Lord Grey replied. "They were abducted."

Catarine glanced toward where the royal couple had been escorted away. "By whom?"

"I do nae know, but I must f-find out." On a curse, he tried to sit up.

"Do nae move. You are wounded," Catarine said as she knelt, placed her palm against his shoulder, and held him down.

His body trembled. "My men?"

Heart in her throat, she took in the bodies strewn about, the scent of blood strong against the fresh Highland morning. "I am sorry, they are dead."

"God in heaven," the earl hissed.

Atair stepped toward her. "Catarine, we must go."

With a frown, she met her friend's gaze. "With his wounds, if I leave him he will die."

Frustration darkened her senior fey warrior's eyes. "And the tracks of the English knights we must follow?" Throughout her life she had been confident in her decisions, a trait the fey guards appreciated; but for the first time, she felt unsure. Neither did she forget Sionn's mention of the Otherworld law forbidding her to aid Lord Grey. 'Twas her choice, one filled with ramifications once her father learned of her actions—if she decided to remain and offer the earl aid.

"Atair, take Kuircc, Magnus, Ranulf, and Drax to the stone circle and spread out," she said. "If you find any trace of the English knights' passing, return to me."

Atair nodded, his mouth grim. "And when we return, if we have found a trail, you will leave with us?"

She stiffened. "Your question is unseemly."

"Aye," Atair agreed, "as is your request to remain and aid a huma——"

"Enough," she said with a covert gesture toward Lord Grey. They knew nae this human, nor could they trust him enough to speak freely of any mention of the Otherworld.

With a frown, Atair waved the four men to follow him. Their steps soft upon the earth, they hurried toward the towers of timeworn stone.

Sionn nodded. "I will remain nearby." He moved several steps away.

"En-English knights?" Lord Grey asked, his confusion evident.

"Do nay talk or move about," Catarine said, settling beside him. "I need to tend to your wounds."

"No time," he gasped, his face strained as he tried to sit up. "Mu-Must save my king."

Irritated, she held his shoulders to prevent him from moving further. "If you attempt to follow your king now, with your injuries, you will die."

Die, mayhap, Trálin mused, but if he did nae attempt to follow whoever had abducted King Alexander III and Queen Margaret, the royal couple's lives could be in danger.

Still, if whoever had stormed Loch Leven Castle last night sought to claim the crown, why had they nae killed the king and queen in their bed? Naught made sense, but by God he would learn the truth, and set them free.

He shifted and pain slammed in his head. Trálin fought for consciousness. Bedamned, he must leave.

"Lord Grey?" the soft, lyrical voice called.

Through the murky haze of agony, Trálin focused on the woman. As if a spell cast, beneath the sheen of the fragile morning sunlight, he stared, transfixed by her beauty. The intensity of her gaze drew him, made him yearn to hold her against him and trust her with his secrets.

Shaken by what she made him feel, he dismissed the unwanted thoughts, ascribing them to his injuries. He tried to move; she held him firm. "I must discover where the men who abducted the king and queen are headed."

"Stirling Castle," she replied. "Now lay back and let me tend you."

Suspicion crawled through him. "How do you know where they are going?"

She hesitated. "I overheard the knights as they led them away."

"What else did they say?"

"Lord Grey," she said, her frustration clear. "If you allow me to care for you, you can ask all of the questions you wish."

"Will you answer them?" he asked, finding himself intrigued by this woman who looked like a fairy, but held herself with the confident grace of a warrior. Neither did he miss her unusual garb. Her gown, a sturdy yet silky material, adorned with a belt holding several gemstones of striking quality. He hesitated. Who was she? From the quality of her garb a person of wealth, or the daughter of a powerful noble. Regardless, she was a stranger he could far from trust. At her silence, he eyed her hard. "You said if I allowed you to tend me, I may ask all of the questions I wish, but will you answer them?"

A smile touched her mouth. Fled. "Mayhap."

"Fine then." Gritting his teeth, he lay back against the cool, damp earth.

"Now, do nae move." With efficient movements, she removed his mail and exposed his wounds. "I will be back in a trice." She started to rise.

"Catarine."

The beautiful woman hesitated.

"I heard one of the men address you as such. 'Tis your name, is it nae?"

"Aye." Her expression cautious, she stepped back.

"'Tis a name befitting your beauty, a name a man savors as it rolls across his tongue."

Any warmth in her eyes faded. "Methinks you have had much practice in wooing a woman. Save your sweetened words for another. You are far from what I seek in a man."

Far from put off, he was left intrigued by her cool dismissal. Regardless of what she believed, never had he spoken to a woman in such regard. "Do you n-nae feel it?"

She shot a nervous look toward a lean warrior with blond hair standing nearby. At his comment, the warrior's eyes narrowed.

The beautiful woman met Trálin's gaze, hers wary. "I feel naught."

From her reaction, he believed she lied. And what of her quick dismissal? She seemed dubious of his compliment. Why? As if he had time to ponder such?

"I will be but a moment," she said. "I am fetching some water to cleanse your wounds."

Curious, Trálin watched for her reaction. "I practice naught but the truth."

"Do you?"

Her skeptical reply intrigued him further, and he watched her, wished for the full light of day to catch every nuance. "Aye."

She studied him a long moment, then left. A short while later she returned with a crude bowl woven from grass. She knelt beside him, tore a strip of cloth from the bottom of her garb, and gently began to rinse his wounds.

The scent of the grass and the soft shimmer of lilac filled his every breath. "What clan are you from?"

She flushed the injury with water, then pressed a damp cloth over his wound.

At the whip of pain he hissed. "Was that my answer?"

A slender brow arched.

'Twould seem the lass was more stubborn than most. Then, as she was the daughter of a noble, he shouldn't be surprised. Exhausted, Trálin laid his head against the cold ground. "The men with you, who are they?"

Gentle fingers cleansed the exterior of another wound. "My guard."

Though they were quiet, he heard authority in her words. "You are nobility."

At his statement, Catarine stilled. "Aye."

Having traveled with the king since his youth, and now as King Alexander's personal guard, how had he missed seeing this stunning woman before? "Who is your father?"

She hesitated, then cleared her throat. "You would nae know him."

Blackness threatened. Trálin MacGruder kept conscious, barely. "Lady Catarine, as a Scottish noble in high standing, I have met all nobility in Scotland and most in England and France as well as several other countries. No doubt during my travels, at the very least, I have heard of your father."

Her full lips tightened.

"Is it such a mystery?" he asked, curious at what incited her reserve. By her burr she was Scottish, and by her speech, learned.

"How did you come to serve the Scottish king?" she asked.

Scottish king? Why would she refer to King Alexander III as the Scottish king and nae *our* king? God's teeth, mayhap her loyalties lay with another sovereign?

With the abduction of his sovereign this day, dare he answer her? More worrisome, he was the only person left from the king's personal guard who had seen them abducted from Loch Leven Castle. And what of this woman's reservation in telling him from which clan she hailed or who her father was? Something was amiss here, and he would bloody well find out what.

"Lady Catarine," he said, his words cautious, "you stated you overheard the men who abducted King Alexander say they were taking him to Stirling Castle."

She stilled. "Aye."

"What else did you hear?"

"That . . ." She looked away.

By God he would know. "Tell me!"

Anger darkened her gaze as she faced him. "That if King Alexander doesna comply with their lord's request, he will die."

Chapter Two

Though it was slight, Catarine caught the flicker of distrust in Lord Grey's eyes. As he was a warrior, a man loyal to his king, she understood. He held suspicions of her being in league with those who abducted his king.

She worried her finger across the leather sheath of her dagger. Never had she considered that Lord Grey would question her about her family. Then, she'd nae considered they'd speak for any length. Regardless, whatever mayhem was about with Scotland's sovereign, 'twas nae a concern of the fey.

But the Scottish lord would offer her little trust without some admission. "I am of nobility."

Lord Grey arched a brow. "As you travel with your guard, 'tis obvious."

Catarine ignored Sionn's frown. "You stated you are the king's personal guard."

"Aye," Lord Grey replied.

From his hesitation, there was more. "And?"

A ruddy hue darkened on his face. "And he is a man for whom I would give my life."

A friend. Interesting.

Shrewd eyes studied her. "Who is King Alexander III to you?"

Though soft, demand echoed in Lord Grey's question. "A man whom I have heard much about, that for one of his age he is a man of wisdom, and as a king it is said he garners many a loyal alliance."

"It is said?" he asked.

She must watch her words. The man was too quick. "I misspoke."

A shrewd look settled on his face. "And your father is?"

"A man I doubt you have ever met," she replied.

"Why do you evade my questions?" the Scot asked, his pain-ridden voice gruff.

She ignored Sionn's grimace. "I am nae from your country." The truth, but how would he react if she informed him she was a fairy from the Otherworld?

A shiver visibly wracked his body. The Scot's fisted hands turned white and he closed his eyes.

Catarine withdrew a blanket from the roll she carried and covered him. "Please do nae speak more. You must rest."

His eyes opened, narrowed. "Do you s-support my king? I must know." His last words fell out in a rough whisper.

Catarine nodded. If nae from the Otherworld, his king was a man she could give her allegiance to.

"Aye," he rasped, "that I believe." He struggled to speak, but with a fractured breath, his lids fluttered closed.

She moved closer.

After several moments, his breathing grew even.

"Lord Grey is unconscious," she said. "With how he is suffering, 'tis for the best."

"Catarine, what is going on?" Sionn asked.

At the soft concern in her friend's voice, guilt wove through her. She met the fey warrior's querying gaze and stood. "I do nae know, but I sense he is important to me."

"Important to you, how?"

"I canna explain, but I feel it," she replied. "I must stay until he is well enough to move."

"You promised Atair if they picked up the trail, you would leave."

"I know." Guilt swept her as she glanced to where her senior fey warrior and the others searched the area around the stone circle for any sign of where the English knights had passed. "If . . . any sign of a trail remains."

"From the frustrated look on Atair's face and the erratic angles they are walking around the tall grass," Sionn said, "it looks as though they are having little success."

"So it seems." Unease slid through her. "Sionn, why do I find myself caring what happens to this human? Do you think that, like the spell-tipped arrows that killed my uncle, my draw to Lord Grey is another ploy cast from magic?"

Lines of worry marred his brow. "I do nae know. If whoever is behind the attack has the ability to bring humans to the Otherworld as well as erase the English knight's trail, then their power is great."

Scraping her teeth across her lower lip, Catarine studied the unconscious lord. An ache built in her chest. Was it a spell? Never had she heard of a fairy being attracted to a human.

A yell sounded.

Had they found the trail? She glanced toward the stone circle.

Atair waved the fey warriors to him. The men gathered around him. A head shook, then another. A frown deepened on his brow as Atair stepped from the group and strode toward Catarine and Sionn, the others following suit.

Frustration built within her. "They have found naught."

"Who has found naught?" Trálin asked, his voice rough as he fought his semi-conscious state.

The woman hesitated, then a smile touched her mouth. "You are awake."

"Aye," he replied, refusing to have his question dismissed. "Who has found naught?"

The steady pad of steps upon the grass grew.

"My men are returning. Stay still, please." She turned toward her incoming warriors.

Stay? Like bloody hell. He shoved the blanket away. His body trembling, Trálin shoved into a sitting position.

At the soft scrape of his body against the frozen ground, she turned. Her eyes widened. "What are you doing?"

"Standing." Pain burst through Trálin as he struggled to his feet. His vision blurred, and he wavered.

Catarine caught his forearm, her hold gentle. "Please lay back down; your wounds are serious."

Thankful his eyesight was clearing, he ignored the pounding in his head and focused on the approaching warriors. "Mayhap, but I have suffered worse." Nor would he lay helpless around strangers, more so those who would nae reveal their full names.

The soft crunch of grass sounded nearby.

A fierce-looking man with coal-black hair secured behind his back met his gaze, glanced at her hand, then frowned. "He is awake, then."

"Aye." Red touched her cheeks as she withdrew her hand from Trálin's arm.

"'Twould seem he will recover," the dark-haired man stated, little welcome in his voice.

She cleared her throat. "He will need to rest."

Uneasy silence fell between them.

"Atair," Lady Catarine said, "did you find anything?"

The dark-haired man grimaced. "'Tis best if we speak in private."

"Nay," Trálin stated, anger storming past the pain. "You will speak here."

The woman whirled. "You will nae——"

"My king and queen have been abducted, you avoid telling me who your father is, nor have you told me from what clan you hail," Trálin stated, far from giving a damn if his outburst pleased her. "I demand an answer."

The hiss of a blade echoed in the air as the dark-haired man stepped forward. "You will nae speak to Pr——"

"Atair!" Lady Catarine ordered. "Enough."

The warrior muttered a curse. With a cool look, he sheathed his sword. Her face paled. "My regrets, Lord Grey."

"Do nae apologize, my lady. Your knight but defends you," Trálin said. "If I stood in his stead, I would do the same."

Sunlight flickered over the horizon, the golden rays shimmering off the mist-laden grass. Time was passing. He must give chase if he was to save his king and queen. "My lady, you seek English knights, why?"

The dark-haired warrior stiffened at her side.

Her wary eyes studied him. "The reasons are my own."

"Nae if they involve my king," Trálin stated.

"They do nae," she replied.

Lord Grey hesitated. "You are sure?"

"Tell him nothing," the dark-haired warrior stated.

With a frustrated sigh, she faced the man. "Atair, did you find any sign of the trail?"

The dark-haired knight shot Trálin a cool look before turning back to her. "Naught. 'Twas the same as before."

Her shoulders sagged. Lady Catarine met Trálin's gaze, the anger and pain in them stealing his breath. However suspicious he was of her, she struggled with whatever conflict she dealt with.

"My lady," Trálin said, his voice softening. "I do not mean you, nor your men, any harm. Neither do I know, or am I in league with, the English knights."

The man she called Atair grunted.

Trálin ignored him. "My lady, are you sure the men you seek are English knights?"

A light breeze kicked up, tossed her blond hair against her cheek. "Aye."

Why would the English be this far north? King Alexander had received nay writ from King Henry of his intent to send his men into Scotland. As the Scottish king's personal guard, his sovereign would have informed him of news of such import. Unease swamped Trálin like a cesspit. Unless King Henry was involved with whoever had abducted the royal couple and sought to increase his power. Bloody hell. With each thought, he found naught but more questions.

Catarine rubbed her arm. "Why do you ask?"

Trálin grimaced as he shifted the weight off of his injured leg. "There is no reason for English knights to be on Scottish soil."

"We had hoped to follow them to discover who had sent them," she explained.

"For what purpose?" Trálin asked.

She paused. "They will lead us to whoever sent them to murder my uncle."

"I am sorry, lass," Trálin said, too aware of the difficult emotions one struggled with after the loss of one you loved.

"My thanks," she replied. "We caught sight of them as they were leaving and have trailed them to the stone circle. Now, we canna find any trace of them."

"Lady Catarine," the knight with the black hair said. "I ask that you use caution in what you share."

Trálin held the man's gaze, far from intimidated by the fierce glare. The warrior she'd called Atair didna like him, which was fine with him. "My lady, what was your uncle doing to raise ire so that the English knights would be sent into Scotland with lethal intent?"

She hesitated.

The lass held secrets. Nor would a lone man against her and her warriors find out.

After a long moment, she nodded. "I do nae know who sent them or their reason for taking his life, but I must discover both."

As much as he wanted to ask more, with each question she gave him little in reply. For now she'd tell him little more about her uncle's murder or her. Regardless, he found her words sincere.

"Are you sure the men you chase are English?" Trálin asked.

"Aye," she replied. "One of my guards caught a glimpse of the men as they were escaping."

Trálin mulled over the information. "Do you believe the knights were sent by King Henry?"

She shrugged. "I am unsure."

"My lady," Trálin said. "If I am to help you—"

"My lord, you would help us?" she asked.

He needed to discover if a connection existed between King Henry, her uncle's murder, and King Alexander's abduction. God in heaven, all thoughts pointed to the English king preparing to make a bid to lay siege and claim Scotland. Except, that made little sense. King Henry was a man of peace. But then, many a man was lured by the temptation of power.

"Aye, I will help you," Lord Grey replied, "But first you will help to free my king."

Atair grunted. "We do nae need delays."

"'Twould be but days." Alone he could nae challenge the abductors and free his king.

"Why would you want us to help you first?" Catarine asked.

"Blast it," Atair said. "You are nae considering his request?"

Shrewd eyes studied Trálin. "Atair, I want to hear him out."

Her lead warrior's mouth tightened. "If we help Lord Grey, by the time we return, any trace of the English knights' trail would be long past."

"And what have you found now?" Trálin asked, tired of his suspicion.

"Naught," Catarine replied, "but how could you help us days from now if we have nay trail?"

Trálin glanced toward the stone circle where her men had searched, then back to the woman. "Once King Alexander and his queen are freed, with his gratitude at your assistance, I am confident he will agree to assign me a contingent of knights to help find the English knights you seek." More so if he suspected the English king was plotting to seize Scotland.

The black-haired man cursed. "We do nae need this Scotsman's aid."

Her ire building, Catarine turned to Atair. "And what are we to do, return to our home and pray that no one else dies?"

Her senior fey knight's mouth tightened. "You would be safe."

"Would I?" she demanded. "Without us knowing exactly who is behind the assassination as well as the extent of their plans, my entire family's lives may be in peril."

"We canna find a trail, which leads me to ask why? 'Tis nae natural," Atair said with emphasis. "So how is having this Scot or more men going to help us find what we canna see? In a sennight, the weather could easily have washed away any wisp of a trail."

The Scot's jaw tightened. "I know the land, the people who live here. If Englishmen have passed through, I will find out."

Atair rounded on the Lord Grey. "If we help free your king and queen, then after you find naught, we will be left with but mere words."

"And if we do nae try, we will be left with the same," she stated, her heart aching. "Listen to me. By helping Lord Grey, we have a chance to find who is behind this treachery." Eyes angry, Atair held her gaze, but Catarine refused to look away. "Tell me," she whispered, damning that they had little but hope to risk their lives upon, "do we give up the slightest chance to find whoever murdered my uncle?"

Her senior fey warrior's jaw tightened. "This discussion is moot. You promised after we searched for the trail, you would return . . . home."

"I agreed only if you found a sign of the English knights," Catarine replied, her voice crisp, "which you didna."

Atair muttered a curse beneath his breath. "What if the reason is one we did nae consider——'tis erased?"

"Erased?" she asked, a sickening in her stomach.

"Aye." Atair replied, "erased by whoever allowed the English knights entrance to our"——he glanced at the Scot——"castle."

Atair meant the Otherworld, a fact he didna wish to disclose to the human. Blast it, he believed whoever led the English knights had enough power to erase the trail with magic. Angry tears burned her throat. If Atair was right, Lord Grey would be of nay help, and their aiding to free his king would be naught but a waste of precious time.

"Catarine," Atair said, his words rough. "We must return. The risk is too high for us to remain *here*."

She nodded. "Come, let us——" Wait! Why had she nae thought of it before! Mayhap the human was immune from fey magic and could indeed help?

"What is it?" Sionn asked her.

As if she could discuss anything about the Otherworld with Lord Grey standing where he might hear? They dealt with someone holding powerful magic, a fact proven by the English knights' ability to enter the Otherworld as well as the spell-tipped arrows designed to kill the fey. But the spell that was cast to erase the trail was intended for the fey. A chance existed that the human was immune to its powers and could help.

"However slight," Catarine said with emphasis, "a chance exists that Lord Grey can aid us in our task. And, 'tis a chance I am willing to take."

Atair arched a doubtful brow, and Drax crossed his arms. The other fey warriors watched her, equally as unconvinced.

"I will explain more later." And she prayed she was right.

Chapter Three

Catarine faced Trálin. "We will aid you in freeing your king, but you must give me your word that after, you will help us as well."

Though relieved, neither would Trálin let down his guard. Whatever the lass wished to explain to her warriors, she wanted to ensure he did nae hear. Secrets. Still, among the questions her actions raised, he sensed she was a woman he could trust, which made nae a whit of sense. But his instincts had saved his life in the past, and he'd heed them now.

He scanned the woman and her five knights. Whatever their relation, 'twas none like he'd ever witnessed between a noblewoman and her guard. "You have my word."

Her shoulders sagged with relief.

"Since the knights who abducted the royal couple have taken them to Stirling Castle, then we will head west." Trálin scanned the rough terrain they must cross. "On foot, 'twill take two days of hard travel."

Lines of concern deepened on her brow. "With your injuries, a day's rest would serve you well before we departed."

"Mayhap," Trálin replied, "but 'twill nae aid my king."

"'Twould seem the Scot is as stubborn as you," a blond-haired man said. He nodded to Trálin. "I am Sionn."

"Sir Sionn," Trálin replied.

"Our lead warrior"—Sionn gestured toward the outspoken black-haired man—"is Atair."

"Sir Atair," Trálin said, nae surprised to find the man who advised the woman and watched him with distrust was her senior knight.

Atair gave him a curt nod.

"The rest of the men are," Sionn gestured to a red-haired man with a thick beard, "Kuricc." With a wave, he introduced the bald warrior with a Celtic tattoo on the back of his head. "Magnus." The man at the end of the group with his long black hair secured in a thong at his back nodded, "Ranulf." He motioned toward a man with brown-red hair. "And Drax."

"Good to meet you as well," Trálin said, "and my thanks for helping free my king."

A raven called in the distance.

Senses on alert, Lord Grey scanned the field. Emotions stormed him as he caught sight of his men slaughtered. "Before we leave, my lady, I seek your men's aid in giving my knights a proper burial."

Grief darkened her eyes. "Of course. I am sorry for your loss."

The depth of her sincerity touched him. "My thanks, my lady. And I deeply regret the recent loss of your uncle as well."

Her lower lip trembled, and she gave a solemn nod. "Lord Grey, we will be together for several days. I ask that as I bid my warriors, you call me Catarine."

Atair's mouth tightened with displeasure.

"Lady Catarine, 'tis my honor." A smile touched her face, one he found he enjoyed causing. "And please, my lady, call me Trálin."

A slight red hue slid up her cheeks. "Aye."

"Let us begin so we can be on our way." With somber steps, he walked with the others to where his men lay.

Hours later, the icy whip of wind cut through Catarine's cape like daggers. Fatigue weighing her every step, she tugged the woven wool closer and continued up the steep incline. The rich tang of pine and the hint of snow filled her every breath as she moved. With her next step, she shoved aside a tree limb, pushed forward.

A gust of wind shook the limbs above.

She glanced skyward. Dark clouds thickened overhead. "'Tis going to snow."

His breath rushing out in puff of white, Trálin nodded. "'Tis my worry. The trek to Stirling Castle will be dangerous enough without a storm slowing us down. Nor will we want the tracks we will leave in the snow exposing our approach."

"Tell us about Stirling Castle," Catarine said. "'Tis best if we know what we are up against."

"'Tis a formidable stronghold," Trálin explained. "Surrounded on three sides by cliffs. Our best hope, if we have time to wait, is to slip in beneath the cover of the night."

"You know of a way to get in the stronghold then?" Drax asked.

"Aye," Trálin replied.

"With Scotland's king in residence," Atair said, "'twill be heavily guarded."

"Mayhap," Trálin replied, "or confident any who witnessed the abduction are dead, they will nae bolster the strength of their guard. Regardless, 'twill be dangerous."

"Do you know where they will be holding the king and queen?" Sionn asked.

Wind whipped past Trálin, cool air rich with the promise of winter. "I believe they would place them in the upper tower."

A fat flake twirled past, then another, the late afternoon light shimmering through the thin weave of ice in a fluttering prism as if a spell.

As if a spell? Bloody hell. An odd thought. Nor had he seen a fairy hill. As if he believed that the fey lived beneath the large mounds of dirt? A smile touched his mouth. Aye, he believed in the fey, but as for them living beneath the earth, 'twas naught but a bard's tale.

Trálin glanced at Catarine. "While your warriors and I go inside Stirling Castle, you remain hidden in the forest."

With a dismissive glance, she kept walking. "We all go together."

"Aye," her men agreed.

Anger swept Trálin. He shot each of the warriors a cool glance. "By God, she is a lass. I refuse to endanger her life."

The slide of steel sounded as Catarine whirled and laid the blade against his neck. Flakes of snow plopped on the forged metal as she lifted his head slightly with the honed tip. "And a woman who can wield a weapon as well as any man."

Stunned by the press of cold iron against his neck, Trálin stared at her. "Blast it, lass, where did you learn to handle a blade like that?" Except for the swoosh of the sword, she'd moved too quickly for him to catch her intent. However much it hurt his pride to admit, if she'd have wanted, he would now be dead.

With an indignant sniff, she withdrew her blade, then secured it in her sheath. "I am a warrior and have trained with weapons since my youth."

From the first, he'd noted her lithe movements, and the confidence when she spoke, but he'd nae made the connection to weaponry training. It was his penance, if he was truthful, for allowing his mind to linger on the curves of her body and a voice that would seduce a saint. At Atair's soft chuckle, he glanced at the warrior.

"Mayhap you have learned that next time you *ask* Lady Catarine, nae order her about," the lead warrior said.

Trálin grimaced. 'Twould seem there was good reason the men hadn't hesitated in having Catarine along. "Though the lass is quick with a blade, it still doesna mean I wish to place her in danger, nor can I forget she is nobility."

"Enough," Catarine stated. "I will go inside Stirling Castle. More important, the sun will be down soon. We need to cover as much distance as possible before then."

As Trálin reached the bottom of the brae, fat flakes of snow began to fall at a steady rate covering their tracks. The land angled up. Muscles aching, his wounds throbbing with pain, he pushed on. With his next step, dizziness swept him, and he stumbled.

Drax reached out, caught him. "Steady there, Lord Grey."

Trálin nodded. "A bit winded. My thanks."

"Winded?" Catarine halted. "A fool can see you are weak and in pain. We will make camp here."

"We can travel another league, mayhap two, before we lose daylight," Trálin stated.

She angled her jaw. "We can, but I have doubts of you lasting that long before you pass out. Nor will I have my men carry you."

"Blast it, has anyone ever told you that you have a penchant for ordering people about?" As quickly as he spoke, Trálin regretted his terse words. He needed their aid to save his king. "My lady——"

She chuckled, a wee bit at first, then gave a full-fledged laugh.

Smiles broke out on her warriors' faces as well, except for Atair, whose grimace remained.

Irritation smothered Trálin's regret. "I see naught that is funny."

"You do nae know me," she said, a smile in her eyes, "but my men do. Aye, you have the right of it. At times I tend to have my say."

"And then some," Sionn added, a twinkle in his eyes.

The warriors chuckled, and the tension hanging between them since they'd met lightened.

Though he appreciated the levity between her and her men, neither would Trálin relax his guard. Too many questions stood unanswered, and at every turn, he discovered that Catarine was nae the woman he'd first believed her to be. But, with his body trembling from pain and weakness, a rest would do him well.

"We will continue at first light," Trálin agreed.

"A fine choice," Catarine replied. As if the Scot had another? If Lord Grey had tried to continue, he would have passed out before they reached the bottom of the brae. She turned to her men. "Make camp."

In short order, Lord Grey and her warriors used limbs to craft a large angled overhang beneath which they could all sleep. They wove boughs of fir and limbs to shield any breaks. Several times, she caught the Scot stumbling, but she held her tongue. The man did nae know that in the Otherworld, women held the same authority as men. Nor with his stubbornness would it do any good to ask him to sit down and let them finish. For the meager time they would be together, 'twas best to nae raise further questions.

As her men finished covering the top of the makeshift shelter, Catarine carried a heap of dried moss inside, and began spreading it atop the snow-dusted ground. As she patted down the last bit, the crunch of snow beneath boots sounded behind her. A smile touched her mouth. Atair had come to speak with her.

"That should give us a bit of comfort this night," she said as she wiped her hands, stood, and turned.

Stilled.

Trálin MacGruder stood in the doorway, his gaze riveted on her, nae a man with a question, but with a look of passion. As if realizing he was staring, red slashed his cheeks. He cleared his throat. "Forgive me lass. I startled you."

"Na-Nay." She gave him a confident smile while her insides

churned with awareness. His muscled body told of a man who handled himself with pride and care. With his deftness with a blade, he was a man who none except a fool would challenge. But to a woman he offered a quick mind, protection, and a body so tempting 'twas as if carved by the gods. "I was just finishing spreading the last of the moss." And she needed to leave before she made a foolish mistake. Like move closer.

"And doing a verra fine job," he said, his words soft. "'Twill serve us well this night."

Us. The intimacy of his words wrapped around her like a warm blanket, ignited images of his mouth covering hers, and of his hands slowly caressing her with deft intent. Her body ignited with need.

Stunned, she blinked. What was going on? Never had a man affected her like Trálin. And blast it, he was a human.

And forbidden.

As if her attraction to Trálin MacGruder mattered? She was promised to Zacheus, Prince of Olghar. With the arrival of Beltane would come the time for her vows, ones nae for love, but for duty.

She forced a smile and stepped back. "We are all tired and in need of a good night's sleep. With the falling snow, the morrow and the travel ahead will be arduous."

"Aye, 'twill," Atair stated from behind her.

Guilt swept her as she composed herself. "Is everything finished?" Catarine asked as she nodded to the lead warrior. He was upset to find them alone, as she should be. Except she wished for a few moments with Lord Grey, to discover the taste of his kiss.

"There are several things that I must speak to you about," Atair replied, his voice gruff. "In private."

Trálin stepped to her side. "My lady, do you need me to come?"

The lead warrior crossed his arms. "Nay."

"Lady Catarine?" Lord Grey repeated, his voice hard.

Her guilt escalated. From the roughness of his voice, he wanted her still, and blast it, she wanted him as well. She forced a smile. "Nay. I will be away but a brief while." Before she said something she'd regret, she left.

Snowflakes fat and wet spiraled before her as she stepped outside.

"This way." Atair turned on his heel and headed toward a stand of trees a short distance away. "Everyone is awaiting *our* arrival."

In silence she walked by his side, the blasts of snow-ridden wind a stark reminder of her reason to be here. Shame filled her. How could she think of Lord Grey as anything but a means to find her uncle's killer? Limbs rattled overhead battered by another gust, and she tugged her cape tighter.

Atair glanced over, his face drawn. "I thought it best for you to brief the fey warriors on your suspicions."

"My thanks."

Atair sighed. "Catarine, he is human."

"I know what he is."

Her senior fey warrior slowed. "I know you care for him, as I understand you are well aware to consider helping—much less being with—a human is forbidden."

Though her senior fey warrior, Atair was a friend, one who she turned to when she needed advice. "Our situation is critical, and my decision is one I am confident my father would make. As for my duties, I will handfast while the sun rises on Beltane."

Sage eyes met her. "A wise decision to follow the dictate of necessity, nae that of the heart."

"'Tis the way of my ancestors."

He shrugged. "It does nae mean you canna wish for someone to love."

"Like you?" she asked.

"We are nae speaking of me," Atair replied, his voice soft with concern. "Catarine, I do nae want to see you hurt."

"Nor will I be. We will remain away from the Otherworld for a sennight, a fortnight at most."

"Attraction can happen in a moment. For everyone involved, I pray yours with Lord Grey will pass."

"I will do my royal duty when the time comes."

"Of that I have no doubt."

Exhausted, she scanned the sky. Her mind churning with unwanted emotions for Trálin MacGruder, Catarine studied the top of the ben to the west where jagged peaks scraped the low sky like angry fingers of grey. A shiver whipped through her.

"I prefer the spring," she said, "The long days of sunlight and how the sun seems to hang in the sky like a battle with the night."

Atair raised an amused brow. "A battle with the night, is it? Are you practicing to be a bard?"

At his teasing, she laughed, thankful for their friendship. However much they disagreed, she could always count on Atair to be a voice of reason. Though she didn't love the fey prince, he was a man she respected. For the sake of peace within their realm, that had to be enough.

"Come, 'twill be dark soon." Snow crunched beneath her boots as they walked through the forest to where her men stood.

Atair studied the churn of clouds overhead. "I fear the snow will be heavy by morning."

"Aye," she agreed, "and 'twill make travel difficult."

"Or impossible," he added.

She caught a limb, shoved it aside. "I will give Tra—Lord Grey chamomile this night to help him sleep."

"He is fortunate to have your aid. 'Twas me, I would give him naught but a boot in the arse."

Far from intimated by his gruffness, she chuckled. "You would give him chamomile as well."

"Mayhap."

Warmth touched her heart. A fair man, Atair would, nae that he would admit it now.

At their approach, the fey warriors nodded their welcome and widened their circle to allow them entry.

"My thanks for meeting me here," Catarine said. "I couldna speak freely around Lord Grey."

Understanding in their eyes, her warriors nodded.

"It concerns the stone circle," she said. "Atair believes the trail is there, but is erased by magic."

Surprise widened Sionn's eyes. "Magic?"

"Aye," she replied.

"Magic from the Otherworld has been used on Earth before," Atair said.

"Never for evil," she said. Gusts of wind spun snow around them in hectic spirals.

Kuircc drew his hand through his thick beard. "What do you think it means?"

She shrugged. "I am unsure, but whoever is behind the foul deed at Preswick Castle is someone who has powerful magic. A point proven by the knight's use of spell-tipped arrows, their allowing humans into the Otherworld, and our inability to track the English knights once they traveled through the stone circle and into Scotland."

Atair and the other fey warriors nodded.

"My thought is that the magical power affects the fey, but mayhap the humans are immune," she continued. "I believe the trail exists, but through magic we canna see it."

Sionn frowned at the thick snow completely covering the grass. "So why didna we ask Lord Grey to find the path while we were there?"

"We know nae what other spells have been left if we try and follow the assassins, spells that I believe willna affect Lord Grey and other humans. If this is correct, we need his aid. A bargain he agreed to if we helped save his king."

Drax rubbed his jaw. "Why do you think the spell would nae affect them?"

"Because," she replied, "whoever is behind this will never expect us to join with humans in our search."

Magnus crossed his arms. "Your reasoning is sound, but what if you are wrong?"

"If I am wrong, we have lost a few days. But," she said, refusing to give up hope, "what if I am right?"

Atair grunted. "Regardless, if we find whoever is behind the assassination, we face someone of formidable power. Do you think 'twill be a force we can defeat?"

Dread curled up inside her, cold and dark. A question she'd considered throughout their journey, one even now that overwhelmed her. Her lower lip trembled as she met his somber gaze. "I am unsure."

Chapter Four

The first rays of morning light sliced through the cloud-laden sky as Trálin leaned against the boulder and mulled the challenges of the mission ahead.

"You are up early for a wounded man."

At Catarine's lyrical voice, his body tightened. Bloody hell, the last thing he needed was to be alone with her in the forest. Had she nae noticed his attraction to her last night?

"I am."

"You couldna sleep?" she asked.

He kept his focus on where the sun peeked over the ben—a safer choice. "I slept well enough." A lie, one he would hold to. Throughout the night he'd dreamt of her. Hot, seductive images of her that had awoken him several times. And coming out of an erotic dream to the soft breaths of her warriors sleeping between them had doused his need as fast.

A light wind swirled past, thick with snow that'd fallen throughout the night, layers which would make their journey this day treacherous. The churn of dark skies overhead held the promise of more. For his king's safety, it was a journey they must make, regardless of the danger.

"I heard you tossing and turning," she said. "'Tis nae the sounds of a man in deep rest."

Irritated by the way her voice wove through him, igniting unwanted need, he turned, riveted his gaze on her. "And 'twould seem if you heard me moving about, you were awake as well."

At his curt reply, turquoise eyes brimming with concern faded. She stepped back. "Forgive me. You wish to be alone."

A fine way to treat the lass, especially one whose aid he sought. Caught up in his own frustration of wanting Catarine, he'd hurt her. "Wait."

She halted. Strands of blond hair tossed by the wind fluttered against her cheeks, her gaze hesitant.

Moved by the depth of feeling she inspired, he steadied himself. "I am sorry."

A weak smile worked its way to her mouth, fell. "'Tis for the best."

An odd answer. One mayhap he shouldn't seek further explanation. Still, something about her drew him. Blast it. He needed to know. Trálin pushed himself away from the stone. "What is for the best?"

She took another step back. "My leaving. We shouldna be out here together alone. 'Tis imprudent, nor a choice I would normally make. But I had dreams."

As if her revelation helped anything. Pulse racing, he stepped toward her.

She remained still.

"I dreamt of you as well," he whispered.

Her face paled, and she shook her head. "You do nae understand; this, us, canna be."

She turned to leave, but he reached out, caught her wrist.

"I should nae have come," she said.

Nor should he keep her here, but 'twas as if a man drowning, he needed to know. "What did you dream about?"

Catarine's hand trembled within his.

Throat dry, he swallowed hard. "Did you dream of my kissing you?"

For a long moment she watched him. Then, hesitantly, she nodded.

And his last defense tumbled. Trálin claimed her mouth, and heat stormed him at her taste. At her soft moan, at how she pressed her body flush against his, he took the kiss deeper, his tongue taking, commanding hers to respond, and she gave. Images of him stripping her, touching her everywhere, roared through his mind.

"Release her!"

At Atair's brusque voice, Trálin's mouth broke free, then he stepped back.

Guilt swept her as she stumbled away, glanced toward her senior fey warrior. "'Tis naught what it seems." Nay, 'twas more. Never before had a man made her feel so much. God in heaven, had her friend nae interrupted them, what would she have allowed?

His face drawn in a fierce frown, that of a protector—or a lover—Trálin stepped to her side, held Atair's cool gaze. "Leave us."

"Nay," she rushed out, struggling to find a rational explanation. As if such was possible? 'Twas she who'd stepped across forbidden boundaries by nae departing before.

Trálin's eyes riveted on her. "We are nae finished."

The rough desire in his voice shook her further. How she wished it was true.

Hand on the hilt of his blade, Atair walked closer. "Catarine wishes to return to camp."

The Scot rounded on the warrior. "Bloody hell—"

"I am betrothed to another," she blurted out, damning that she'd allowed their time alone to deteriorate to this moment—and, against the Otherworld laws and her promise of marriage, wanted Trálin still.

Shock widened Lord Grey's eyes, then they darkened to anger. "Betrothed?"

At the condemnation in his voice, anger that she deserved, she nodded. "Given the circumstance, 'twas wrong of me to come here. I am sorry, more than you could ever know."

"Sorry?" Trálin cursed. "And that is supposed to make what happened between us right?"

"Nay," she whispered.

"Catarine," Atair said, his voice gentle. "Go. I will speak with Lord Grey—alone."

"She will remain," Trálin snapped, the irritation in his tone making it clear he wanted her to face the chaos she'd created.

The warrior stepped forward. "If she chooses—"

"Why come here this morning aware that I want you?" Trálin demanded of Catarine.

"I did nae mean for this to happen," she said.

"Catarine," Atair said, "leave us, I beseech you."

Hand on his sword, Trálin stepped toward the warrior. "And what will you do once you and I are alone?"

"Enough, both of you," Catarine said, frustrated at the entire situation.

Both men glared at her.

As if she didn't deserve such? "I have wronged him, and I owe Lord Grey an apology. And, another to you, Atair."

"Regardless," her fey warrior stated, "'tis done."

Heart aching, she shook her head. "Nay, I forgot my place, my promises made."

Her friend's mouth tightened.

Thankful for his silence, Catarine exhaled, focused on the earl. "With my thoughts muddled with sleep, I didna weigh the possibilities of my actions."

"Why did you come here?" Trálin demanded.

"To talk," she replied. "Aye, it sounds foolish now, but as I explained, I heard you tossing and turning throughout the night. With your wounds, and knowing you struggled with the loss of your men, I wanted to check on you. Then, when I saw you and . . ."

Atair muttered a curse. "'Tis unseemly for you to be alone with this man."

Hands on hips, she faced her senior fey warrior. "As if I am nae alone with five men on regular occasion?"

"'Tis nae the same," Atair replied. "We are with you for your protection."

"You are," she agreed. "And your remaining here is stirring an already agitated situation." She paused. "I need but a few moments with Lord Grey. Alone."

Atair's mouth turned into a deep frown. "You must return to camp."

"I will," she replied, "in a few moments, once Lord Grey and I talk."

Her fey warrior's eyes narrowed. "I do nae like it."

"I know," she replied, softening her voice, understanding that her friend tried to do naught but protect her. "I will be but a moment. I promise."

"I will await you through the thicket. Any longer and I will return."

After a warning glance toward the Scot, Atair shoved aside the thick boughs of green and stepped past.

One upset man dealt with, now on to the other. Catarine drew a steadying breath and met Trálin's hard gaze. "I know you are displeased with me, but no more than I am with myself."

A muscle worked in his jaw. "Your guard should have stayed."

Unbidden, laughter bubbled up, cutting away a layer of tension.

"You find this amusing?" Trálin demanded.

"Nay, 'tis that I find you as stubborn and protective as Atair. Traits I greatly admire." She sobered. "Never did I mean for our attraction to happen."

"But it did."

His gruff tone assured her that he still struggled with his feelings. A fate she too shared. "Aye, it did."

Green eyes darkened. "Do you regret that we kissed?"

Another wave of guilt poured through her as she savored the memory of his mouth taking hers. "I should."

"Blast it, you are betrothed. Do you think my knowing how you feel about me will make our time together easier?" He stalked toward her. A pace away, he halted.

Her body trembled with awareness.

The hard edge of his gaze softened. He lifted her chin with his finger.

Desire ignited, burned within.

"From the first moment I found myself attracted to you," he breathed, "and last night, if we hadna been interrupted, I would have kissed you. And now, with the taste of your mouth storming my mind, I want you more."

Unsure how to reply, or if it was too dangerous, she remained silent.

His mouth tightened. "I want you, lass, make no mistake of that." His thumb across her full mouth, then on a sigh, he stepped back. "But you are nae mine to have." He stilled. "Do you love him?"

She looked away. "My feelings toward my betrothed change naught."

Hope flickered in his gaze. "Catarine, I am a powerful lord, one who holds the king's ear. If you do nae love this man, we can—"

She looked at him and swallowed hard, wishing it was that simple. "Do naught." She stepped back. "I must go."

He closed the distance.

"Do nae touch me again," she whispered.

"Because you want me?" he demanded.

"Aye." She closed her eyes, slowly opened them, regret making her heart ache. "And because any chance for us can never be."

Anger darkened his eyes, and he caught her hand. "Why?"

"Catarine?" Atair called from behind the brush.

"One more moment," she said.

A muttered curse sounded.

Thankfully her warrior stayed out of sight. "Lord Grey," she started, needing formality between them, "we come from different worlds."

"Our clans may be different," he stated, "but 'tis nae a challenge with the king's decree we canna overcome."

Catarine gave an exasperated sigh, and for the first time in her life wished she was nae a fairy. And what would her father and mother think of this mayhem? With the necessity for her marriage to bring peace between their realms, any intrigue at her dilemma with this human would fade as fast.

Shrewd eyes studied her. "Does he love you?"

Her brief meeting with Prince Zacheus of Olghar came to mind. Though amicable, they had little in common. "Nae, 'twas an engagement made to bring peace across the lands. As I, he agreed to wed out of duty."

His face somber, Lord Grey nodded. "Such arrangements are common within nobility."

"They are," she replied. "But with the risk of lives at stake, our upcoming marriage is one that canna be broken."

The tension in his face ebbed. "Lass, 'tis normal for upheavals within the realm. I am confident with King Alexander's intervention, we can bring peace between your lands and the betrothal will become unnecessary."

Wonder rolled through her at the thought of being free to choose whom she would wed, then reality crashed with a horrid jolt. She was fey, and he, human. A man forbidden. Nor could she forget the recent clashes between her family and Prince Zacheus's, or a tentative peace inspired between their kingdoms with the announcement of their marriage. A peace the dismissal of the betrothal would destroy.

"Nay," she replied, a wisp of regret slipping through, "your king can be of little help."

Trálin gave a soft chuckle. "You make the situation sound so dire, but lass, do nae doubt a king's might."

"I wish 'twas so simple." The mirth in his eyes faded, and her heart broke. She should have left before he had kissed her, before she had allowed him to believe that between them there could be more.

"Who is your father?"

Panic swept her. She was making a muddle of this. Or was she? How would he react to the truth? Would he believe her? Or, would he think her daft? Dare she tell him? Dare she nae?

On a trembling exhale, she braced herself. "My father is King Leod MacLaren."

"Play no games, lass."

He didna believe her? Hurt tore through her. "I play naught."

"Nay? Never have I heard of a king named Leod MacLaren."

"Nor would I expect you to," she replied, unsure how to convince him of her heritage, but needing to try. A long moment passed, then another, before she gathered the courage to explain. "My father is, as I and my warriors are, from the Otherworld."

Chapter Five

Trálin waited for Catarine to smile, to expose her claim as naught but a jest. At her silence, a low pounding built in his head. With a muttered curse, assured he was as loony as the old man secluded in the northern bens, he rubbed his temples. He scowled. "The Otherworld?"

"A sword's wrath, lass," Atair spat as he stepped through the thicket, his boots crunching as he walked through the snow. "What have you done?"

"'Tis foolish to keep the truth from him," she stated. "In the end, 'twill serve naught but cause more problems."

Atair's mouth tightened. "'Tis a mistake to tell Lord Grey anything more."

Suspicion filled Trálin as he took in the warning glare from Atair to Catarine. What in bloody hell was going on? First the lass dare tell him that her father is a king he has never heard of, that they were from the Otherworld, and then her knight warns her to say nay more? 'Twas naught but a well-planned ruse.

"He risks his life in helping us," Catarine defended. "Do you nae think he deserves to be told the truth?"

Trálin's mind spun. Her anger appeared real. As did her knights'. Were they from the Otherworld? Nay, he was going mad. Enough. "The Otherworld is the home of the fey."

At his interruption, her worried eyes rested on him. "Aye, because that is what we are."

He shot a glance from one, then to the other.

Neither smiled.

"You and your knights are from the Otherworld? Impossible."

"'Tis possible," she replied, her voice quiet, "Very much so."

Anger slammed him. He stepped back. "I am nae sure what mischief is about, but by God I will nae stand here and be made a fool of."

"Wait!" Catarine rushed out, "I will prove it to you."

"Do nae," Atair warned.

"How?" Trálin asked, ignoring her guard's comments, skeptical such a feat could be achieved.

"As long as I hold my breath and think it," she explained, "I can remain invisible."

Trálin laughed. "Lass, I have heard many a bard's tale, but never have I——"

Catarine inhaled.

Fat flakes of snow swirled down where seconds before she'd stood.

Stunned, Trálin gasped. "It canna be."

Catarine reappeared, her eyes searching his for belief.

"God in heaven," Trálin whooshed out. "You are telling the truth?"

"Aye," she replied.

"A fairy," he stated, needing to say the words, struggling to find fact in what should be but a tale. "How did you come to Scotland?"

"We travel through stone circles," she replied.

The sturdy pillars near where he and his men had fought came to mind. However outrageous her claim, a moment before he'd witnessed proof. He scrubbed his face again. 'Twas already a long day, and 'twas but morning.

"'Tis much to take in," she said, a smile curving on her lips.

"For a human," Atair added, his voice dry.

"The English knights you chase," Trálin asked. "Is that the truth as well?"

Her smile faded. "Aye."

Scraping for coherent thought, struggling to accept what he'd witnessed as real, he focused on logic. "How did English knights travel to the Otherworld?"

"A question we are anxious to solve," her senior warrior replied, "and the reason we must find them."

"Your uncle?" Trálin asked Catarine.

She gave a shaky exhale. "He was murdered by the English knights yesterday past."

Trálin rubbed his chin, mulled the situation. "I didna know 'twas possible for humans to enter the Otherworld."

Catarine glanced toward Atair. "We didna either, nor do we believe 'twas without aid."

"They were helped by another of the fey?" Lord Grey asked.

"'Tis the only explanation," she replied. "We believe the English knights were allowed into the Otherworld through a spell."

Could this day could grow stranger? *Magic?*" Trálin asked.

Hope illuminated Catarine's face. "You believe me?"

"It should be impossible." But the image of her disappearing, then reappearing was etched in his mind. "Aye. Please, start from the beginning and explain."

In short—and beneath Atair's disapproving look—Catarine related all that'd taken place and their journey since yesterday.

Trálin weighed her words, her explanation still a touch hard to accept as real. "So you believe when we return to the stone circle, I will see the English knights' trail, because whoever is behind this has cast a spell erasing the tracks to fey eyes?"

"That is what we are hoping," Atair grudgingly agreed.

"What of the snowfall since we departed?" Lord Grey asked.

"'Tis unfortunate," Catarine replied, "but if the land remains undisturbed and the snow has melted, there still may be tracks you can see."

"Regardless," Trálin said, his mind working through the glut of information, "I know many people throughout Scotland. If English knights pass, they will tell me."

She gave a relieved sigh.

"Once the king and queen are freed and if I canna see any tracks, once I can reach trusted sources, I will send runners to search for information." He paused. "I will try my best, but I can nae promise we will find the men who killed your uncle."

Her face solemn, she nodded. "We understand."

A thought occurred to him. Stunned, he stared at Catarine. "You said your father was a king?"

Confusion wrinkled her brow. "Indeed."

"Then you are . . ."

"A princess," she said.

"A princess," he repeated, the words tasting like dust. Though he was a noble high in the ranks, she was the daughter of a king. "And the man to whom you are betrothed?"

"A prince," she supplied. "And instead of the formalities while we travel, I ask again that as my men do, call me Catarine. And unless a formal occasion, 'my lady' works as well."

Lord Grey's eyes clouded. "'Tis nae—"

"Proper?" she interrupted. "'Tis the way of the Otherworld."

The grimace on his mouth tightened. "If you wish."

"I do," she replied.

Atair cleared his throat. "We must inform the men that Lord Grey knows who we are, then leave."

Catarine nodded.

His each step as if laden by stones, Trálin walked beside Catarine toward their makeshift camp. A fairy princess of the Otherworld. Never would he have believed such a fact. Except she'd proved her claim.

And what of his attraction toward her? As if it mattered? She was engaged to a fey prince. And he was committed to serving his king, one who if he didn't reach him in time would be dead.

Snow, fat and thick, plunged down around Trálin. Long past were the light flakes of this morn that were swept away by the wind. The sun's warmth had done them little favor. Another burst of icy wind battered him, and he shielded his face as he trudged forward.

At his side, Catarine glanced over. "How far are we from Stirling Castle?"

He scanned the mountains looming before them. "As long as we have no delays, at best, another day's hard travel."

Fir branches weighed by a thick blanket of snow swayed against the wind. Trálin shoved aside a branch, and was rewarded by a blast of hard-edged snow. With a curse, he wiped the icy shards from his face, and pushed onward. Soft crunches of the fey warriors moving behind him blended with the wind.

"There is a pass ahead," Trálin said.

She shoved aside another limb. "Would it nae be faster to cross the open field?"

"Nae with the snow so deep," he replied. "Nor is it safe. This high up, there are many openings in the cliffs. We have no way of knowing what dangers the snow is covering and must take every precaution."

As they topped the next hill, the two peaks framing the pass came into view. The fierce crests of stone and ice stood like ominous guards to the break in the land he'd so often used.

She gasped. "'Tis beautiful."

"It is," he replied, as he took in the steep snow-covered peaks, "and dangerous. A footpath skirts the cliffs, but we must be careful." He glanced at her and arched a brow. "You can nae cast a spell to bring us to Stirling Castle?"

A smile tugged at her mouth. "Nay, nothing so grand. A love spell, mayhap giving someone meddling a twinge or two, but naught more."

"I thought the fey held many powers?" Trálin asked, thankful the tension between them had eased.

Amusement sifted in her eyes. "The bards of your world find many a tale to spin of our abilities."

"Alas, I have been duped," Lord Grey said.

She smiled. "You and many others."

"Nor should he be telling anyone else of our origin," Atair said, shooting her a warning look.

The lightness of the moment faded.

Trálin nodded. "I will say naught." In silence, he trudged forward, fighting to ignore the pain in his side. Without the white willow bark Catarine had given him to ease the pain, he would never have been able to continue.

As they neared the top of the heavily wooded land, the rush of water echoed from far below. He shoved aside a large limb. "Blast it."

"What is wrong?" Atair asked, moving to his side.

"Look ahead." Trálin pointed to where large limbs smeared with snow hung like broken arms across a narrow expanse above a gorge.

Atair shielded his eyes, studied the landscape. "I see naught but fallen trees and snow."

"Look farther to the left," Trálin said. "There is a narrow path that follows the cliff, connected by a wooden bridge."

"I see it now," Atair said.

"Since I was here last, there must have been a landslide that covered the entrance to the bridge." Frustrated with the delay, Trálin searched the sheer cliff and the sharp angle of the mountain on either side, then met the lead warrior's hard gaze. After their confrontation this morning, he'd made no friends with this man. "We will have to climb over the debris to reach the bridge. With the snow atop, 'twill make the crossing dangerous."

"But navigable," Atair said.

Trálin glanced toward Catarine. "Do you think you can make it?"

"I can hold my own," she replied.

"Stay behind me." Trálin stepped into the clearing and started up the steep incline. His boot slipped once, then again. On the third try he found a solid foothold. "Careful, the rocks are covered with ice."

Without the shield of trees, wind thick with snow rushed past.

As Catarine stepped forward, she slipped.

"Careful now," Trálin said as he caught her arm and steadied her.

"My thanks." She glanced back, struggled to see the last warriors in the line. "The snow is falling harder."

"Aye," Atair agreed. "A storm is moving in."

Uneasy, she studied the bulky limbs covering the ancient wooden bridge rocking to and fro.

"What is wrong?" Trálin called back.

"The bridge is swaying," she replied.

Concern darkened Lord Grey's eyes. "Are you afraid?"

"Nay." The truth. The bridge didn't terrify her. 'Twas heights.

"Come," Trálin urged. "We must reach the other side before the worst of the storm hits."

With a fortifying breath, she shoved up the slippery incline.

Trálin reached the first fallen tree, caught a gnarled root, and pulled himself up. He reached down. "Give me your hand."

The twist of roots of the fallen tree reached into the snow-thickened sky like bony fingers. She shivered, moved closer to the time-battered bridge. "I can make it."

A look of pure exasperation settled on his face. "Aye, of that I am confident. Now let me help you."

He must see her nerves. So be it. Catarine laid her hand in his strong one. Wind tugged at her hair and with his aid, she half-climbed, half-pushed through the tangle.

"Steady now," Trálin said as she halted on the trunk, and stared at the wooden bridge.

A strong gust of wind pummeled her, and she started to slip. She clutched a nearby root and kept her balance. Barely. She refused to give in to her fears or to look down. Her realm depended on the success for their mission.

Trálin's mouth thinned. "Hang on to me as we cross."

Her body trembling, she nodded. Snow-drenched gusts of wind battered her, the hard flakes like needles upon her skin. With her free hand, she caught the thick braided hemp rope secured along the bridge posts. Half-bent to keep her balance, step by treacherous step, she followed Trálin as he worked his way across the wooden bridge.

Wind howled past.

The bridge rocked in a frenzied dance.

A loud crack echoed from behind.

Catarine whirled. The limb of an enormous fir broken by the fierce wind swung wildly high above the warriors. Another gust of wind tossed the half-torn branch up. With a snap, the large limb tore, then fell.

"Sionn, watch out!" Catarine yelled.

The fey warrior glanced up. With a curse, he dove to the side.

Snow spewed as the bristled branch hit, the whip of wind hurling away the flakes.

Her heart pounding, she searched the mottled bank for her men. All there. "Sionn, are you all right?"

Snow dusted his blond hair as the lean warrior met her gaze. He nodded.

Thank God.

"Hurry," Trálin yelled back.

Her entire body trembling, she stepped forward. The wood groaned, held. She slowly made her way, climbing over fallen branches, several half-caught and twisted in the hemp. Holding the rope tight, she took another step. As her foot settled on the next slat, the wood gave.

She screamed.

Trálin reached back, caught her hand, and helped her climb back on the bridge. "The falling limbs must have damaged the wood. And with the blasted snow and branches, you canna see." He frowned at where the fey warriors had started to make their way onto the bridge. "Atair," he called, "pass to the others that the bridge is damaged in places."

Her senior fey warrior nodded.

Her body trembling from her near accident, she glanced down. Stilled. Far below, the churn of water pounded with angry slaps against the banks. With each slam against boulders littered within the surging water, the spray hurled up, hard blasts of white to coat thick icicles longer than a man.

"Catarine?"

At the concern in Trálin's voice, she met his gaze.

"We are over halfway," he said as he gave her hand a squeeze. "You can make it."

She nodded. If she spoke, he'd hear the fear in her voice. With her hand tight in his, she made her way across, each step as if a miracle given.

Several paces from the opposite ledge, a gust of wind slammed them.

With an ominous groan, the bridge began to rock.

"Hold the rope tight!" Trálin ordered.

Catarine's grip on the weathered line tightened. In moments, the swaying began to gentle.

He tugged her hand.

Relief swept her as he stepped onto the opposite ledge of the gorge. Now to—

A loud rumbling echoed from above.

She glanced up.

From the top of the mountain, a huge mass of snow and debris raced down the slope, growing with each moment.

"Avalanche!" Trálin pulled her toward him. "Catarine, jump!"

Fear tore through him as Catarine's fingers clutched his, her eyes wide with terror as the avalanche grew closer. "Move, lass!"

Her body shaking, she started forward.

Snow and debris crashed against her, jerked her from his hold, and hurled her onto the rocking bridge. Bloody hell! Trálin dove. Snow slapped his face as he grabbed her hand. He caught a post wedged in the sheer rock behind him, and clung tight.

"Hold on!" His arms aching, he pulled her toward the ledge.

Clumps of snow pummeled the wooden slats of the bridge as they moved back.

A loud groan echoed.

Hemp snapped. The wood beneath her shuddered, sagged.

God no! "The bridge is going!" he yelled. Adrenaline pumping through him, Trálin wrapped his free arm around a sturdy pole, shoved to his feet, tugged.

Catarine's body jerked against him.

He hung on.

Barely.

The slide of snow surged around them with a thunderous roar. The upheaval slowed, then another clutter of debris-laden snow plowed into her.

Muscles in his arm burned as he strained to hold her as she was tossed out, then slammed back against the ledge.

Swinging wildly from the end of his arm, she screamed. "Trálin!"

"Hold on, lass!" He clung tight, the churn of the river raging far below like a mutilated wash of death. He would nae lose her! "Dig your foot in the snow on the side of the cliff and push!"

Through the clearing tumble of snow, dazed eyes stared at him.

Blast it. She was in shock. "Lass," he yelled, his breaths rolling out in puffs of broken white, "Dig your foot into the bank. When I tell you to, push!"

Catarine blinked. Terror widening her eyes, she dug her boot onto a half-crumbled ledge.

"Now!" He pulled.

Face strained, she shoved. Her upper body slid up.

"Again!" he urged as he tugged.

Her breaths coming fast, she wedged her foot on a higher stone and pushed up.

Wind, bitter and cold, battered his face. He gritted his teeth, and inch by painful inch, he hauled her up.

Her foot digging closer into the top of the bank, Catarine shoved, came over the edge, and collapsed against him.

They tumbled back. Body trembling, he held her tight. He'd almost lost her. "Th-thank God you are safe."

"I . . . My warriors!" On unsteady limbs, she pushed herself up.

He shoved to his feet.

Through the thick whirl of snow, on the opposite bank, the remnants of the wooden bridge slapped the wind-battered rock in hopeless disarray. Several warriors lay sprawled along the cliff's edge. Sionn clung to the top of the bank, and Atair clutched a half-broken post, his feet hanging off the cliff. Atair caught Drax's offered hand. The warrior pulled him to his feet, then both scrambled away from the ledge.

Trálin did a quick count as on the opposite bank, snow blustering past. "Miraculously, they are all alive."

Her body trembling, Catarine cupped her hands over her mouth. "Is anyone injured?" she yelled.

One by one the warriors shook their heads.

"Thank God," she whispered.

The image of her hanging over the ledge left Trálin shaking. "How fare thee?"

Her breaths coming fast, she nodded. "Fine."

Worry dredging his face, her senior warrior looked across the gorge. "Any injuries?" he yelled.

She shook her head. "Nay."

A blast of snow-laden wind battered her senior fey warrior's face as he took in the broken bridge twisting in the wind. Then he scanned the sheer sides of the gorge before looking back. "Where can we cross?"

"You and the others will have to backtrack," Trálin yelled back. "Once you are at the bottom of the ben, make your way around the base and come up from the south."

A strong gust thick with snow howled past, temporarily blinding his visibility across the gorge.

When the sweep of snow cleared, Atair held his hand up to his ear. "What?"

Blast it. 'Twas difficult to talk, much less hear. Trálin gestured toward the valley from where they'd traveled, made a big half-circle with his hand. "Backtrack!"

Atair grimaced. "What about Stirling Castle?"

At the lull of the wind, Trálin cupped his hands to his mouth. "You will arrive at the base of the cliffs below Stirling Castle. Meet us there at the copse of trees."

Atair glanced toward Catarine. "Take care!"

"I will be fine," she called.

Atair hesitated, then gave a curt nod toward Trálin. "Keep her safe!"

Lord Grey nodded. 'Twas nae as much the fey warrior's worry over her safety as much as her being alone with him that bothered the man. As if their separation was by choice?

With a wave, Atair turned and motioned for the fey warriors to follow. Wind swirled around them as they trudged down the icy incline toward the protection of the forest.

When the last warrior had disappeared into the thick firs, Trálin faced Catarine. "You hit the cliff hard. Are you sure you have no injuries?"

She gave him a flicker of a smile. "I am a bit shaken, but fine."

Fine? Had he nae held her as she'd slammed against the cliff? Odds were she was injured. "Would you tell me if you were hurt?"

Blond hair torn from her braid extended against the sharp breeze in wild disarray as Catarine watched him. And remained silent.

"Blast it, being stubborn will do naught in the end but endanger your life. Lass, if you are hurt, tell me."

"My injury is nothing so dramatic."

As if he bloody cared about drama. "Where is it?"

She pointed to her upper right thigh. "When I slammed against the ledge, I hit a rock. I believe 'tis naught but a bruise. Had it been any more, I couldna stand."

Stubborn to the last. "Walk with me a few steps. Tell me if you feel any sharp pains."

Turquoise eyes narrowed. "I know how to check for injuries."

"Do it."

With a scowl, she took several careful steps, then shook her head. "Naught but deep soreness."

Neither had he caught her wincing with any seriousness, exposing the sign of extreme pain. "As we travel, let me know if your injury feels worse."

Her eyes narrowed. "Do you always give such dictates, Lord Grey?"

At the irritation in her voice, he shoved away a smile. "Only to those I care about."

Frustration shadowed her eyes. "I thought we clarified that 'tis a poor decision to care about the other."

Trálin arched a brow. "Did we agree on that?"

"We must." Regret weighed in her voice.

"'Twould be wise." But he found thoughts of nae thinking about her, caring, far from a choice. Nor would he reveal as much. Both had their own lives, destinies made, hers nae in this world.

With a hard swallow, she tugged her cape tighter against the slash of wind. "How long will it take my warriors to reach Stirling Castle?"

He rubbed his fingers through his beard. "Given the conditions, if they make good time, two days."

Her face paled. "If your king does nae heed his captor's wishes, by then he could be long dead."

As if he bloody wasn't aware of the fact. "Aye."

"Do you think King Alexander will cede to his abductor?"

"Nay," Trálin replied. "King Alexander is a proud man. He would die first."

"Which is what is going to happen if we do nae reach him." Catarine scraped her teeth over her lower lip. "What are we going to do?"

"I refuse to believe we will nae arrive in time," he said. "Come, we have little time to waste. If your leg begins to hurt, tell me."

Her mouth tightened. "There is no time for delay. If I canna keep up, leave me behind."

He rounded on her. "We will discuss that *if* it becomes an issue."

An issue? Her life against his king's? Nay, the decision 'twas simple. Regardless of Trálin's wishes, if she became a detriment to their reaching his sovereign in time, he *would* go on alone. Nae that she would tell him that now. He would waste precious time and argue.

Lord Grey started forward.

With a shaky exhale, Catarine followed as he climbed over the large banks of snow. She'd come so close to dying. When the wooden bridge had collapsed, she thought she'd fall to her death.

But he'd saved her life.

Humbled by his selfless action, she kept pace, ignoring her leg that throbbed as if beaten. 'Twas lucky an injured leg was all she suffered.

A strong gust pummeled them.

Trálin glanced up, frowned. "I had hoped to make it to shelter before the storm hit," he shouted, his voice broken by the rush of wind.

She squinted as she searched the blur of white. "I see naught to take cover in."

"I know of a place nearby."

Nearby? Again she studied the battered terrain, saw naught to offer shelter. And what of those who had abducted the king and queen? Had they reached their destination? She prayed they were slowed by the storm as well.

Step by step, she forged against the howl of wind. Dark, angry clouds thickened overhead, and the light darkened to a murky gloom.

A distance down the trail, Trálin veered away and started to climb.

"Where are you going?"

"'Tis hard to see," he called back, "but up a ways lies a cave where we can rest."

A distance up the incline, against the blur of tossed snow, she caught the slight outline of an opening. Exhausted, Catarine followed, stepping where his boots had broken the snow.

After climbing over several large rocks, Trálin turned, extended his hand, and shot her a frown. "I know your leg is bothering you; do nae refuse my help."

"Why would you think I would?"

He arched a brow. "Because you are stubborn, proven overmuch this day."

She tried nae to be charmed by his concern, failed. "So I am." She laid her hand in his.

Trálin helped her up. "Duck," he cautioned as he led her below a large rock overhang.

They stepped inside. Blocked by the timeworn rock, the blast of wind ceased. Thankful, she took in the surroundings. At the entry of the cave, snow tumbled past, but deeper inside, a layer of dirt covered the floor, the cave large enough to fit her warriors if they had made it across. Where were they now? Had they made it to the base of the mountain? Wherever they were, she hoped they, too, had found a place to keep out of the weather to rest this night.

"Sit and rest, lass."

With slow, aching steps, she walked toward the back of the shelter. Trálin hurried to her side. "Let me help you."

"Thank you."

He wrapped his arm around her waist and led her to the back.

A soft groan fell from her lips as she settled on the flat rock. Body throbbing, her mind weary with exhaustion, she closed her eyes.

Pebbles and dirt shifted, and she felt the solid warmth of his body, alerting her that he'd settled next to her. "How bad does your leg hurt?"

"A good bit. After a night's rest, I am confident I will be able to continue."

A muscle worked in his jaw. "We will see how your leg feels in the morning. At best, 'twill be sore and stiff."

And if she was nae fit to travel, she would remain behind.

Eyes dark with concern, Trálin watched her. "You have had a rough day of it."

She'd fortified herself to maintain her composure, to try and keep the mayhem of this day from her thoughts, but the exhaustion and the soft concern in his voice unleashed the terror churning in her mind.

Tears burned her eyes, and her entire body trembled. "I almost d-died."

Firm hands drew her against his chest. Tender fingers stroked her hair. "But you didna. And miraculously, no one was hurt."

Images of the splintering bridge, the hurl of snow as the river churned far below, ravaged her mind as if a curse. A shudder tore through her. "Had we been a moment slower in crossing, had my men been closer to us——"

"But we were nae and everyone is safe." Outside, the rush of wind roared as if a battle fought. "You are cold." He released her and stood. After he'd removed his cloak, he tucked it around her, then sat beside her and drew the remainder around him.

"M-my thanks," she said as she snuggled closer. "The warmth is welcome."

"Aye."

"As is the company."

Desire flickered in his eyes, and her body stirred with need. With their awareness of each other, she must choose her words with care. Now was nae the time to think of him, or of their kiss. She was promised to Prince Zacheus. A fact which, when around Trálin, seemed to fade.

Shaken by the depth Lord Grey made her feel, she shifted back to the safer, however unnerving, topic. "I still canna believe the bridge collapsed."

"The falling trees must have weakened it," he replied, his voice grim. "Against the weight of the avalanche, the aged bridge had nay chance."

And she had almost died. She shivered. After such a terrifying event, how could she nae relive the near fatal moment? She would have nightmares, of that she had no doubt.

A blast of snow swept past the entry, erasing the forest or any other discernible feature. The howl of wind quieted, and the forest below came into view.

"Trálin?"

"Aye, lass?"

She replied, trying to keep her focus off their being alone, or how she wanted him with each breath. After saving her life this day, however much they'd tried to fight it, they'd formed a bond, which served to further complicate everything.

"You said there is a secret tunnel through which we can gain entry and reach the king?"

"Aye, once inside Stirling Castle, normally 'twould be easy to find where the king and queen are held," he replied. "But as the king's personal guard, if anyone is about there is the risk that I will be recognized."

"How can we disguise you?"

He gave her a dry smile. "We?"

Realization hit her of his intent "You will nae leave me outside while you risk your life."

"Catarine," he said, his voice soft, "'tis too dangerous for you to come along. There is a place inside the tunnel where you will stay until my return."

She crossed her arms. "We made a deal."

"One that still stands."

She stared at him in disbelief. "You think I would expect you to assist me in finding the English knights if I do nae help you?"

"Aye. You need me to see if I can find any tracks."

She shot him a withering look. "Like it or nae, I am going inside with you."

Anger sparked in his eyes hot and quick. "You will remain hidden near the entry. 'Tis too dangerous, and I will nae risk your being hurt or worse."

"And your life means naught?"

A muscle worked in his jaw. "'Tis my king."

"And my oath I have given you, one I canna break." She unfolded her arms. "With my father a king, do you nae think I know the dangers, the risks involved?"

"Nay," she said when he made to speak. "I am a warrior, trained to fight."

"Bedamned, in Scotland women are nae warriors."

"Exactly," she replied, "so we have the advantage. The men who abducted your king will expect me to be little threat."

"I—"

"What?" she demanded.

He arched a weary brow. "I do nae like it."

A smile touched her lips. "Nor, as a stubborn Scot, would I expect you to."

He grunted. "I may be stubborn, but I scrape the surface when compared to you."

"You agree I will go inside with you then?"

After a long moment, he nodded.

Satisfied on this point she'd won, Catarine leaned back. "I assure you, you will nae regre—"

"As my wife."

She stilled, the thoughts ignited by his words dangerous. Forbidden. "What?"

Laughter twinkled in his eyes. "Nae as my real wife, only a claim for the sake of cover."

Unease flickered inside. "I do nae like it."

He frowned. "Why?"

Did he nae understand? "While we are inside Stirling Castle, I can never agree that I am your wife. If so, we would be handfasted. The consequences of such to the peace in my realm would be devastating."

Trálin stroked his beard. "You are a fairy, and nae bound by Scottish law."

"But I am," she replied. "Handfasting originated in the fairy world."

A smile tugged at his mouth. "You jest?"

Wind howled, and an errant burst of snow whirled inside as she stared at him. How she wished she did. "Nay, 'tis the truth."

His smile fled. "How can that be? Handfasting has been a law of the Celts since before annals recorded the event."

"Aye. 'Twas during the time when laws were passed by word of mouth that a fairy placed the notion in the mind of a sleeping laird."

Trálin raised a doubtful brow.

"'Tis true. Though," she said, recalling the tale told around a fire late in the night, "I would nae have wanted to be the culprit once the queen found out of their deed."

"Why?"

"The law is sacred," she explained. "One reserved for the fey. 'Twas never supposed to be shared with humans."

He again drew his fingers through his beard. "Did they ever find who told of the tradition?"

A shiver swept through her. "Aye. He was banished from the Otherworld to Scotland," she explained, her voice grave. "Never again did he see his family, those he loved."

"He was banished to outside the Otherworld?"

The surprise in his voice was overshadowed by hope. Hope she didna wish to hear, or cling to. She nodded.

"Would a life in Scotland be so horrible?"

Nay, with you 'twould be a gift. Words she could never say. "'Tis a different life."

"Mayhap." He lifted her hand in his, pressed a soft kiss upon her hand. "If you were nae promised to another, and I asked you to remain with me in Scotland, would you?"

Chapter Six

If you were nae promised to another, and I asked you to remain with me in Scotland, would you? At Trálin's question, Catarine stilled, shaken by the pang of longing that filled her.

"But I am promised." Nerves rattled her voice. As if she could remain unmoved at such a question? From the first they'd made a connection, one that with each day together grew stronger.

Their kiss held but temptations of what might be, and a hint of the possibilities. Possibilities, aye, and so much more she ached to know.

His gaze holding hers, he lifted her hand to his mouth and pressed a soft kiss upon her knuckles. "Why are you avoiding answering my question?"

Shaken by what he made her feel, she withdrew her hand. "'Tis unfair to ask me." More so with them alone inside this cavern as the snowstorm raged outside and trapped her with him to face the dangerous truth.

Silence stretched between them, broken by the howl of wind and rattle of distant branches. "Because you are betrothed to Prince Zacheus?"

"Aye, but more, because 'tis forbidden for one of the fey to be with a human, or help them."

He hesitated. "But you agreed to help me free my king and queen."

"We are desperate to find who is behind the murder of my uncle, and I believe due to circumstance, my decision will be supported by my father."

"And what of my question?"

She shook her head. "Regardless of my wishes, with the upheaval between the realms, 'tis a marriage I canna change."

Tender green eyes watched her as he stroked the soft curve of her cheek. "But what if you could?"

Images of them living in Scotland flickered through her mind, of their laughter, the joy of waking up each morn by his side, and their nights of making love. She exhaled a shaky breath. What was she thinking?

"We met but yesterday," she replied, frustrated she'd allowed herself to consider his words, more to be enticed by them. "I know little about you. By your actions I believe you are a man I can trust. But"—she shot him a warning look—"do nae think my attraction to you keeps me from noting your other less desirable characteristics."

"My other less desirable characteristics?" he asked, the hint of a smile driving her frustration deeper.

"Aye, one being your arrogance."

His smile faded. "Arrogance?"

Fine, let him be upset, 'twas safer. "Arrogant if you would think I would sacrifice my realm's peace for you."

A slash of red colored his cheeks. "My question nae has any consequence unless 'tis your desire as well in wanting what I ask."

"I . . ." Her anger fell away. She was ashamed she'd become unsettled on but supposed circumstance.

He muttered a curse. "My apologies, 'twas nae my intent to upset you."

Lord Grey was right. If her desire wasna the same, his question wouldna have mattered. "I was being foolish."

He watched her for a long moment as if deliberating the safest way to reply. With a sigh, Lord Grey laid his head back and closed his eyes.

Frustrated at his silence when her mind lay in turmoil, she tugged the cape tighter. "Are you going to sleep?"

He peered out of half-open lids, then closed them. "Nay, I was thinking."

"About?"

"How to conceal my identity."

"Oh."

"Methinks," he said in a teasing tone, "'tis a prudent topic."

And one *she* should have raised. 'Twas dangerous to linger on topics of *them*.

"I will shave my beard," he said, "which should change my image enough for the brief time we will be in Stirling Castle." He opened his eyes and drew his hands through the well-groomed curve of rust-colored hair. "Though, I will miss its warmth."

His last comment pulled a smile to her lips.

"You find my freezing funny, lass?"

At the false despair in his voice, her smile grew. "'Twill grow back quick enough."

He shifted to his side. "Easy enough for you to say, you have never had the luxury of a beard, nor the irritation of having to regrow one."

A laugh slipped out. "Nor would I. 'Twould stir more than one tongue."

A smile, full and wide, curved his handsome mouth. "It would."

Her thoughts shifted to Stirling Castle. "If the castle is a massive labyrinth, how will you find out where King Alexander and his queen are being held?"

"I believe they will be held in the royal residence."

"And if nae?"

He shrugged. "Then we will have to search, which is why I mentioned before that 'tis best to slip inside Stirling Castle late at night. There will be minimal guards about and most residents will be abed. The last thing they will expect is but a man and a woman to try and free King Alexander and Queen Margaret."

True. Catarine took in the fading light outside the snow-smeared opening, the rough chill that, despite her every attempt to block it, slipped through her cape. She shivered.

"Are you cold?"

"A bit. More concerned for the safety of your king and queen."

His mouth tightened into a grimace. "As am I. King Alexander will never comply with the abductors' demands."

And he and his wife would be murdered. Coldness swept Catarine, understanding too well the dangers a sovereign faced, her uncle's murder and the current threat to her family proof.

"Are you hungry, lass?"

At the reminder of food, her stomach growled. Heat slid up her cheeks. "Forgive me."

"'Tis naught to be embarrassed about." He reached beneath his cape and withdrew a small wrapped leather bundle, then unrolled it.

In the dim light, she tried to discern the contents. "Bread?"

"Oatcakes," he replied.

"I have never heard of them before."

"A staple of Scotland. They will sate the worst of your hunger." He glanced outside, where the wind howled. "As much as I would prefer a heartier fare, with the storm blowing and the snow cutting off any ability to see more than a pace ahead, 'tis foolish to try to weather the storm to snare a rabbit."

She took the offered round, took a bite, and chewed. "They are made with honey?"

"Aye, to help bind the oats when they are baked."

"My thanks." She took another bite.

In silence they ate. Every so often, a blast of wind hurled errant flakes into the cave's entry.

Another gust of wind swept past, and a large flake whooshed inside, spiraled deeper, and one landed on the tip of her nose.

Amused, Trálin reached over and wiped the flake away. "You look like a pixie," he teased.

"Mayhap because that is what I am."

The humor of the moment faded. "That you are." In silence, Trálin ate his last bite. As if knowing she belonged to another made him want Catarine less? He cast a covert glance toward her.

Alone.

With naught between them but long dark hours ahead. And to stay warm, they needed to lay with their bodies close. Before, they'd had the warriors' presence to smother any desire. Now, they had no one.

Catarine cleared her throat and edged closer. "'Tis best if we conserve our body heat."

His body stirred, and he struggled to tamp down the desire. Failed. Bloody hell, they'd lain here but moments and he was in pain. By morn he would be in agony.

Tense silence fell between them.

She shifted. "The snow is coming down fast."

Working to ignore the softness of her body against his, he studied the steep slope, the buildup against the large angled rocks. "'Twill be difficult travel for us and your warriors."

"I pray they have found shelter as we."

"If nae," Trálin said, "no doubt they have built one similar to that we made last night."

"Though I know my men will be fine, I canna help but worry."

He sat up, secured the cape around her.

"What are you doing?" she asked.

"Too much wind is coming in from the side," Trálin said as he walked to the exit. "I need to stack a few rocks and sticks to make a windbreak." And however practical, also to take a reprieve from lying next to her.

Boots upon rock scraped as she tossed aside the cape and started toward him. "I will help."

An argument came to mind, but he dismissed it. She'd long since assured him of her independence and would nae appreciate his gallantry.

In short, they worked together to haul loose rocks and sticks to the western edge of the overhang, the icy wind quickening their pace.

As they settled back on their pallets, he reached inside his cape. "Did you want another oatcake before you go to sleep?"

"I am fine." Catarine loosened her braid. Her blond hair spilled out in luxurious disarray.

Images of her naked and in his bed slammed into his mind. His body hardened. Bloody hell.

Her hands slowed. "What is wrong?"

Her innocent question served to fuel his lust-filled fire. "Wrong?" Trálin asked, fighting to sound normal.

"You look as if you are in pain."

Pain? Nay, 'twas a poor choice of words for the way his body was burning for her. "'Tis only that I am exhausted," he replied. "Naught that a good night's sleep willna fix."

"You are sure?" she asked, her voice sincere.

Blast it. If he caught more than a whit of sleep with her body flush against his, 'twould be a miracle. "Aye."

She slipped beneath their makeshift pallet, tugged the cape up to her chin.

He gritted his teeth, lifted the cape, and climbed beneath. As if bloody decorum served him well when 'twas freezing? He lay with his body flush against hers. Heat, warm and luxurious, enveloped him—along with her scent of woman and innocence. He gritted his teeth. He could do this. Aye, he was a man who'd fought many a war, faced the toughest warriors.

Catarine snuggled closer.

Desire surged through him. "Lass," he all but roared.

She sat up, the cape spilling to her lap. "You are hurting?"

"Nay," he said, his voice a bit rougher than he'd meant. "Why are you shifting about?"

She hesitated.

"Tell me," he said, frustrated with himself. 'Twas nae her doing that'd landed them here alone.

"I am cold."

He almost laughed. Warmth, she sought but warmth, nae his touch or to have him slip deep inside her wetness, a sure way to forget the cold. He almost groaned at the thought.

"Come back under the cape, lass."

"After you."

"I am nae the one sitting up."

"Oh." With an exhale of exasperation, she lay beside him.

He tugged the cover back up over them both. "Good night, lass."

Catarine turned her back to him. "Good night." After a long moment, her soft sigh wrapped around him like a caress. What would it be like to go to bed each eve with her by his side? To have her turn to his touch? *A fine dream, lad. She's a fairy and you're a human.*

"Trálin?"

Her sleep-thickened voice was a luxury unto itself. One that he could listen to forever. "I thought you were going to sleep?"

"I will," she replied. "But I just realized I have nae asked about your family. Do you have brothers?"

"Why do you ask?"

The cape rustled as in the dim light, she turned to face him. She shrugged. "Curious."

"One. Faolan."

"Gaelic for wolf," she said.

"It is," Trálin replied. "On the night he was born, a wolf was howling outside the castle. Our father thought it an omen. Hence his name."

"Are you close to your brother?"

Memories of him and Faolan growing up flickered through his mind. "Very much so. Though I am firstborn and inherited the title of earl along with Lochshire Castle, 'tis nae a point of contention between us. He lives there now, caring for our home while I am away."

"I am pleased to hear such," she said. "Many a time the lust for power ruins a family's close bond."

Wind roared outside as Trálin folded his hands behind his head, laced them. That his brother chose to remain at Lochshire Castle and ensure it was well guarded pleased him, but how long would that be? Though their bond was strong, his brother had made known his wish for his own title and lands. Nor could he blame him.

"Trálin?"

The soft wisp of her voice wrapping around his name made him shudder with need. "Another question?"

"But one. Is there a . . ."

"On with it, lass."

"Are you engaged as well?"

Stunned by her question, he stared at her murky form in the fading light. "You are a fairy and engaged, you know that I am attracted to you, and you want to know if I am betrothed?"

Catarine cleared her throat. "I never should have asked."

Understatement. As if he needed a reminder that they were damnably attracted to each other.

Catarine rolled over, again putting her back toward him.

Thankful, he started to tug the cape up, when she inched back, her beautiful bottom a hair's breadth away. As if a man sentenced, he exhaled. "Are you settled?"

"Aye."

"Get some rest, lass. With the upcoming trek in the morn, we both will need all we can get."

Silence, fractured by the howl of the wind, echoed through the chamber.

"Catarine?"

Her soft breaths fell out.

Hair slightly mussed, in the fading light, she looked every inch the fairy. Except, he'd witnessed her wield a blade. A fairy mayhap, but far from the delicate image from the tales bards told around the campfire. And for the next few days they'd be together. After, she would return to her world. Sadly, however much he wished otherwise, he'd have to let her go.

Catarine opened her eyes.

Blackness.

Curious what had awoken her, she pushed on the cold stiff cloth and sat up, bumped something firm. Memories rolled back in.

Of Trálin.

Of their sleeping together throughout the night for warmth.

"Are you okay, lass?"

His sleepy burr rumbled through her, and awareness ignited. She shoved the dangerous thoughts away. "Aye. I woke up and for a moment wasna sure where I was."

He shifted closer. "'Tis cold. Come back beneath the cape."

With a shiver of need, Catarine slid beneath the thick cover.

The wind howled outside.

"No, I have no woman I care about."

Heart pounding, too aware of him in the dark of the night with naught around them but each other, she stilled. "Why are you telling me now?"

"You asked."

As if knowing there was no other woman in his life helped put him out of her mind? "I asked you hours ago. You are a frustrating man, Trálin MacGruder."

"So I have been told."

The smugness in his voice ate at her composure. "And may I add charming," she said dryly.

"And what did you expect my mood to be hours before the sun rises?"

A valid point. Outside the entry, as her eyes adjusted to the darkness, meager moonlight reflected off the vast expanse of white, the shadows of the forest as if smears against the pristine swath.

She glanced at the Scot, found hints of moonbeams slipping across his handsome face. "What is the favorite place you have visited?"

"You are still awake?" Lord Grey asked, his voice gruff.

"We will soon be with my men and the chance to talk about your past will be lost."

"Mayhap for the best."

Sadness touched her. "Is it?"

He hesitated. "Catarine, do you think 'tis wise for us to share more about ourselves?"

She lay back, closed her eyes.

"Catarine?"

"I am thinking."

He laughed.

"You are making fun of me.

"Nay," he replied. "I am trying to decide if I am going crazy."

She turned, touched his mouth to feel his smile.

He stilled, gave a slow exhale, and his smile fell away. "'Tis dangerous."

Her entire body vibrated with awareness. "I only wanted to feel your smile."

Trálin shifted, his body now aligned with hers, his breath warm and soft upon her brow. With a slow, delicate sweep, his thumb slid across her cheek.

"That is nae my mouth."

"Aye," he replied, "with how I'm feeling about you this moment, I dare nae be foolish enough to touch it."

Too aware of him, Catarine swallowed hard. "Why?"

"Because I might kiss you, and with as much as I want you," he replied, his voice rough with desire, "I am unsure if I would stop."

Chapter Seven

As Trálin forged through the snow, his words from last night to Catarine rolled through her mind. What would it be like making love with her? Though she was innocent of a man's touch, with the depth of her feelings for him, how could it nae be amazing?

"'Tis knee-deep up here," Trálin called.

"Better than the thigh-deep snow we traveled through earlier this morn," she replied.

Against the morning sunlight crafting prisms in the new snow, he scanned the trail ahead. Since they had departed at first light, wind continued to whip the frozen slide of the ben, shaking the leafless branches with brutal disregard. "Aye," he replied, tugging his cape closer, "but we still have a long way left to travel before we reach Stirling Castle."

"How close are we?"

The hope and fatigue in her voice made his frustration grow. When she'd agreed to aid him in setting his king and queen free, 'twas but a short journey. Instead, she'd become separated from her men and had almost died. Neither did the attraction flaring between them help an already tense situation. "With our slowed pace," Trálin replied, "mayhap another day."

"I will pray that like us, the abductors have been slowed by the storm," Catarine said.

A hope he held as well. Trálin turned and trudged forward. His boot slid on the slick surface, then caught purchase. With a crunch his foot sank into the snow as it had with his every step since they'd departed the cave.

He scanned the crisp layer of snow. Throughout the night the air must have warmed and allowed the surface to begin to thaw, but the sharp drop in temperatures early this morn had hardened the surface into a blanket of thin ice as they'd traveled. As if they needed the blasted hindrance? They'd barely made half the distance they needed to this day.

At his next step, the crusted snow splintered beneath his step, slid over the side. With a shuddering scrape, the fractured chunk plummeted toward the bottom. As if an omen, it slammed against a ledge far below and shattered. Catarine stared down to where the shards lay. "'Tis a long way to the bottom."

Trálin damned the worry in her voice.

"Is there a shortcut we can take?"

"None that I would consider," he replied.

"Because of me?"

Bedamned, why did the lass have to press? "Because 'tis too bloody dangerous."

Shrewd eyes studied him. "Would you take the risk if you traveled alone?"

"Why are you pushing this point, lass?"

"There is a shortcut," she stated.

He muttered a curse beneath his breath. "As if you bloody well do nae know the answer?"

Catarine arched a brow. "And you dare call me stubborn?"

"'Tis naught to make light of."

"On that we agree." Hands on hips, she glanced up the slope, turned. "If we travel over the top, will that take us to Stirling Castle?"

A muscle worked in his jaw. The lass would rile the calmest man. "Aye."

"And 'twould be faster?"

"Indeed."

Catarine arched a questioning brow. "Did you want to lead, or should I go first . . . being a wee lass?"

At her bravado, a smile tugged at his mouth. "Pushy as well."

"Lord Grey, I have been around stubborn men my entire life."

With a frustrated sigh, he studied the steep incline. She was right. If they crossed over the top of the ben, they should make up a good portion of the hours the abductors had ahead of them. 'Twas not the time to ponder how they would free the royal couple, then meet up with the fey warriors, nor the hard travel to bring the king and queen to safety after. Those challenges would come soon enough.

"We will go over the top," he said, "but I will lead."

She remained silent.

He grunted. Wise as well as stubborn—a smart lass indeed. Snow reached his knees as he moved from the trail and started up.

Sweat drenching her brow, Catarine followed Lord Grey's tracks. From his grim expression, he worried for her safety in taking this shortcut. Regardless of the dangers, 'twas the prudent decision.

The sun's golden rays glistened off the hard surface of the snow as she continued, crafting rainbows along the curves of the half-ice-covered rock. For a moment she took in the unexpected beauty, then pushed on. Her breaths coming fast, she shoved her foot upon another rock.

At a staggered crop of rock, Trálin turned. "Take my hand."

Snow whipped her face as she glanced up.

Wedged at the base of a rock, he clung to a sturdy limb, his hand outstretched.

Thankful, she laced her fingers in his, pushed off. Her boot landed next to his.

A grimace on his face, he nodded. "We can take a break here."

Her every muscle ached. "Nay."

"We have made good time."

"Mayhap," she replied, "but until we reach Stirling Castle, 'tis nae good enough."

His mouth a hard line, Lord Grey turned and started up.

A short while later she followed him around the last few boulders to the top. Fatigue weighing on every limb, Catarine halted next to him on a flat snow- and ice-covered rock and stared at the impressive outline in the distance.

Framed by the roll of snow-laden hills and mounted upon a crag stood a fortress of grand magnificence. Culled stone borne by hundreds of men rose into the air with sheer defiance. A shudder wove through her as she looked past the intimidating structure and studied the flat of land beyond, cut by a river that wound in a lazy flow.

"Stirling Castle." Pride filled his voice.

"'Tis stunning," she said. "And as fine as any castle in the Otherworld."

"Indeed?"

Somber, she nodded, well aware that battle-trained men had crafted the design. "With the castle's strategic position, a guard could easily see any who approached."

"Which is why we must keep to the shadows and glens during our descent. However quickly I wish to travel, we must take every precaution to ensure we are nae seen." He rubbed the back of his neck. "At least we have the angle of surprise. Few would dare to cross over the ben."

With the steepness of the slope and the slick crust of snow, 'twas dangerous. "If by chance we are seen, that we are but two will nae offer a threat."

"Normally I would agree," he said. "Because they hold the king and queen hostage, due to the direction we came from, our presence will raise their suspicions."

"We could tell them we risked crossing the top of the ben because we are freezing."

Trálin wiped the snow off of his cloak. "'Twould be the blasted truth."

"Though I have cursed it all day, the wind will keep any loose snow in the air and offer, however thin, a shield." Catarine glanced toward the clear blue skies bright with sunshine, fierce with the whip of cold wind. "But if the wind dies with the night, without clouds and a full moon as we approach, we could easily be seen."

"Then," he said, "we shall hope for the skies to become overcast."

Though Lord Grey made light of the challenges they faced, however much he tried to shield her from it, it was clear he was worried. As if she didna hold the same concerns?

He gestured forward. "On with you now. Lagging behind like a lame mule."

Unbidden, she laughed as she followed him down. "Lame mule?"

He glanced back. "I was trying to charm you. How did I do?"

At the desire in his eyes, the moment shifted to something dangerous. A moment where she could envision him in her life forever.

Catarine halted.

His expression a mix of desire and frustration, Trálin closed the distance. "I find it hard to be with you and nae kiss you."

Her pulse raced. "'Tis a fact I find myself struggling with as well."

Green eyes darkened. "'Twould make a mess of an already convoluted situation."

Throat dry, she nodded. "It would."

On a ragged breath, he lifted her chin. "And be bloody worth it." His mouth claimed hers, hot and hard. As quick he broke the kiss, then stared at her a long moment. "Ah lass, I wish we had met under different circumstance."

Aching at his words, Catarine shook her head. "Trálin, why did we have to meet now? Here?"

Sadness shadowed his gaze, and he stepped back. Wind spiraled between them as if in a myth. "I dinna know the why of it, only that you and I can never be." Regret wrinkling his brow, he turned on his heel and started down the ben.

And if all went well, this night they would free his king and never again would they be alone.

For the best.

Except his passionate kiss lingered on her lips, his tenderness exposing how his feelings were growing toward her. More unsettling, though innocent, Trálin was a man who lured her to give in to temptation, and tread on a forbidden path she'd heard whispers of from women within her castle.

"'Tis a mistake."

At his gruff voice, she jumped. Heat stroked her cheeks as she'd nae noticed he'd halted and was staring at her, his face rough with desire. "What is?"

"By the look in your eyes," he replied, "'tis safer to nae answer."

It was, but often those who took the risks of life were rewarded the most. "Why must we come from different worlds?"

The hard line of his mouth tightened. "And if I came from the Otherworld, with your pledge to handfast with Prince Zacheus, how would it change anything?"

"'Twould nae." She swallowed hard. "'Tis best if we move on."

"Catarine."

The soft burr of his voice slid through her like warmed wine. "What?"

"That you are happy in your life is what I desire. Never can it be more."

Tears burning her throat, Catarine stepped past him and started down the perilous trek. She would focus on their reaching Stirling Castle, on saving his king and queen, then on discovering who had murdered her uncle. To mull over thoughts of a life with Trálin would invite naught but angst.

She stepped around a large boulder. Time would help her forget him, forget the feelings he inspired, forget that for the first time in her life she'd found a man who made her feel complete. As she took her next step, her boot landed on an ice-covered rock and she slipped. Arms flailing, she tried to regain her foothold.

Trálin's hand caught her shoulder. "Careful, lass. 'Twill be slick the entire way down."

Her pulse racing, she nodded, refusing to look at him and allow him to see her tears, the foolish reason for her near tumble. "It will."

"Let me go first," he stated.

"What does it matter?" she asked. "If either of us starts to slide down, neither of us will be able to stop the other."

He strode past her. "Nor will walking with your emotions mulling your thoughts allow you to make wise choices in your steps."

His expression taut, he turned and started down the steep incline.

Trembling, she followed.

Streaks of orange-red sheeted the sky as, halfway down, they reached the clutter of boulders jutting out in a reckless array. Beyond the snow-covered shield rose the land embracing Stirling Castle.

"Do you need to rest?" he asked.

However much she wanted to agree, she shook her head. Except for stopping for short breaks on their way down and a few oatcakes she'd eaten as they'd walked, they'd continued at a grueling pace. Nor did it help that she'd slept little last eve. But, with Stirling Castle in sight, 'twas worth every step.

"Careful," Trálin cautioned as he glanced back. "Though the slope appears smooth, there are many drop-offs hidden beneath the thick snow."

Exhausted, Catarine wiped her brow and nodded. "'Twill be nice to get out of the cold."

"Aye." He started forward.

Shielding her face against the wind, she began her descent. With her each step, clumps of snow broke free, then tumbled down the steep incline before they hit errant rocks to shatter into a mist-laden smear.

Ahead, Trálin navigated the knee-deep drifts. As he passed a clump of shrubs half-covered in the deep snow, he glanced back. "How fare thee?"

"I am fine."

A frown dipped his mouth as he studied her. "Are you sure, lass?"

She forced a smile. "Aye."

Legs trembling from fatigue, she took another step. Snow broke off the edge of the bank before her, then rolled down to slam against a sturdy shrub. Horrific memories of the avalanche and her near death assailed her. Her body tense, she made to take another step; her foot slipped. Catarine steadied herself, barely.

Trálin whirled. "What is wrong?"

Embarrassed to be caught up in her musings, she shook her head and straightened. "Naught. I was but——"

The snowbank beneath her gave way. "Trálin!"

He grabbed for her.

Their fingers touched.

Broke free.

She screamed. Air, cold and brutal, rushed down her throat as she slid down the slope. Blurs of white and dark swept past. "Catarine!" The wind mutilated Trálin's distant shout.

Snow clogged her throat as a shrub down the slope came into focus.

She reached out.

The leafless branch whipped her hands.

Missed!

Ahead, the frozen snow curved over a partially exposed bolder.

Struggling to keep her wits, she shifted her weight to avoid the half-barren ground. She missed the first jut of rock, then was again thrown up. She slammed to the ground.

And began to roll.

Panic tore through Trálin as he hurried down the battered snow trail in her wake.

Far below, Catarine's body continued to roll.

Bedamned! Trálin lunged over the broken bank. Snow battered him as he slid, rocks threatened his precarious balance, but he used his arms and legs in a controlled slide, his fear for Catarine's life growing with every second. He shifted, barely missed a dense leaf-less thicket sprinkled with barren rock.

Far below, Catarine's body came to a halt.

She lay still.

Fear tore through him. Damning the risk, he leaned forward and lifted his legs to increase his speed. The rush of snow hurled past him. Every jolt and bump tossed him, but he shifted his weight and arms to slide faster.

At the bottom as the land began to curve up, he slowed to a stop. Frantic, Trálin jumped to his feet. He stumbled, caught himself, and bolted toward where she lay. Breaths falling out in bursts of white, he knelt beside her, lay his palm on her shoulder. "Catarine?"

She moaned.

Emotion choked him. Thank God she was alive! With a gentle touch, he moved his hands over her body to ensure nothing was broken. A miracle that he felt naught out of place.

"Catarine," he urged, needing her to open her eyes, to talk to him. Too many times had he witnessed knights injured in the cold who'd fallen asleep never to awake. "Catarine, can you hear me?"

As if a gift, turquoise eyes met his. "I-I lost my footing," she breathed. "I tried to catch myself but . . ."

Her pain-filled whisper shook him to the core. "Where does it hurt?"

"Everywhere," she rasped.

"When I checked you, I did nae feel anything broken."

She closed her eyes, and then opened them. "Bruises, then." A whisper of a smile graced her mouth. "I should have been more careful."

"Careful?" he muttered, anger taking hold that she'd blame herself with the dangerous footing. "'Tis icy and the wind is howling like an ornery old woman. In the slippery conditions, you did the best you could."

Another shiver tore through her body. "So c-cold."

Bedamned, she needed to be out of this wind. Trálin glanced toward Stirling Castle seated on the hill above them. Once inside the secret passage, he could use his body heat to warm her.

"Do you think anyone saw us?" she asked.

He glanced toward the castle, caught no sign of moment. "Nay. If so, we would have heard them sound the alarm by now. Can you stand?"

"I-I think so."

Ignoring the aches battering his body, Trálin helped her to her feet. "Take it slow. You had a hard fall."

As she pushed up, her legs gave.

He caught her, set her on the ground. Blast it, he'd missed an injury. "Where does it hurt?"

She rubbed her right thigh. "When I tumbled over the stones, I must have hit my leg."

"Aye, you had a rough fall. Unfortunately, 'twill hurt for several days." Trálin slid his arms beneath her, then picked her up.

"What are you doing?"

"Carrying you into the secret passage."

"I can walk."

"Aye," he agreed dryly. With her shivering in his arms, he started walking.

With a groan, she laid her head against his chest. Her teeth began to chatter. "How much farther?"

"See the large fir ahead?"

She nodded.

"The secret entrance lies behind it." Once inside and safe, if she was too sore to move, he'd leave her with oatcakes and water, then set about freeing the king and queen. Once they'd returned, they'd decide the best way to meet the fey warriors.

"There is a lot of snow around the fir," she said.

He scanned the drifts over their destination, frowned. "Aye." More than he wished to see.

"There is a road beyond. It leads to the castle, does it nae?"

"It does," he replied. "Once we make it past this tree, keep watch for a stone that looks as if it is a cross."

"A stone that looks like a cross? Wouldna such a bold display be noticed by the castle guard and under suspect?"

"The stone stood here long before they built Stirling Castle. The weave of rock was crafted by wind, rain, and time," he explained. "Any suspicion held is long past."

"Interesting."

He shrugged. "It is. Some say 'twas left here by the fey."

"You jest?"

"Nay," he replied, "the Scots are a suspicious lot."

Catarine shivered.

Bedamned, she needed to be warmed. What he wouldn't give for a fire within a chamber awaiting them. Except little time remained for such luxury. The entire mission must be finished before the break of dawn. "We will be inside the secret passage soon."

She nodded.

His admiration for her grew. Few women would endure what she had without complaint. Relief swept him as they reached the firs. Soon he'd have her out of the wind. He ducked beneath the thick, needled branches, and snow shuddered like a white mist around him.

She gestured ahead. "Is that the cross over there?"

He glanced to where she pointed. As he'd remembered, a stone jutted from the earth, now white beneath the assault of winter. Halfway up the stone, chiseled pieces crafted the upper half of a Celtic cross. Every time he'd seen the stone, it always reminded him of forbidden worlds merging. With her explanation of some of the fey cast out of the Otherworld for revealing the secret of handfasting, 'twould seem the mystery behind whoever had made this was solved.

At the half-carved cross he halted. Wind whipped loose snow against his face as he set her on her feet.

Except for a slight grimace, she stood fine.

"Wait here," Trálin said.

She looked around. "Where is the entry?"

"See the large boulder by the firs?"

Catarine nodded.

"'Tis ten paces to the west from the cross."

Intrigue lit her face. "Where no one would ever think to look."

"Aye." He stepped back. "'Twill take but a moment." He headed to the back of the cross, started walking. Ten paces in, he leaned down, brushed away the snow.

The crunch of steps sounded behind him.

He glanced over, found Catarine walking toward him. Trálin focused on digging deeper in the snow.

She halted at his side.

Against his ministrations, the ice-crusted snow broke into little chunks. He muttered a curse, removed his dagger, and jabbed it into the frozen mix.

"Do you want me to help?"

"Nae." Beneath his blade, the icy snow gave way to a slick sheet of ice. His gut sinking, he sat back. "The entry is frozen over."

"Will you be able to open it?"

Frustrated, he glanced up, her face barely visible in the dimming twilight. "Aye, but 'twill take a long time." Time—with her shivering from the cold—they didna have.

Teeth chattering, she knelt and withdrew her blade. "Then we will work together."

Trálin hesitated, then nodded.

Shards of ice flew beneath their daggers, but as the last of the daylight gave way to the haze of night, a thick slab of ice still lay between them and the opening.

"Catarine, stop."

"What?" she asked, her voice weary.

He blew out a rough breath. "We canna get inside."

"Then how are we going to get into Stirling Castle?"

Damning the entire situation, he took her hand. "The only way left."

"And that is?" she asked.

He helped her stand. "Through the castle entry."

Chapter Eight

A pace away from Lord Grey, Catarine stared at him in disbelief. Was he daft? Her body shaking against the cold of the night and aching from her terrifying slide down the steep incline, she shoved to her feet.

"You expect to enter Stirling Castle th-through the main entry?" Catarine shook her head. "'Tis insane."

"And the only way."

She shivered as the snow swirled past, the bitter wind relentless. "As if the guards are going to let you in with but a wee request?"

"Nae for me, but us. And," he said before she could speak, "they will."

The determination in his voice shook her. Concerned for her, and with little hope of protecting them if the guards became suspicious, he feared for her life to where he risked capture, or even death. Her throat tightened at his selflessness. Humbled by his caring, more by his bravery, she nodded.

He withdrew his dagger.

Confused, she frowned. "Why do you need your weapon now?"

He placed the blade in her hands, curled her fingers around the hilt. "As we discussed before, I must change my appearance to nae be recognized. Though far from the place I'd choose, I need you to shave my beard."

Her fingers trembled on the forged handle. "I said naught before as I believed we would have the advantage of the secret tunnel. Already if a guard sees you alone in the castle, more so with the king and queen held within, they would challenge you if nae raise the alarm."

"I expect as much, and while inside I will try to ensure I am nae seen."

"How can you avoid being seen by going through the main entry? I think 'tis p-prudent that we continue breaking the ice away from the secret entry."

"And chance your freezing to death?" he asked, anger storming his voice. "'Tis a risk I refuse to take. Begin shaving me, lass."

As if the blasted, stubborn Scot would see reason? In the first shimmers of moonlight beneath the clear sky, she placed the honed blade against his skin and scraped over his firm jaw. The first lengths of his beard curled free, then were swept away by the wind. With each stroke his squared chin came into view. As she finished, she studied his face in the growing moonbeams, the strong lines a fine portrayal of this warrior. Too aware of him, Catarine continued in silence.

As she took the last stroke, a chill swept her. Fingers trembling, she wiped the blade upon a bit of cloth, then handed it to him. "'Tis done."

With a curse, he sheathed his blade, then swept her into his arms.

Catarine tried to fight him, but she began to shiver uncontrollably. For a moment the newborn night blurred, then her lids drooped. Groggy, she laid her head against his chest.

Trálin muttered a curse as he continued to walk. Her body was growing too cold. "Do nae go to sleep."

She shuddered in his arms, her lids threatening to again slide down. "I find myself so tired."

At her weakening voice, terror ripped through him. "Aye, and we will be before a warm fire soon enough, and then you can sleep." A lie, but he'd tell her anything to keep her awake. Naught guaranteed the guard would allow them in. "You must stay awake."

Silence.

"Promise me," he stated, his voice firm.

"I—I will."

As if he bloody believed her? With her shaking in his arms, he hurried up the slope toward Stirling Castle. With each step along the snow-covered road, he prayed she'd live; with each league closer, he worried they might be killed by suspicious guards upon their arrival.

He cast aside the tale of them being married. If the guards did nae believe him, he wanted no tie of her to him. But what? A simple story would do. He'd explain how he found her freezing and wandering about. As long as the castle guards thought her nae with him, they would give her shelter. And in time, her fey warriors would find and rescue her. In brief, he described his plan to Catarine.

Her moves sluggish, she gave a slow nod of understanding.

Bedamned, never should he have asked for her and her warriors' aid. He'd done naught but put their lives at risk.

The curve of ground angled up, and captured by the sheen of the moon, the daunting fortress he'd visited many times came into full view. Except this time, if the guards learned who he was, he could very well be killed.

Catarine shivered in his arms, and he glanced down. "Are you awake, lass?"

In the moonlight, dazed eyes stared at him.

"Lass?"

"Aye," she replied, her voice slurred.

Bloody hell! Many a time in the winter he'd witnessed warriors taken over by the cold. Slurred speech and the inability to stay awake often foretold their freezing to death.

His legs protesting, he pushed up the steep incline faster.

Cast in the moonlight, fierce stone walls towered before him, imposing culled stone designed to intimidate.

Wind whipped past as he approached the gatehouse.

"Halt, who goes there?" a guard yelled from the wall walk above.

Trálin stopped, looked up. He made out a faint outline of the guard. "A trader. I came across this lass on the icy roads early this morning. Her wagon was destroyed, and her horse had run away. Due to the length we have traveled, she is near frozen and needs warmth posthaste."

Silence.

"Please, let us in," Trálin called up. "If she remains outside much longer, she will die."

"Is anyone else with you?" Suspicion echoed in the guard's voice.

"Nay." And why would their appearance nae raise doubts? The guards held Scotland's king and queen inside and would have been warned to be on alert for anything suspicious.

Long moments passed.

"Open the gates," the guard yelled from above.

Thank God.

A creak, then a telltale rattle of chains echoed into the windswept night. With a clunk, the forged-iron gate clamored closed.

Catarine groaned as he hurried forward. "Steady now, lass, we are almost inside."

"Halt!" a deep voice boomed.

Trálin stopped inside the gatehouse. At least they were out of the wind. "The lass is freezing."

"I know what you stated," the guard replied. "Remain there." The slap of footsteps on cobblestone echoed as he drew close. Fractured light from the torch scraped the curved walls with ominous lashes at his approach. Several more paces and the guard paused. He lifted the torch high. Wary eyes scoured Catarine's pale face, then shifted to him. "Your name."

"Fergus Anecol," he replied, remembering having met a trader in a Highland village who had helped him many times over. If the name was recognized, odds were they would remember the man being a trader. But, with Fergus selling his wares to the north of Scotland, they would nae know the man's description.

The guard grunted. "Never have I heard your name."

Terrified he would refuse them entry, Trálin allowed his fear to reach his voice. "The woman is dying. I will answer any questions later. Please, let us inside. She needs warmth."

A muscle worked in the guard's jaw. "There is little room inside for travelers."

Aye, the guard was under orders to use caution with who was allowed within Stirling Castle. "Please, anyplace where she can be warm will be enough."

With a suspicious eye, the guard scanned the road beyond, a wash of yellow torchlight flickering across a long scar over his left cheek that'd long since healed. Far from looking pleased, he spun on his heel, started off at a fast clip.

"Follow me," the guard snapped.

Relief swept through Trálin as he hurried after the guard.

Inside the bailey, instead of turning toward where the horses were bedded where he'd expected they would be settled, the knight headed toward the keep.

Thank God in heaven. Within she would have heat. He glanced at Catarine. Her pallor beneath the torchlight ignited a new round of fear. "Lass, wake up."

Tired eyes flickered open. "Where are we?" she whispered.

"Stirling Castle," he replied in a low voice. "Soon you will be warm."

She started to nod, but ended up shivering.

Bedamned! At the top of the steps, the guard swung the keep door open, gestured them inside.

Grateful, Trálin carried her in.

"Go near the hearth," the guard said, his voice gruff. "You will sleep there for the night."

"My thanks," Lord Grey replied.

The guard's face grew taut. "Do nae go anywhere else until you depart."

"We willna." *Until Catarine is able to move.*

The fierce-looking man watched them for a long moment. "If I find you have left the great room, regardless if you do nae know the woman, you both will be killed."

Trálin gave a curt nod. Aye, the man was nae taking any chances.

The guard opened the door, strode out, then slammed it shut. Against the torchlight spilling from the sconces on the wall, snow that'd slipped in near the entry spiraled in a hazy wash, then drifted to the floor.

With Catarine trembling in his arms, he walked toward the roaring fire in the hearth. As he neared, several dogs lying near the flames raised their heads, sniffed. With no food offered to them, the mongrels settled back onto the floor and closed their eyes.

In the flicker of light, he noted that scattered about, several women along with their children lay nearby. With the chores finished for the night, the staff would seek the fire's warmth to sleep.

As he neared, he caught the scent of meat and herbs from the earlier meal. His stomach growled. The last time they'd broken their fast had been midday with oatcakes. Mayhap he could talk one of the women within the chamber to fetch Catarine some warm food? 'Twould help her recover.

At their approach, the woman closest to him with her grey hair braided stood and gave them a measuring look. "Who are you?"

At the suspicion in her voice, nerves edged through him. "A trader. I came across this woman on the icy roads early this morning. It took most of the day, but we were able to make it here."

The aged lines on her face settled in horror as her gaze shifted to Catarine. "With the bitter wind, the poor lass is half frozen." The woman hurried over.

Thank God she'd believed him. "She is, which is my greatest concern."

"Come with you now." The woman motioned them forward. "'Tis colder than a beggar's wish outside. While the fire warms her, I will fetch her a bit of wine." She tsked. "Once she is lucid, I will bring you both some stew."

Humbled by her generosity, he nodded. "'Tis deeply appreciated."

"I have stood in her shoes," the woman said. "'Tis a nasty thing to survive such a fate." She motioned to Catarine. "Remove her boots and rub her feet. I will return in a moment." With one last worried look, she crossed to the other side of the hearth to a small pixie-looking girl no more than eight summers and knelt before her. After a few hushed words, the woman rose and hurried off.

Beneath the curious eyes of the surrounding staff, Trálin gently knelt with Catarine beside the hearth.

"Me mum said you would be needing this," a small girl's voice said.

He glanced to his side. The child the woman had spoken to now stood beside them holding out a tattered woolen blanket. Trálin glanced over to where they had made their pallet, and noticed several more blankets still remained spread out for the child and woman.

"My thanks, lass."

The girl's eyes widened, and then she scurried off to her bedding spread near the hearth.

Catarine trembled.

"Easy now." With gentle movements, Trálin removed her cloak, then wrapped her in the blanket. Once he had Catarine settled, he tucked her cloak atop her trembling body, then removed her boots as instructed and began to rub her feet until warmth came to her skin. With everyone in Stirling Castle believing them strangers, he must ensure his actions toward her raised nay questions.

When Catarine's shivers began to lessen, he sat back and breathed a sigh of relief. A part of him found comfort in tending to her, another found regret that their time together would soon end.

Soft steps echoed on the stone floor.

He glanced up.

A goblet of wine in her hands, the woman returned. "'Tis warmed."

Grateful she'd taken time to heat the wine, Trálin nodded as he accepted the handcrafted goblet. "My thanks."

"If you need anything else," she said, "do nae hesitate to ask."

"You are very kind."

She hesitated as she stared at him, and a blush touched her cheeks. "As are you." She turned, walked to where the girl lay curled on the blanket.

An odd comment. They'd never before met. With his beard shaven, mayhap he looked as someone she'd seen before? Catarine moaned, and Trálin dismissed his musings to worry. If the woman recognized him, she would have sounded the alert.

Lord Grey lifted the goblet to Catarine's lips. "Drink, lass."

Sleep-laden lids fought to open, fell back. "W-want to sleep."

"In a bit. For now you must remain awake." He nudged the cup against her mouth. "Take a drink. Please."

Trembling fingers lay atop his. On a soft exhale, she tipped the mug up. Her throat worked. After several sips, her hand fell to her side. "Nay more."

"You must."

Thick lids lifted, and in the murky torchlight, confused eyes met his.

Bedamned, she would comply! "Finish the goblet."

Hands trembling, she raised her hand to the cup and took another drink.

Long moments passed as he coaxed her until she drained the

wine. "Well done." He set the forged cup aside and prayed they'd reached the castle in time to prevent complications from the cold.

She shivered and the confusion in her eyes cleared. "The fire f-feels like heaven."

"Indeed." He gave her a tender smile, and wiggled his pinkie before her. "I had thought never to feel my fingers again."

A soft laugh fell from her lips.

Thankful for the sound, he relaxed a degree. "Tell me a story."

Sleepy eyes met his. "If I did nae know better, I would think you mean to keep me awake."

He arched a brow. "'Tis necessary when one becomes too cold."

Her expression grew somber. "Thank you."

"If the situation was reversed, you would do the same for me."

"Aye." A tender smile touched her mouth, and she laid her hand upon his. "I know nae what I have done to deserve you."

Heart aching, he swallowed hard, wishing they had the luxury of time, that of years to be together. "We have naught but a fortnight at most before you must return to the Otherworld," he whispered.

She started to look away, but he caught her chin.

"But we have now, and I willna allow the precious time we have left together slip away without knowing more about you."

"But——" Panic widened her eyes, and she sat to sit up.

He held her. "What is wrong?"

She shot a covert look around. "Your king," she mouthed. "We must find him this night."

Moved that when she should be worrying about herself she was concerned for others, he nodded. "Aye, we will, but first I will ensure that you are warm and rested."

"We do nae have time to wait," she insisted.

"'Tis foolery for you to try and travel so weak from the cold, nae to mention after your fall."

Regret touched her gaze. "You are right, I am but delaying you. Leave me and save your king and queen."

He wanted to shake the lass. "I willna leave you," he returned, his voice as quiet as hers.

Her lower lip trembled. "Mayhap there will come a point when you have no choice. Too well I understand how at times a difficult choice must be made."

Anger stormed through him. "I forget naught."

In the glow of firelight, a frown wedged in her brow. "And what if the guard finds us gone when he returns on his rounds?"

With a grimace, he glanced toward the entry. Concerned that if they talked too much it might raise suspicion, he subtly raised his finger to his mouth.

Understanding dawned in her eyes, and she shifted to a more comfortable position.

Long moments passed, and he absorbed the warmth of the hearth. He waited a while longer, then turned to her. "Before we make any move, we must learn how long each pass takes, then we can plan the best time to leave to search the keep."

Catarine shifted to her side. "Where is the royal chamber?"

"'Tis on the upper floor, and is where King Alexander has stayed on his previous visits. And, 'twill be the easiest place for the guards to ensure that he and Queen Margaret do nae escape."

"If they are on the upper floor, and with the hidden tunnel entry route frozen, how will we escape?"

"Sterling Castle has several secret tunnels. I was only privy to the one location," he said in quiet reply. "I believe the king will know others."

"But you are nae sure?" she whispered.

He damned his reply. "Nay." And what of the others within the great room? When they departed, would they alert the guard of their disappearance? Blast it, once they headed to find the king, they would have but one chance to escape.

"Trálin," Catarine said, "we are to meet the fey warriors at the base of the cliff. What if they didna—"

He gave her a subtle nod. "Do nae invite worry. They are well-trained and I am confident they will be there." And he prayed they'd reach their meeting point unharmed.

Eyes unsure, she watched him.

God help them if the fey warriors didn't make it. Their absence meant one of two things—they'd been caught, or, in the brutal snowstorm, they'd died. Neither did he wish to consider.

The crackle of wood burning in the hearth filled the tense silence. What more was there to say? Once they escaped this night, numerous challenges lay ahead.

A creak sounded. A burst of cold air whipped into the great room as the door opened wide.

With a curse at the bitter night, the guard who'd brought them to the keep stepped inside the great room and shoved the sturdy door shut. A dark scowl creased his brow as he scoured the room. As his gaze rested on Trálin and Catarine, he paused. In the flicker of torch-light and the flames from the hearth, the guard's eyes narrowed.

Panic swept him. Had the guard recognized him? Beneath the tunic, keeping his movements slow, he clasped his dagger.

The guard grunted in disgust, then scanned the remainder of the great hall. As if satisfied naught was amiss, he strode to the turret and entered. The thud of his steps echoed up the winding stairs and, moments later, faded.

"With the way he looked us over," she whispered, "I worry he suspects something."

"As I." But he wouldna linger on the discussion and concern her further. He studied her face. "You have color on your cheeks. A good sign."

She gave a shudder. "Never have I been so cold."

"And I pray you are never so cold again."

Soft steps echoed toward them.

He glanced up. The woman that'd helped them earlier headed toward them with two bowls of stew and a hunk of bread. "We are in luck, lass. Warm food."

The woman smiled as she halted before them. "You looked like you both were ready to eat."

"We are, my thanks," Trálin said.

"A pleasure, my lord," she replied.

Trálin stilled. "What?"

A soft chuckle fell from her lips. "Nae worry," she said in a low voice. "Many a time you have visited, but with you busy with your affairs with the king, I doubt you would have noticed me."

God in heaven. "What do you mean?"

"With your beard shaved, Lord Grey, at first I didna recognize you." She shook her head. "I will nae be informing the guards. Nasty business they have done, abducting King Alexander and Queen Margaret."

Hope soared. "Do you know where they are?" he whispered.

"I do." She laid out a platter before them. "The stew is hot, so do take care when you eat. 'Twill do you both good. As for the king and queen, they are in the royal chamber on the top floor, but under guard."

As he'd suspected. If their luck continued, they'd all escape this night. "You are loyal to King Alexander then?"

"Aye," she replied. "Upstarts the Comyns are. They think they blasted have a right to the throne and can manipulate a king with threats."

"They plan to nae manipulate him," Trálin whispered, "but kill both King Alexander and his queen if he does nae comply with their demands."

The woman gasped. "That explains the activities since their arrival earlier this day."

"What happened?" Trálin asked.

"I was nae privy to it all," the woman replied, "but I heard whispers that the king had until tomorrow morning to make his decision. I didna know that if King Alexander refused their demands, 'twould cost him and the queen their lives." She made the sign of the cross. "God help us."

Indeed, the king's men would attack Stirling Castle and many innocent people would die. "We are here to free them," Trálin explained. "And when we return with substantial guard, we will ensure the Comyns receive their due."

The woman nodded. "If you have need of anything, let me know. Several others beside myself were outraged when we saw our king led here beneath guard. Treasonous, it is. I assure you, if asked, they will offer their aid as well."

"Your bravery along with that of others who help us will be remembered," Trálin whispered.

Gratitude shone in the woman's eyes. "King Alexander's freedom is payment enough. Sleep well, my lord." The woman returned to her daughter.

Catarine shook her head. "She recognized you," she whispered.

"Aye." He rubbed his clean-shaven jaw. "I thought shaving my beard would conceal my identity for the wee bit of time we are to be here."

"It fooled the guard." Catarine said.

Unease cut through him. "Nae completely. Something about me seems familiar, but for now he has nae connected a name to my face."

"But he will," she said, her words filled with worry.

"Indeed, we must be long gone by then." He studied her in the shimmers of firelight. Though her face was regaining color, 'twould take time for her to regain her full strength. Time they didn't have before they must leave. "Will you be fit enough to travel this night?"

"Aye."

Blast it, as if he expected her to say otherwise? She was a warrior, a woman of fortitude, and a woman who made him want her more than was wise. Shaken by the enormity of what she made him feel, he gestured to the steaming stew. "Eat, lass. We will be needing all of the strength we can have this eve."

Several hours later, fed, warmed, and rested, Catarine and Lord Grey slipped from the great room. The soft tap of his boots echoed in the silence as Trálin walked beside her up the spiral steps.

Catarine's breath caught in her throat as she peered up the wash of torchlight spilling upon the timeworn steps. "'Twill be dawn soon."

"Aye," he whispered, damning the passing hours. "The guard has made his rounds often. I worry my true identity will soon come to him. Neither can we delay in freeing the king. The Comyns will soon be demanding King Alexander's answer. Then, any chance of saving my sovereign will be lost."

In silence, they continued up. Near the top of the steps, Trálin held up a finger to his lips.

She nodded.

Gut churning, after one glance down the turret, he crept up the last few steps. He peered down the long corridor, pulled back. Be-damned!

Soft steps came up behind him. "What is wrong?" she whispered.

"Three guards are posted at the royal chamber's door. The distance to them is too far to have the element of surprise."

"How will we get past them?" she asked.

Several thoughts stormed him, none of which held any appeal.

"Trálin, what if I go and—"

"Nay."

In the spit of torchlight, her face grew taut. "I will become invisible and knock all three of them out. The guards will nae know I am there until 'tis too late."

He wanted to argue, refuse to endanger her life. What man allowed a woman to face a guard even if invisible? "I canna, 'tis nae my way."

"You are right," she replied, "but 'tis the way of the Otherworld."

Silence thrummed between them.

"For your peace of mind," she said, "if I do nae come back in ten seconds, come after me."

A muscle worked in his jaw as he glared at her. And in seconds she could be dead. "I do nae like it."

A soft smile curved her mouth as she laid her hand over his. "I wouldna expect you to."

Far from amused, he narrowed his eyes. "Nae think tenderness will soften me."

Catarine shot him a wink. "Mayhap it will." She inhaled a deep breath.

Disappeared.

Blast her! One. Two. Three. Fo—"

A guard grunted.

"What in blasted—ugh," the other guard groaned. A thud sounded.

Bedammed, he'd nae wait until the count of ten. Sword drawn, Trálin bolted around the corner.

At the doorway, the third knight crumpled to a heap.

With a confident smile on her face, Catarine appeared and sheathed her blade.

Stunned, he took in the three highly trained guards who lay sprawled as if after a night of too much drink. "How did you knock them out so quickly?"

"The hilt of my sword," she beamed.

He shook his head as he sheathed his blade. "Remind me never to upset you."

The humor in Catarine's expression fell away. "Never would I use it to harm anyone who didna deserve it."

"That I believe," he replied, humbled by her at every turn. "You are an amazing woman. One who I wish was human."

For a long moment she held his gaze, her desire easy to see. She cleared her throat, and waved him forward. "Come, we need to awaken your king and queen."

He shoved aside his own longings. "Let me go in first in case a guard is inside."

With a brow raised in amusement, she stepped back.

On alert, Trálin slowly opened the door, peered inside. A candle burned on each side of the massive bed where the king and queen slept. No guards stood inside. The lack of protection within was easy to understand. With three guards outside their door, the Comyns would nae suspect someone would ever slip inside this near impenetrable fortress to try and free the king.

He waved Catarine to follow him. Once inside, he shut the door. "Wait here." Trálin walked over to the bed. "Your Grace."

King Alexander sat up, his eyes thick with sleep, widening with surprise. "Lord Grey?"

"Aye, Your Grace. I am here to help you and Queen Margaret escape."

Emotion swept the king's face, and he shoved the covers aside, stood. "I—I thought you were dead."

Images of the massacre swamped him, and Trálin's throat tightened. "I survived, Your Grace."

"And your men?" the king asked, his voice rough.

Trálin shook his head.

"A sword's blood," the king spat. "The Comyns will pay for this." Rubbing his eyes, he paused. "Your beard is gone?"

"A necessity for us to enter Stirling Castle unrecognized," Trálin replied.

The king started to speak. Hesitated. "Us?" He glanced behind Trálin, frowned. "A lass?"

"'Tis a long story and there is no time to explain," Trálin said. "Your Grace, we must hurry."

"Aye, the bastard Comyn is to come at first light for an answer to his demands." He turned to the queen who had been listening to his explanation. "We must leave now."

With a nod, Queen Margaret hurried out of the bed.

While the royal pair dressed, Trálin pulled the unconscious guards into the chamber, removed their weapons, then hid them behind the massive bed. "Where is the escape tunnel, Your Grace?"

King Alexander shook his head. "'Tis blocked."

Chapter Nine

The escape route was blocked? The anger in the king's voice matched Trálin's. This explained why they hadna escaped prior to his arrival. Queen Margaret was a strong-willed woman who would follow her king into the harsh weather without hesitation. So like Catarine.

"The Comyns made a wise decision to nae underestimate you, Your Grace." Trálin turned to Catarine. "Before we leave, I wish to introduce you to Lady Catarine MacLaren." 'Twould raise too many questions to reveal her title as princess.

King Alexander's brows raised with surprise. "My sincere pleasure to meet you, Lady Catarine."

"And mine," the queen replied.

"I wish 'twas under difference circumstance," Catarine replied.

"Indeed," Trálin agreed, "but now we must leave." He glanced toward the window overlooking the castle ledge. As quickly, he dismissed the idea of crafting a makeshift rope and attempting to reach the ledge below. Even if they had enough material, with the length of time the climb would take, the cold, brutal winds could easily mean death. "Is there another way we can escape Stirling Castle?"

The king shook his head. "None except through the gatehouse or a side door, but for either, first we would have to reach the bailey."

Bedamned. Without the added ranks of his men, or the fey warriors, little hope existed to challenge the castle guards. Catarine's ability to become invisible came to mind. Except she would have to hold her breath the entire way across the bailey to remain invisible and reach the guards and render them unconscious. He shoved aside the thought. 'Twas too dangerous.

"Trálin," Catarine said. "We also have help from the servants."

"Help from the servants?" the king asked, his voice skeptical.

"Aye," he replied. "Your Grace, a servant below recognized me." At the king's horror, Trálin shook his head. "Nay, she kept her silence and explained that she and others in Stirling Castle are outraged by the Comyns abducting you and Queen Margaret. And, if we needed their aid, they would be there."

King Alexander frowned. "If so, why have those in the castle who support me nae banded to free us before now?"

"Your Grace," Trálin explained, "though substantial in number, they are afraid to confront a well trained and very large guard."

The king's mouth tightened. "That makes sense. The Comyns will regret using their men for their own greed." King Alexander glanced toward the door. "As for our escape, while those loyal to me distract the guards, if we don common garb, we could slip out the castle gates."

"In the dark of the night with naught but torchlight, I believe it will work," Trálin agreed, thankful he'd nae asked Catarine to endanger herself by facing the guards alone. "One more thing, Your Grace." In brief, he explained about the guard who had allowed them entry into the castle and had warned them nae to leave the great room. "Once he returns on rounds and finds us gone—"

"He will sound the alarm," the king finished, his expression grim.

"Aye, 'tis why we must hurry." Lord Grey met the queen's worried gaze. "Your Grace, will you be able to travel?"

A determined grimace tightened Queen Margaret's lips. "None will stop me."

Aye, she was Scotland's queen indeed, a woman her knights were proud to follow. Trálin handed the king a sword, then a dagger before handing a second dagger to the queen. "For your safety, I will go first."

King Alexander nodded.

With a glance at Catarine, Trálin led them from the chamber. The batter of wind against a window echoed through the corridor as they hurried toward the steps. At the entry to the turret, he halted and raised his hand. With a prayer nay guards ascended the curved steps, he peered around the corner.

"'Tis empty," Lord Grey whispered.

"Good," King Alexander replied.

Torchlight scraped the hewn stone like angry claws that left ominous swaths of black twisted light on the curved walls as Trálin led them down. The soft pad of their steps echoed against the silence, each moan of wind, each distant call of a castle guard leaving him further on edge. Blast it, time was running out. They must escape. To fail meant they all would die.

Near the bottom, the murmur of voices echoed with a soft whisper.

Trálin raised his hand and halted. On edge, he leaned forward and scanned the great room. Against the glow of flames burning in the hearth, he made out two women sitting on the floor together in quiet conversation. The others within the massive chamber lay tucked beneath their blankets in haphazard groups.

Relief swept through him. "No guards are about, Your Grace."

"Excellent," the king replied.

Catarine exhaled with relief.

"Your Grace, "Trálin whispered. "I will be but a moment."

The king nodded.

With quiet steps, he started across the great room. As he passed the two women in discussion, the woman with red hair glanced over, stiffened.

Trálin nodded at her, kept walking toward the woman who'd offered help before. From the corner of his eye, he saw the red-haired woman hesitate. *Please let her return to her discussion.*

Shrewd eyes narrowed as she continued to stare at him. After a long moment, the red-haired woman returned to her conversation.

Thank God in heaven. Lord Grey glanced toward the entry.

The heavy wooden door remained closed.

Except the guard would soon make his rounds. Several steps later, he knelt beside the woman who'd offered aid. "Are you awake?"

Groggy eyes opened, looked up. She quickly sat up. "My lord."

He placed his finger over his lips. "I need your help."

Her eyes widened. "The king and queen?"

"Aye," he replied. "They are hidden in the turret with the woman I came with."

Trálin made a quick scan around the chamber to ensure they remained unwatched, then faced her. "We all need common garb. Warm cloaks to travel. Can you procure them?"

"Aye, Lord Grey."

"You said there are others who would help us as well?" Trálin asked.

"They will, my lord," she replied.

"Excellent," Trálin said. "Once we have donned our garb, we will need you and the others to create a disturbance while we escape."

The woman hesitated. "My lord, regardless of our distraction, the gatehouse will remain guarded."

"It will, but the guards' attention will be on the mayhem, and give us the opportunity to knock them out and escape."

She nodded. "My Lord, I will be but a moment." After a quick look around, the woman stood. Dust motes swirled in her wake as she hurried toward the two women still deep in conversation.

Trálin curled his hand on his dagger. Had he misjudged her?

At her approach, the two women turned. The woman with the red hair motioned them closer. After furious whispers, the two women hurried down a corridor.

Trálin exhaled, released his hold on the hilt.

The elder woman returned to his side. "My lord, the women are gathering others and will set a fire in the upper rooms of the castle. Posthaste, tell King Alexander and Queen Margaret to follow me."

He nodded and rushed to the turret. "Everything is set. Come." He led them toward a darkened corridor where the woman waited.

At their approach, she curtsied to the king and queen. "This way, Your Grace." She guided them along the passageway.

A creak sounded. Yellow candlelight spilled out of a door near the end.

"Quickly," the woman urged.

Trálin followed, thankful to find the woman he'd seen talking earlier shaking out simple gowns and thick undergarments along with serviceable common garb.

"Your Grace," the red-haired woman called, "I will help the women. Please follow me."

Without hesitation, Queen Margaret and Catarine dashed into a private area to change.

"This way, Your Grace, Lord Grey." The other woman led them to a small chamber, handed them the serviceable garb. "The thick wool will help keep you warm as you travel."

"My thanks," King Alexander said. "Your loyalty will be remembered."

A blush darkened her cheeks in the candlelight. "'Tis an honor to help you, Your Grace." With a bow, she turned and departed.

Once they'd finished securing their garb, Trálin and the king rejoined the others.

A shuffle at the entry sounded, the door shoved open, and a dark-haired woman rushed inside, her face flushed. "The fire is set."

"Excellent," the woman helping the group replied. "Your Grace—"

"Fire!" a woman shouted from the great room.

Screams echoed within the keep. Doors thumped, and guards shouted for water.

"This way!" the woman helping them called.

Keeping Catarine close to his side, Trálin followed the woman. As if in an odd maze, they wove through half-lit blackness, the scents of aged meat alerting him they passed through where they cured the venison and boar. A door creaked open, and he stepped out.

Distant torchlight exposed the bailey. Trálin flattened himself within the shadows of the building. "Catarine."

"Here," she whispered.

"Please check around the corner to ensure no guards are about."

"I will." She touched his shoulder. "Thank you for your trust." Catarine crept to the corner. A step away her vague outline disappeared. A moment later, she came into view.

"'Tis so dark," the king whispered as he halted beside Trálin, "for a moment I lost sight of Lady Catarine."

"Indeed." A smile tugged at his mouth. If only he knew the truth.

"The guards have made a line from the well and are passing buckets of water to the keep," Catarine explained as she halted beside Trálin.

"Do we have a clear path to a side gate near the gatehouse?" King Alexander asked.

"Regardless," Trálin said, "we must keep close to the walls and use the broken shadows."

"'Twill take too long," Catarine whispered.

A muscle worked in Trálin's jaw. As if he didna know the risks? "'Tis the safest to lure the guards at the gate."

Catarine leaned closer. "Remain here. I will go alone."

He caught the emphasis in the word *alone*. She meant she'd become invisible. Bedamned, she'd risked her life enough. "Nay!"

"What is wrong?" the king asked.

"Your Grace," Catarine said before Trálin could speak. "I will take out the guards at the gatehouse. When I—"

"With the distance necessary," Trálin interrupted, upset she'd nae discussed it with him first, "'twill take you too long to—"

Catarine bolted deep into the shadows.

Bedamned! Trálin started after her, caught a vague shimmer, then she disappeared. With a muttered curse, he glanced toward the guards at the gate. With the yells from the top of the castle, their attention was focused on the fire.

"Lord Grey," the king softly called.

Trálin cursed, slipped back beside the king.

"Is the lass insane?" he asked.

Nay, a fairy. "In part," Trálin replied.

"Never have I seen a woman with such bravado," King Alexander said.

"She is a trained knight," Trálin explained.

"A lass is a knight?" the king stated, the shock in his voice expected. "Never have I heard of such."

"Nor I." Neither would the king learn more. Trálin scoured the bailey. Where was she? Blast it, if he could reach her, he'd throttle her. "I do nae see her," the king whispered.

"She is in the shadows," Trálin replied, and prayed she could hold her breath that long.

A blur came into view paces away from the first guard.

"There she is," the queen said.

Catarine's form faded.

"What the bloody devil?" The guard yelled as he withdrew his blade. "Behind you," he shouted to the other sentry.

The other knight whirled. "Bloody hell, 'tis a sword in the air." He stumbled back, grabbing for his blade.

"'Tis a curse!" the other guard called.

Fear for her life tore through Trálin. "Follow me." He bolted across the bailey.

Blade drawn, her form becoming visible, Catarine swung.

The knight gasped, angled his blade. Steel scraped. The knight's sword flew to the ground.

As she rounded her blade for her next swing, her entire body came into view.

Fear tore through Trálin. "Leave her be!"

The guard met her swing with a solid blow. He shoved her back and rounded on Lord Grey. "What blasted trickery is this?"

In the wash of torchlight, her body wavered.

Bedamned, she was too close to the knights to become invisible! Furious at the risks she was taking, Trálin shoved her aside and deflected the knight's next assault, caught the man's sword with his own, shoved.

The knight stumbled back.

Protectiveness pouring through him, Trálin charged, swung.

Sparks glittered in the night, the shouts of the men trying to put out the fire echoing behind them.

Trálin angled his hilt, slammed it against the knight's head.

A curse echoed, then the guard's body slumped to the ground.

In the dim shimmer of distant torchlight, Catarine's eyes blazed. "Why did you shove me out of the way?"

"Nay time to discuss it now." With a quick glance behind to ensure they had nae been spotted, Trálin unbarred the door, jerked it open. Wind, thick with the cast of snow, hurled through. "Go!"

She shot him a cool look. As Catarine made to pass, he caught her arm. "'Twas a foolish risk."

"Nae, necessary." She jerked her arm free and ran through the entry.

Footsteps echoed behind him; the king and queen hastened past.

"The king has escaped!" a man's voice boomed in the distance.

Blast it! He'd hoped they'd had more time. "Run!" Trálin yelled.

At his next step, a gust of wind hit him thick with flakes of white. In the gloom of night with only the meager reflection of the moon through the clouds, he lost sight of everyone ahead of him. A moment later, the wind slowed, and he caught their outline.

"The door to the side gate is open!" another man shouted.

Trálin cursed, shoved the door shut. "Run toward the cliffs!" Wind-fed snow pelted him as he pushed forward, the crunch of the iced surface giving way to a thick powdery white that slowed his each step.

Catarine dropped back. "The cliffs?"

"I know of a trail." The gloom of night enveloped Trálin as he reached Catarine, then caught up with the king and queen. "Follow me!"

Yells echoed from the entry. Hinges creaked. The scrap of the iron sounded with a treacherous groan.

Catarine half-stumbled as she glanced back. "They are opening the portcullis!"

"We must make it around the side of the Stirling Castle," Trálin called, "before they—"

"There they are!" a knight in the distance behind them yelled.

Catarine halted.

Trálin whirled. "What are you doing?"

Clouds broke overhead, and a shaft of moonlight illuminated her as if a magic spell cast. "I will slow them," she replied. "Go, take the king and queen."

"Catarine, you will—"

"Catch up with you."

Snow whipped Trálin's face as he caught Catarine's hand. "Are you daft? Nay," he muttered as he dragged her with him as he followed after the royal couple, "do nae answer that."

Orders for more men to help find the royal couple rang out in their wake. The fierce gong of a bell sounded, backed by calls awakening those who still slept.

The king and queen hurried around the corner of Stirling Castle.

"Halt!" a distant guard yelled.

"This way. There is a hidden path down the cliffs." Trálin headed toward a thicket of trees. As he neared, the limbs of the tree shook.

A burly guard leading several men brandishing swords stepped from the thick swath of firs before them. "Halt or be killed."

Chapter Ten

The burly guard moving from the thick fir stilled. "Catarine?"

At Atair's voice, her entire body sank with relief. In the racing clouds above, moonlight streamed through a break, exposing her senior fey warrior along with her other men moving out of the trees.

"Halt!" a deep voice boomed from near the castle walls.

Her breaths rushing out as puffs of white, Catarine sprinted toward Atair. "We escaped with the king and queen and are being chased. They must be taken to safety!"

Against the sparse moonbeams, a grimace flattened Atair's mouth as he waved the men forward. "Drax, escort the king and queen down the trail. We will follow as soon as possible."

"Aye." Drax motioned for the king and queen to follow him. "This way, Your Grace, quickly."

"Nay, I will fight." The king gestured for the queen to follow Drax. "Go!"

Terror slid through Catarine. What was King Alexander doing? He could nae remain. "Your Grace, we are greatly outnumbered. Your safety is imperative."

King Alexander withdrew his blade, "By God, 'tis my country, and I will face those who want me dead."

A part of her damned the king's decision of putting his life at risk, another held respect.

The queen hesitated, then nodded. "Be safe."

King Alexander faced Catarine as the queen followed Drax through the fir boughs and out of sight. "Lady Catarine, go with her."

"With respect, Your Grace," she stated as she withdrew her sword. "I will remain and fight with my men."

King Alexander stepped toward her. "'Tis nae——"

"Seize him!" the castle guard yelled as he closed.

With a curse, the king lifted his blade and joined the fey warriors as they charged the oncoming men.

Her mind shifting to tactics, Catarine followed. Wind hurled snow in her face as she met the first aggressor. She swung.

The screech of steel pierced the air.

She clenched her teeth, rounded her blade, swung. Metal slammed with a hard scrape.

The guard stumbled back.

Without hesitation, Catarine lunged forward, drove her sword into his heart, then withdrew. She whirled to face her next attacker. The cacophony of blades echoed around her as she delivered a fatal blow.

Her challenger crumpled to the smear of white.

Breaths coming fast, with no castle guards nearby, she glanced behind her. Near the trees where the queen and Drax had entered, Sionn was battling a tall knight, with Trálin engaged in a vicious clash of blades nearby.

Another knight ran around the castle corner, bolted toward Trálin. Panic swept her. "Lord Grey, behind you!"

Trálin dispensed the knight before him with a savage blow, rounded on his heel, and angled his blade as the castle guard charged.

Steel scraped.

On a curse, Lord Grey shoved his attacker back.

"You will die for your treachery!" the knight roared as he swung.

Trálin's sword caught the man's blade at the hilt. He tossed it aside, then drove his sword deep. "Nay, 'tis your dishonor for which you will now pay the price."

In the moonlight, the guard gasped, sank to his knees, then collapsed.

Sword readied for the next assailant, Catarine scanned the fractured moonlit area around him.

Several castle guards remained engaged in battle, but the king and fey warriors quickly finished them off.

"Your Grace," Atair called, "we must go before reinforcements arrive!"

The king withdrew his blade from his attacker, sheathed it. "Aye."

He followed the senior fey warrior toward where the queen had entered the forest with Drax.

Breaths coming fast, Trálin ran to Catarine. "Are you hurt?"

"Nay," she replied, her voice shaky.

"Thank God." Trálin gave her shoulder a squeeze. "Come, we must hurry."

Moonlight glittered upon the snow around her like fairy dust as she followed her fey warriors, Trálin at her side. As she reached the trees, she shoved aside a limb, ran through. A cloud of snow showered her, and she pushed forward.

Inside the cloak of trees, illuminated by wisps of moonlight, she navigated the needle-covered limbs, keeping up with her men ahead. With the grueling pace, she was thankful that the queen had a head start. They would need to keep moving throughout the night. Soon castle guards would arrive and find their men dead. Furious, they would send the full guard to recapture the king and queen—a fate she and her fey warriors could never allow, regardless the cost.

She rounded a large boulder, and the trees began to thin. In the distance, with the clouds clearing, she made out her warriors and the king as Drax led Queen Margaret down a narrow path.

Atair slowed. "We were to aid you in freeing the king," he said, his voice cool, "nae meet you outside the castle walls after the fact."

"Catarine had an accident and almost died," Trálin stated without apology. "We were fortunate to be allowed inside Stirling Castle, more so that a few hours of rest, warmth, and food allowed her to recover."

"God's sword," Atair rasped. "How fare thee now?"

In the shimmers of moonlight, Catarine pushed aside another bough of fir, the scent rich. "I fought well enough."

"Stubborn lass," Atair muttered.

"An opinion you and Trálin both hold," she replied.

Atair dodged a tree. "As if you do nae hold the blasted trait?"

"Mayhap." Her breaths coming fast, a smile touched Catarine's mouth. Both men were——

"They have killed our men!" a man's deep voice boomed from behind them.

Fear tore through her. "The reinforcements have arrived."

Trálin caught her arm, shoved her ahead of him. "Go. Now!"

Aware now was nae the time to argue, she bolted forward. Moments later, the fey warriors aided the king and queen as they hurried into shadows of rock and began their descent down the dangerous cliffs.

Catarine didn't peer over the edge, didn't think, but focused on each snow-laden step. She refused to ponder her near fall from the wooden bridge spanning the gorge, or the mind-numbing fear. That her guards had made it to Stirling Castle safely, and that they had a path down the precarious cliffs, was more than enough reason to give thanks.

"If only our shield of invisibility would cover humans as well," Catarine whispered to Trálin as she wedged her foot into the next rocky jut.

He angled his body, reached the next step down. "Aye."

Weary, she clutched a sturdy branch, stepped down.

Throughout the night, beneath shimmers of moonlight mixed with shadows, they worked their way down. At times the sounds of the castle guards searching for them grew close, at others their shouts echoed from afar.

Wisps of purple gold illuminated the sky as Trálin held onto a sturdy limb, climbed down another precarious step of the treacherous ledge. He glanced up.

In the meager light of dawn, a mask of weariness painted Catarine's face. Regardless, she pushed on without complaint.

Blast it, the lass would nae ask to halt unless she collapsed. Though she'd recovered from near freezing, another day's rest would do her well. Nae that they had time for such luxury with the castle guards on their heels.

"The sun is beginning to rise," Trálin said. "We must find a place to hide and rest."

With a frustrated sigh, Catarine searched the rough trail ahead. "No doubt the king and queen are unused to such demanding travel. Do you know of anywhere nearby we can take cover for the day?"

"Nay," Lord Grey replied. "The few times I passed this way, I did nae have a need to ask. But, below is a ledge hidden by boulders. 'Tis enough room for us all to take a break and discuss our next move."

Her body trembling with fatigue, Catarine stepped down onto the rocky shelf. Wind swept snow rushed past as she followed Trálin to where the angled rock broke the gusts of windswept snow.

Amidst the swaths of orange red illuminating the morning sky, one by one, her men reached the landing.

The first rays of morning sun slipped through the crevices, leaving an unsettling glow around him as Catarine waited for everyone to gather.

"How fare thee, my queen?" King Alexander asked as he guided his wife toward the clearing.

Queen Margaret gave him a wilted smile. "Well enough."

As the king reached the awaiting men, he nodded to each one, his expression fierce. "With Comyn's guards out en force, we must decide our best strategy."

Trálin rubbed his chin. "Your Grace, the Comyns will believe that you will attempt to reach Scone Castle."

"Aye," King Alexander agreed. "Instead, I will return to Loch Leven Castle."

Stunned, Trálin shook his head. "Your Grace, with my knights slaughtered and only the castle guard to protect you, 'tis too dangerous to return."

"I too believe 'tis wise to return to Loch Leven Castle," the queen stated. "Those who abducted you will think that with the lack of your security, you would hesitate to return. Fools that they are, they do nae know you." Her mouth thinned. "Evident by their brazen abduction."

"A point well made," the king agreed. "Nor are the Comyns aware of the secret chambers within Loch Leven Castle. From there, I can send runners to lords I trust to deal with the Comyns' treachery."

"Aye," Trálin agreed, then met Catarine's gaze. "Your Grace, 'tis one other issue I wish to discuss."

King Alexander arched a thick brow. "Go on, Lord Grey."

"Your Grace, while I lay wounded and dying on the field outside Loch Leven Castle, Lady Catarine and her men saved me. 'Twas due to their help that we were able to set you and the queen free."

His gaze somber, the king nodded. "My deepest thanks to you all. Your brave actions saved a man who is like a brother to me, and freed the queen and I."

Heat swept Catarine's cheeks. "'Twas my honor to aid you, and the queen, Your Grace."

"Your Grace," Trálin said. "I mention their brave actions as they have need of your aid."

"Indeed?" King Alexander asked. "Explain."

"Lady Catarine and her men were en route to complete their own task when they came upon my men and I fighting after your abduction," Lord Grey replied. "For the risks she and her men have made in your behalf, I ask that you grant them aid in completing their quest."

The king's somber eyes focused on her. "Lady Catarine, ask what you will, and I will grant it."

The image of her uncle sprawled on the floor came to mind, and emotion stormed her. "Your Grace, my uncle was murdered," she explained, avoiding any mention of her being nobility, or that she and her warriors were fey. "We were following the attacker's trail in the vicinity of Loch Leven Castle when we lost it near where Lord Grey and his men were attacked." She took a calming breath. "We believe with Lord Grey and several of your knights helping us search, we can pick up the trail and find whoever is behind the treachery."

King Alexander rubbed his jaw as he studied her. "Why do you believe Lord Grey and extra men will help you find the trail?"

As if she could admit she believed magic had erased the assassin's tracks to the fey and that 'twas still visible to humans? She shot Trálin a nervous look before focusing on the king. "Your Grace, we have traveled far in our quest. We know nae the land, nor its people."

The king studied her a moment. "A fair request. We will discuss the number of men needed once we reach Loch Leven Castle."

Catarine exhaled with relief. Regardless of the snow covering the tracks, she refused to believe they wouldn't catch who was behind the treachery, more so with Trálin knowing the land and those who lived there. "My thanks, Your Grace. 'Tis generous of you."

"'Tis little for the risks you and your men have taken to free Queen Margaret and I," the king replied.

A gust of wind swept past. Like an omen, snowflakes spiraled around them, then sifted to the ground like fairy dust cast. Nerves swept her. What was her family doing now? Was everyone safe? Had anyone tried to follow her and the fey warriors through the stone circle? *Please let them all be safe.*

The king rubbed his chin. "Who is your father, Lady Catarine? I am sure we have met."

Catarine caught her breath. As if she could answer that? "I——"

"Your Grace," Trálin interrupted, "though we are tired, we must nae tarry. No doubt Comyn's men are scouring the cliffs. We must then find a place to stay during the daylight. Once the sun sets, I believe 'tis best if we continue toward Loch Leven Castle beneath the darkness of night."

She shot Lord Grey a thankful glance.

"Aye," the king agreed, thankfully ignorant to the near disaster of her trying to explain. He took in his wife. "My queen, how do you fare?"

"A bit cold, but no more than anyone else here," Queen Margaret replied, determination riding her voice. "And able to travel wherever we need to go."

Pride swept the king's face. "You are a woman to make your country proud."

Trálin turned to the fey warriors. "In your travels here, did you find anywhere large enough where we can rest for the day that will give us cover?"

"Aye, Lord Grey" Atair replied. "We can stay where we bedded down last night. 'Tis a wee bit farther down the cliffs, but 'twill work."

"Excellent," the king replied.

"Before we depart," Sionn said, "I have a bit of wine if anyone has thirst." He held out a flask.

"My thanks." The king took a long draught, then handed it to the queen.

After everyone had taken a drink, Trálin secured the top of the flask and handed it to Atair. "My thanks."

The lead fey warrior secured his flask, nodded. "Thank you for keeping your word to help us," he said in a low voice.

"You had doubts?" Trálin asked.

His face solemn, Atair secured the flask in his belt, met his gaze. "No longer."

Chapter Eleven

Yellow-purple rays of sunrise spilled over the mountains in the distance as Catarine followed Lord Grey down the treacherous cliffs. On her next step, dizziness washed over her. She grabbed for the weathered tip of stone and struggled to steady herself.

"Catarine?" Trálin called.

Head pounding, she rubbed her brow and she glanced down.

Deep lines wrinkled Lord Grey's brow as he watched her. "What is wrong?"

Tenderness sifted through her at his caring. "A wee bit tired, but I am fine." His mouth tightened. "Last night you were half frozen. Now you have—"

"Recovered with the warmth of a fire and food," she interrupted, refusing to debate the issue. Their reaching Loch Leven Castle and bringing the king and queen to safety was of the utmost importance. "We need to keep moving."

"We do," he replied, his voice firm, "but you *will* tell me if you need to stop to rest."

Tempted to assure him she would do no such thing, 'twould do naught but rile his temper further. Nor could she hide her exhaustion. She nodded.

Catarine focused, stepped over a raised clutter of rock, and moved down.

In the lead as he navigated the dangerous cliffs, Atair paused before two half-fallen boulders. He looked back. "We will rest beyond the stones. You must crawl to enter." His gaze caught hers, then narrowed with worry. Frustration flashed in his eyes, then he knelt and moved inside.

Catarine grimaced. 'Twould seem Trálin had yet another thing in common with Atair. Both worried about her too much. Her legs trembling from fatigue, she stepped down to the flat rock, then crawled beneath the overhang. On the opposite side, she stood. As she surveyed her surroundings, a peculiar tremor of angst swept her. For a moment the view before her blurred.

"Catarine, are you coming?" Atair asked.

Startled, she glanced around. The others were gathering near the center, except Atair, who was striding toward her, eyes dark with worry.

"How did you find this place?" she asked.

Atair gave her a hard look, then exhaled. "Last eve while we were searching for a safe place to hide, Kuircc discovered it."

"Discovered it?" Her disquiet grew. "How, when 'tis all but hidden?"

Atair shrugged. "I do nae know. Fate mayhap?"

"I . . . Nae, 'tis magic," she whispered. Uneasy, she scanned the sweep of protective rock. "A foolish notion. We are many leagues away from the stone circle." She took in the shadows and light of the surrounding stone. Or, was the magic from an unwanted source?

"What is it?" Atair asked.

Images of her uncle murdered flashed in her mind. Their chase when they'd seen the guard. The man's tracks disappearing once they'd entered Scotland and departed the stone circle.

She swallowed hard. "I believe our finding this hideaway is nay accident."

Atair's eyes narrowed. "What do you mean?"

A chill swept through her, and she rubbed her arms. "I sense magic here. And, I am unsure if it is good."

Atair closed his eyes for a long moment, swore as he opened them. "Bedamned, you are right. Why did I nae sense this before?"

"Tired mayhap? Worried?" She shook her head. "I am unsure why I picked it up now, but I will be happy when we are gone from this place."

Her lead fey warrior grimaced. "On that I agree."

"Is something wrong?" Trálin asked as he strode over, his gaze intense.

She caught Atair's warning look. "I was asking Atair how they'd found this hideout." Catarine forced a smile. "I agree with him, 'tis indeed fate."

Trálin shot Atair a curious look, then focused on her. "Is it?"

She nodded. "Aye." To consider otherwise invited unpleasant thoughts she'd prefer nae to ponder.

"But you are nae sure?" Trálin asked.

Catarine hesitated, then shook her head. To head off further questions, she turned and walked to join the others. As she moved, she surveyed their temporary hideout. Caught in the murky morning light, a massive slab of stone jutted from the cliffs. Beneath an almost hidden opening lay a wide cavern. As she neared, the sense of magic lingered, but nae strong enough to indicate anyone was near. Had one of the fey stayed here? Had whoever killed her uncle rested here? Why else would they detect one of the fey's presence or the unsettling notions the discovery brought?

Trálin moved to her side as the others gathered, then looked at Atair. "The shelter will do nicely."

"Aye," the king agreed. "Now to make our plan."

A short while later with the meeting over and unable to sleep, Catarine walked into a shadowed crevice hidden from the others. She leaned against the timeworn stone and stared through the breaks to the valley below.

Smeared with snow, the roll of land descended to the winding river. Beyond, ragged mountains shoved toward the heavens in fierce defense.

"You should be resting."

A smile curved her mouth at Trálin's tender voice. She turned. Watchful eyes held hers as he stepped into the shadowed nook at her side.

"With Drax taking the first guard," he said, "I should say the same about you." Fatigue lined his face as he leaned against the smooth stone near her, winced.

"Your wounds are bothering you?"

He shrugged. "They will heal. And your bruise from the fall?"

"'Tis better," she replied.

Silence fell between them, broken by the whip of wind. Tired and uneasy, she scanned the snow-laden landscape that at any other time that would bring her peace.

"Catarine, I caught Atair's warning look at you earlier when I asked you if something was wrong about this hideout. Do you have concerns about our safety here?"

Frustration swept her. A topic she'd hoped to avoid. "I sensed remnants of magic here."

He studied her a moment. "You think whomever you are chasing rested here?"

She shrugged. "It could be, more so as sensed it, I was uneasy."

"God in heaven, with Stirling Castle nearby, do you think whoever murdered your uncle is in league with the Comyns?"

Shaken, she shook her head. "I had nae considered that. But, why would they?"

"I am nae sure," he replied, "but an association would explain why the King of Scotland would be abducted at the same time as your uncle in the Otherworld is assassinated."

Her mind raced with possibilities, none good. "You think whoever is behind this is making a play for power in both the Otherworld and Scotland?"

"Bloody hell. It sounds incredible."

"Indeed, but it answers many questions."

He rubbed his jaw. "We might be wrong."

"We might be. Regardless, whoever is behind the magic is powerful, and their ultimate intent, frightening." A shiver swept her. "We must find whoever it is."

Lord Grey glanced toward where they fey warriors slept, then back to her. "What did Atair say when you told him about sensing magic here?"

"He is as concerned as I, and will be more so when I explain the possibilities our discussion raised." Catarine closed her eyes, tried to pick up a clear picture of who or what the scent revealed. Naught. She glanced toward him. "Whatever the cause, I sense only a faint hint now, which leads me to believe whoever left it is far away."

"Once we return to the stone circle," Trálin said, "we may find that the trail leads back to Stirling Castle."

A shiver ran through her. "I pray 'tis nae but one of the fey who was cast out of the Otherworld seeking me out for another purpose."

"How would they know you were here?" Trálin asked.

"I . . . Mayhap they saw me and my fey warriors?" A weak reason, but one she prayed was true.

Silence fell between them.

A gust of wind howled overhead, and flakes of snow drifted from above to spill upon them in a soft caress.

Trálin reached over, lifted her chin with his thumb.

She stilled. "What are you doing?"

"This." He pressed his mouth against hers in a gentle kiss, lingered.

Warmth oozed through her, a silky softness that erased her troubled thoughts.

He broke the kiss. "Ah, lass, you should push me away."

Her heart ached at the feelings his touch ignited. "What if I want you to stay?"

A sharp hiss fell from his lips. "A dangerous decision, and one I do nae need to know."

Emotions stormed her——want, need, sadness at what could never be. Her body trembling with awareness, she put much needed distance between them.

With a rough sigh, he peered through a crevice, then stiffened. "Catarine, between the opening in the stones, look toward the copse of trees."

On edge, she peered through the fracture in the weathered stone. A large contingent of men rode across the snow-laden field.

"I can nae see their colors," he said, "but I have no doubt they are Comyn's men."

Hope ignited. "What if they are nae?"

Trálin gave a rough laugh. "How can it be otherwise? None but my men fought Comyn's knights when they attacked and abducted the king. Even if guards from Loch Leven Castle sent for reinforcements, with the snow erasing any sign of our passing, none would know who was behind the abduction or where the king was taken."

She swallowed hard. "You are right."

Trálin's hand settled on her shoulder. "Come, 'tis time to rest. We will be moving with the oncoming night. If we stay here longer, I will be tempted to do something foolish and kiss you again."

"And," she said, "I might do something as irrational as kiss you back."

Thoughts of Trálin incited feelings she'd never known before. It was more than being with a man who moved her, but being with a man who truly cared. A man who if she allowed, she could . . . fall in love with.

Fall in love with Trálin? Ridiculous. She'd known him but three days. They'd kissed, but little more. Yet, deny it as she might, her heart acknowledged what she refused to accept.

She loved him.

Stunned by the realization, Catarine glanced sideways. "I do nae know what to do with you, Trálin MacGruder." Her words fell out thick with desire, betraying what she did nae wanted him to realize.

"I think you do. Giving into your desire canna be a choice either of us can make."

"Indeed." Tears burned her eyes as she took in the sun as it began its ascent over the horizon, spilling its orange-red light over the snow-covered mountains with blazing innocence. Except nothing about what Trálin made her feel was innocent. Nor could her desire for him matter. The Otherworld awaited her, complete with the prince she was to wed.

"What will you do once this is over?" she asked.

"Return to the king's service."

Aching at the thought of their time together coming to an end, Catarine cleared her throat. "You are right, 'tis time to sleep." In silence she walked to the cavern where the others slept, Trálin at her side. She didn't look over, 'twould hurt too much. She lay in the makeshift bed she'd prepared earlier, tugged up her cape.

Clothing rustled. "Sleep well," Trálin said.

She remained silent. If she spoke now, she might say something she'd come to regret.

"I see nothing!" a man's furious yell echoed from above.

Trálin watched from the shield of thick fir, thankful for the progress they'd made throughout the night. With clouds thickening overhead along with the falling snow to cover their tracks, it had allowed them to move from hiding and head toward Loch Leven Castle with minimal risk of being seen. However slow, they'd traveled farther over the past few hours than he'd hoped. Another day, two at most, and they'd arrive. As for the guards ahead, from the sound of their frustration, they would soon move on. He had not expected them to continue their search after the sunset—proof of Comyn's determination to recapture the king and queen.

"I was sure that I saw some tracks," a distant man's voice said.

"You saw naught but that of an animal," the other man grumbled. "With the heavy snowfall, even if it was them, we could nay follow. Come, 'tis time to return to Stirling Castle, unless you would be wanting to freeze to death."

"'Tis blasted cold," the first man grumbled. "We will head back and meet with the others. Mayhap they have fared better."

Wind gusted past, half-smothering the crunch of snow as they headed off.

Trálin sat back, the burn of cold air filling his lungs. "They are leaving."

"Thank goodness," Catarine replied. "The castle guards have searched nearby for the last several hours."

"We could have taken them if we had chosen," Atair said.

Trálin met the lead fey warrior's gaze. "'Twas best to allow them to pass. If the men had nae returned, other knights would have come to search for them."

"The Comyns will have the fight they are seeking, once I return with a full contingent of knights," King Alexander stated. "Let us go."

She slid a covert look toward King Alexander. "The Comyns have made a grave error in upsetting your king."

"Aye." Trálin fell into step beside her, the scent of fir, mixed with that of snow and a hint of cold earth, filling his every breath. Many loved the warmth of summer, but he preferred the fall, thick with the taste of winter and the first blanket of snow that covered the scars of the land.

"You never said where your father is from, Lady Catarine," King Alexander stated as he walked a few paces ahead.

She glanced toward Trálin. "From far away, Your Grace," she replied. "He was a man who enjoyed traveling."

"Your Grace," Trálin said, needing to shift the conversation to a safer topic, "how many men will be needed to retaliate against the Comyns?"

The king's jaw hardened. "Given the force at Stirling Castle, at a minimum, five hundred. As soon as the knights are rallied, we will——"

In the weak slivers of moonlight, a blur moved a distance ahead.

"Down!" Lord Grey warned.

Snow crunched as everyone took cover in the dense thicket of leaves.

His hand on the hilt of his sword, through the cover, Trálin scanned the horizon.

"What did you see?" King Alexander asked.

"Knights in the distance." The slide of blades from their sheaths echoed around Trálin as he removed his.

"How many?" Atair asked as he crept closer.

"Eight," Lord Grey replied, "maybe more."

"Blast it," the king whispered. In the flickers of moonlight spread from breaks overhead, against the slide of wind-flung snow, shadows of a mounted knight came into view over the hill. Then another. More men from the group rode into view.

Trálin's gut sunk. "There are at least fifty men now, Your Grace."

"More," the king replied, his voice grim. "Sir Atair."

The senior fey warrior glanced over. "Aye, Your Grace?"

"Take my wife and Lady Catarine and find safety," the king ordered.

"Your Grace," Catarine said, "I will remain here and fight."

"I need nae go anywhere as well," Queen Margaret replied, anger in her voice. "I have a weapon and can——"

"They are headed this way!" Trálin said!

"Bedamned!" the king whispered. "It looks as though there is no time to flee, and my queen, you will have your wish. If anything should happen to you . . ."

"We will fight together," Queen Margaret said, her voice rich with pride.

"We will," the king agreed.

Shadows moved near the edge of the woods.

"The men are coming into the trees!" Catarine hissed.

"Down!" Trálin whispered.

"You there hidden in the brush!" a deep voice called from the edge of the trees. "Show yourself!"

Chapter Twelve

"Show yourself!" the deep male voice repeated from the edge of the trees.

On a curse, Trálin crept beneath the brush to where the fey warriors hid as his king and queen awaited his report. Fear swept him as he reached Catarine's side, damned that he could nae protect her, damned the words he must say. "We are gravely outnumbered." His whispered words echoed between them like a blast of a mace.

Shards of moonlight exposed the fear in Catarine's eyes. On a shaky breath, she angled her jaw. "We will fight."

Unto the death. She'd nae said it, but Trálin understood. He would do the same, had pledged to protect his king when he'd sworn his oath. But she'd nae asked for this fight, and was in Scotland only to find whoever had murdered her uncle.

He scoured his mind for a way to keep her safe. "You, the king and queen, and the fey warriors slip back. I will create a diversion to allow everyone to escape."

Anger narrowed her brow as she leaned a hand's breath from his face. "Do you think I would leave you and—"

A stick cracked.

Trálin glanced behind him.

In the shadows, King Alexander crept closer. "What is wrong?"

Catarine cleared her throat. "Your Grace," she whispered, "Lord Grey was cautioning me on the upcoming battle."

"Aye," Trálin said, irritated she gave him no quarter. "Your Grace, the odds are greatly against us."

The king peered through the wash of leaves, muttered a curse.

"'Tis a fool's lot to dare challenge such a large force." Surprised, Trálin glanced at the queen noting her grimace to her husband's words. "You will cede?"

The queen moved to her husband's side, laid a hand on the king's arm in a supportive gesture.

"Never," King Alexander spat. "We will fight."

"Whoever hides within," the knight demanded from the outer perimeter of the woods, "come out now. 'Tis your last warning!"

Sword clenched in his hand, King Alexander stood. "We will nae give up but fight!"

Wind shook the thick branches, and in the distance, Trálin caught the murmur of men's voices.

"Why are they nae attacking?" Catarine asked.

"I am unsure," King Alexander replied.

"Whatever they are bloody up to," Trálin ground out, "'tis nay good."

"King Alexander?" a knight near the edge of the woods called, his confusion evident.

"What in bloody hell?" Trálin muttered.

"State your name," the king ordered.

"'Tis Sir Aleyn. The Earl of Torc sent us to rescue you and the queen."

Suspicion ignited, and Trálin leaned close to the king. "Your Grace, though the Earl of Torc is a trusted ally, it might be a trap."

"Aye," he whispered. The king turned toward the knight. "How do I know 'tis nae a lie?"

"Your Grace, a sennight ago, a runner reached Sionnach Castle," the knight replied. "When the Earl of Torc learned of your abduction, he sent us to rescue you."

"If 'tis true, how have you found us so quickly?" the king asked, suspicion ripe in his voice.

"One of my men caught sight of your party in woods, Your Grace," Sir Aleyn replied. "As 'twas but shadowed glimpses of several people, we believed 'twas Comyn's men, which is why we offered a challenge."

Far from convinced, Trálin clasped his hand on his sword as he stood. "How did you know 'twas the Comyns who abducted the king?"

"State your name," the guard called.

"'Tis Lord Grey."

"Lord Grey?" the guard repeated, his voice stunned. "My lord, we thought you dead."

"I lived," Lord Grey replied, "but all of my men who fought at my side were killed."

"Nae all, my lord," the guard replied. "Sir Gyles was able to crawl to a boat and make it to Loch Leven Castle."

Sir Gyles was alive? Thank God. "Tell me," Lord Grey asked, praying more good news would follow. "Did anyone else survive?"

A long silence fell between them, then the knight shook his head. "Nay, my lord."

Bedamned. His heart aching at the loss, he turned toward the king. "Your Grace, I believe Sir Aleyn speaks the truth."

"I as well. Come." King Alexander started toward the knight.

Trálin, along with the others, followed.

Two days later, safe in the confines of Loch Leven Castle, Catarine interlaced her fingers as she and her fey warriors stood in the great room awaiting King Alexander's entrance. The roaring flames in the hearth offered warmth, but did nae penetrate the chill of her thoughts. Had more attacks occurred since they'd departed the Otherworld? Was anyone else in her family dead?

Trálin laid his hand upon her shoulder.

Warmth swept through her at his touch, kindling longings she must forever quell.

"You are worried," he said, a furrow in his brow, "but know I will remain by your side until we find those you seek."

"I canna help but wonder if I was wrong in my belief that you and the other Scots can be of help."

"Lass, do nae invite unwanted troubles," Trálin said. "Regardless of your worries, I have many friends whom I can turn to, and I have sent runners out in search of information."

Nerves shuddered through her. What if they failed? "Trálin, I—"

The door swung open, and the castle guard entered. "I announce the arrival of Alexander, King of Scotland, and his queen, Margaret."

Catarine curtsied as the others bowed their respect as the royal couple entered.

Silence fell throughout the chamber as the king and queen took their places on the dais.

"The queen and I are deeply grateful to each of you for freeing us," King Alexander said. "Without your help, we would be dead."

Her eyes somber, Queen Margaret nodded.

The king's mouth tightened into a hard line. "Know the Comyns will regret their treachery. With the Earl of Torc's support, I will achieve justice. But"—his gaze paused upon Catarine, then on each of her warriors—"'tis nae the reason I have called you here." He stood, straightened to his full height. "I gave my word that I would support you in your quest, a promise I will now keep."

Hope filled Catarine, and she curtsied. "My thanks, Your Grace."

Shrewd eyes studied her. "Lady Catarine, how many men will you need?"

A question she'd given much thought. "Twenty, Your Grace."

"It will be done." King Alexander faced Trálin. "Lord Grey."

Trálin bowed. "Aye, Your Grace."

"I have spoken with the master-at-arms, and he is expecting you," the king said. "He will help your selection of the men necessary."

"My thanks, Your Grace," Trálin replied.

The queen stood. "Lady Catarine."

Curious, Catarine curtsied. "Your Grace?"

"I know you wish to depart this eve," the queen said, her voice gentle, "but our travel to reach Loch Leven Castle has been exhausting. In addition, it grows late. However anxious you are to leave, I request that you and your men take this night to rest. The extra time will ensure Lord Grey has time to prepare the additional men to depart in the morning."

Angst rolled through her as she glanced toward the window. Indeed, the red sunset smeared the handcrafted glass. However much she wished to leave this night once Trálin had selected the king's men, the queen's concern held wisdom. "Of course, Your Grace," Catarine replied. "Your generosity is appreciated."

A smile curved the queen's mouth, her eyes soft with understanding. "I know you are tired, so we will depart. A maid will show you to your chamber." She turned to the king. "I am ready to leave, my husband."

King Alexander stood, and with his wife's hand atop his, he escorted her from the chamber.

Their guard exited behind them, then closed the door in their wake.

At the soft thud of the door closing, Catarine exhaled.

"With the stone circle nearby, I know you are anxious to leave," Trálin said, "but a few hours will change naught."

Atair stepped before her. "Indeed, a night's rest will be welcome to us all." He offered her his arm. "Allow me to escort you to your chamber."

She nodded to Atair as her gaze met Trálin's. "Lord Grey, I will meet you early on the morrow in the stable with the king's men."

Trálin's mouth tightened, then he gave a nod. "I will ensure all is prepared to leave, my lady."

"My thanks." With a long last look, Catarine turned. 'Twas for the best for her to retire to her chamber escorted by Atair. Alone with Lord Grey, with her wanting him until she ached, her choice this night might nae be wise.

Moonlight shimmered over the ripple of waves on the loch as Trálin stared from the wall walk of Loch Leven Castle toward the mountains beyond. He fisted his hands at his side, thankful for the blast of icy cold to numb the dangerous thoughts rumbling through his mind. Neither did he miss the covert looks Catarine had given him when they'd awaited the king and queen's arrival earlier. She wanted him, which helped bloody naught.

Thank God Atair had offered to escort her to her chamber. However much he wanted to be alone with her, with the dangerous attraction between, such folly could invite a decision he might regret.

A decision? Nay, 'twas no decision to be made. He wanted to make love to her. Bedamned her vow, that her realm needed her wedded to the neighboring prince to bring peace, or the fact that she was royalty, he wanted her in his bed.

More important, he could nae forget that she was a fairy.

Errant clouds raced through the sky and splintered the moon's glow, casting the water in a half-shadow, half-silvery sheen. The eerie blend nurtured the mix of emotions searing his mind.

A slow pounding started in his head, and he rubbed his brow, wishing this night long past.

"You are awake?"

At Catarine's soft voice, he stilled. God help him. "I am." He didn't turn. Didn't dare. She was the reason he stood here this night, unable to sleep and struggling between wanting to go to her, and knowing that if he did, 'twould be a grave mistake. The gentle slap of waves echoed from below, lending a soft appeal to the moment. He grimaced. "You should be abed."

The pad of steps upon stone echoed as she moved closer.

Her scent of woman and lilac filled his senses. His body trembled with the need to touch her, to strip her slowly and make love with her until she cried out her release. He closed his eyes.

Bloody hell.

"Trálin?"

"Aye?"

"Will you nae look at me?"

The confusion in her voice eroded his resolve to leave her untouched. "Catarine," he whispered, "'tis best if you leave." Silence filled the night, thick with the scent of the oncoming winter, potent with awareness.

"Trálin, please."

Hurt filled her words, and he damned the entire situation. With a prayer for strength, he turned, met her eyes within the mix of darkness and moonlight. Beyond the worry, in the shimmer of light, he caught the sheen of tears.

"You have been crying." Shaken, he stepped forward and caught her chin. "Why?"

"After this night we will nae have the chance to be alone again."

He forced a smile. "But we will have many moments to talk," he replied, needing to sway her away from the dangerous topic of intimacy on any level.

"You know that is nae what I meant."

Aye, the problem. "If asked, given the strong feelings we hold toward the other, our nae having time to be alone is for the best."

A tear pooled on her lower lid, dripped on her cheek to slide down the curve of her chin, and wobbled onto the tip of his thumb. "It should be."

"God's teeth." Trálin drew her against him, loving the feel of her body against his, wanting her forever. "Catarine, we must think of the time ahead, of the duty we each face."

"Do you think I have nae tried? But each thought fills me with regret." She looked up at him. "I do nae love Prince Zacheus."

Trálin lifted her chin with his thumb. "But you love your kingdom, respect your father, and want peace for your land. And——"

Her body trembling, she pulled away. "Forgive me. You are right. I am being selfish. 'Twas weak of me to come here in such a state."

"You are nae weak, but a woman of passion, one who loves her people, and is torn between the two." Before he did something he would regret, he caught her arm and guided her toward the turret.

"Where are you taking me?"

"To *your* chamber," he replied, the desire in his voice betraying his need.

She remained silent.

Torchlight from the wall sconces flickered against the turret walls in a sensual display as they descended, echoing the fact that never would they have more than the stolen kisses from days past.

As they entered the corridor, he halted before his door, glanced to her entry several doors away. "Good night, Catarine. I will wait here until you have gone inside your room."

Eyes dark with desire met his. "Trálin, I——"

Body aching, he pressed a finger over her lips. "On with you, lass, I will see you in the morning."

A smile trembled on her mouth. "Good night then." She hesitated.

"Go on, we both need our sleep."

She arched a brow. "And will you be able to sleep this night?"

The truth. "Nay."

"Nor I," she said.

The pad of steps echoed up the turret. In the entry, a lone figure came into view.

Panic swept him. "'Tis Atair!"

In the torchlight, her face paled. "He canna see us together. Go inside your chamber, hurry!"

Atair started to turn down the corridor.

Blast it. Trálin hauled her inside his chamber and shut the door behind him with a quiet snap. "Say naught," he whispered.

In the candlelight, wide eyed, she nodded.

On edge, he pressed his ear to the hewn wood.

The sound of steps increased, then moved past. Several moments later, the clunk of a door shutting echoed from down the corridor.

Trálin's entire body relaxed. On an exhale, he turned. "He has entered his chamber."

"Thankfully, he did nae see us together," she replied, her eyes never leaving his.

The moment shifted, grew dangerous. Alone. If they chose, they could fulfill their desires. His throat dry, he held her gaze. "You must go."

"I know." She didn't move.

Awareness burned through him like a heated sword.

"You will be a hard man to forget, MacGruder. I doubt that I ever will."

A long moment passed as he stared at her mouth, the tempting curve that beckoned him to again taste. "Catarine, 'tis best if you leave, before I do something foolish like kiss you."

She pressed her body flush against his, raised her mouth until 'twas a hair's breadth from his own. "'Tis what I would like as well."

Chapter Thirteen

Catarine's full lips glistening in the firelight from the hearth within his chamber, desire seared Trálin, erasing his every good intent. His breath stumbled. Bedamned, just one kiss, one taste, and he would be satisfied.

As if she read his thoughts, her lips parted in seductive welcome.

"Ah lass," he whispered as he claimed her mouth. Her taste infused him, burned his soul until all he could think about was her. Sliding his hands to her waist, he edged her against the door, and with savoring slowness, eased his body flush against hers.

Her soft curves melded against him, her moan drove him wild, and her hands around his neck drawing him closer severed any coherent thought.

Aching with need, he took, tasted her like a man possessed. At her next shudder, he broke the kiss, held her away, his entire body trembling. "What am I doing?" He shook his head. "Never should I have touched you."

Eyes dark with passion watched him with fierce conviction. "Then why does it feel so right?"

He closed his eyes, fought for the strength to make her leave.

"Trálin?"

At the worry in her voice, he opened his eyes. His emotions a complex tangle of need, desire, and duty, he brushed the pad of his thumb across her cheek. "I want you, more than you will ever know."

"I want you as well."

His bed behind them came into focus. *Bedamned!* His pulse

racing, he rested his brow against hers. "Catarine, 'tis best if you return to your chamber."

"Wait," she said, "I have a thought."

With the hint of smoke scenting the chamber, the flicker of flames from the hearth painting an air of intimacy in a shimmering swath, if the situation weren't so dire, he would laugh. 'Twas as if this moment conspired against him.

"A thought?" he asked, curious how that fit into this gut-wrenching debacle. "How does it solve our predicament?"

A flicker of a smile touched her mouth. "Predicament, is it?"

"Aye." Her teasing voice lured him, seduced him to believe she could have conceived an answer to this impossible situation. And, how could she be so calm when their time together must end? Be-damned, the lass was driving him insane.

She stepped closer, pressed her body against his.

"Ah lass," he whispered as he kissed the curve of her neck, savored the pleasure rolling through him. He was playing a dangerous game, but how for this moment could he nae savor what too soon would be lost?

"Now," he said as he continued, "are you going to answer my question?"

"If you keep kissing me," she whispered, "I will nae be able to think, much less talk."

With regret he lifted his head, her taste potent on his tongue.

Face flushed, her gaze dark with pleasure, she watched him. "We are to meet everyone in the great room at the break of dawn, are we nae?"

Enjoying the dangerous game, loving how this one woman challenged him as no other, he laid his palm against the door on either side of her head and lowered his mouth to nibble her lower lip. "We are." He slid the tip of his tongue down the silken curve of her throat, then up to encircle her mouth. After allowing himself the luxury of teasing her a wee bit longer, he claimed her lips in a slow, deep kiss. When her breaths started coming fast, pleased, he lifted his head. "Meeting in the great room is nae an answer."

"Trálin," she rasped, her voice rough with desire, "I am having a hard time thinking."

"Good."

With a laugh, she pushed his mouth away. "I wish to ask you to—"

Too aware of her, he shook his head. "Be careful what you ask for. At this moment there is little which I can deny."

With a hard swallow, Catarine glanced toward the bed, then back at him. "I want to stay with you this night."

Wanting nothing else, he cleared his throat. "As much as I wish for the same, 'tis forbidden that we make love."

"I know, but can we nae enjoy the next few hours together?" She paused, her gaze searching his with needy desperation. "I have heard of whispers of the pleasures a man can give a woman, and a woman a man. For this once, I would like to know if they are true."

Images ignited in his mind of the many ways he could make love to her and leave her a virgin. Of the ways she could pleasure him without risk as well. Bloody hell, what was he thinking? He was a fool to ponder her request. A pignut had more sense. Except the lure of a few hours with her, the knowledge that once wed she would be with a man who made her feel naught, slayed the scales of common sense.

"On one condition."

"Anything," she whispered.

Anything. His body trembled with desire. "Before the others awaken, you must return to your chamber. Never would I want to tarnish your reputation, or harm your promises made."

Relief swept through her eyes. "Thank you for this precious gift."

The sincerity of her reply humbled him. "'Tis you who are the gift." Catarine was an amazing woman, and he regretted her life would be spent in a loveless marriage. However common her fate, he found his heart filled with regret. Before he weighed his decision overmuch, he swept her off her feet.

Turquoise eyes widened, and he caught the hint of nerves.

"Do nae worry," he said as he laid her upon the bed, knelt by her side. Flames from the hearth accented her face alive with a warm glow and wonder. "Never would I hurt you."

"I—I trust you."

Humbled by her words, by her gift of this moment, he pressed a soft kiss on her mouth. "You are beautiful."

Unsure eyes met his. "I am simply a woman."

A smile kicked up on his mouth. "There is naught simple about you, which endears you to me more." Wishing this night could last forever, he traced the neckline of the soft material of her gown. "If I had a wish, 'twould be to see all of you."

Her eyes slightly widened, and full lips parted with an unsteady breath.

"Would you allow me such?"

Catarine gave a shaky nod.

His body trembling with the intensity of this moment, he slid his thumb beneath the material. Paused. He lifted his gaze to find hers dark with curiosity and need. "Tell me if you wish me to stop."

Her lower lip trembled. "With what you make me feel, I doubt I ever will."

Air hissed between his teeth. "One of us will be strong." And with her being an innocent and unaware of the feelings inspired in making love, he vowed 'twould be him. To bring her pleasure, he toyed with the woven edge, wanting to see her passion grow, her body to tremble with need.

"Why are you going so slowly?"

A smile touched his mouth.

Her eyes widened with distress, and she turned away.

He stilled. "Catarine, what is wrong?"

Hesitant, she turned toward him. "I know naught of the ways of intimacy."

Aware of the magnitude of this moment, Trálin paused. "For the next few hours, think about only of what we feel for the other."

"What do you wish me to do?"

"Enjoy . . . as I will."

"Do you nae want me to touch you as well?"

Images of her hands sliding down his skin, caressing him, wrapping around his hard length filled his mind. At this moment, 'twas about her. "My bringing you pleasure is an act that will bring my own as well."

She hesitated as if far from convinced. "Are you sure?"

"Aye." The importance of his every touch, his determination to show her the amazing things her body could feel, focused in his mind. Unless she asked him to stop. A request that, however difficult to fulfill, he would honor.

With painful slowness, he slid the top of her gown aside, exposing her full breasts, sultry curves that would make any man beg. He worked to catch his breath.

"Is something amiss?"

He gazed at her in disbelief. "Do you nae know how beautiful you are?"

The shimmer of firelight across her face exposed the sweep of red over her cheeks.

"Nay, there is naught to be embarrassed about. You are beautiful." He hesitated. "I would like to touch you, everywhere."

She caught her lower lip with her teeth. "I would like that, but however much I am curious to know everything about making love, I must keep my innocence."

A fact etched in his mind with painful clarity. "And you will, that I promise."

Distress clouded her face. "I am sorry I canna give you more."

He gave her a tender smile. "Do nae apologize. Our each moment is a gift I never thought to have." He cupped her full breasts with his hands, enjoyed the transformation of her expression from cautious nerves to immense pleasure. Unable to wait a moment longer, he lowered his head to taste.

"Trálin . . ."

"Just feel." He covered the tip of her breast with his mouth, enjoyed her gasp of surprise that eroded to a low moan. Slow. He had to take his time, ensure this night would give her the memories to savor forever.

At an excruciating pace, he worked his way over the soft fullness of each breast, then nuzzled his way back to the sensitive tip. When her body began to tremble, he moved lower, tasting the flat of her stomach with slow thoroughness, savoring her unique scent of woman and wonder.

Emotions storming him, he lifted his eyes, held hers. "I want to see all of you."

Her pulse raced at her throat, bringing his attention to the sexual flush stealing up her skin. "I would like that as well."

His fingers tense with restraint, he edged the last remnants of clothing aside.

Naked.

In wonder he absorbed her beauty, her every curve that invited and intrigued him and left him aching with need. On a rough exhale, he tamped down the urge to push her back and drive deep inside her. She knew naught of lovemaking, a lesson he would enjoy teaching her.

With a lazy finger, he slid around her sensitive skin.

Catarine's body shuddered.

This time, he swept his finger but inches from her private place, then stroked down her sensitive thigh.

The contrast of his hands against the tender curves of her skin raised his awareness further, and regret filled him that this night would be the last they shared. What it would be like to have each night together. But wishing for the fact would nae make it real.

He slid his hand across her soft wetness, and savored how her body shuddered against his every movement. "Methinks you are liking that."

"As if you did nae know that," she replied in a half moan.

"Mayhap." He made several large circles around her sensitive folds, his each sweep closer, teasing.

As he continued to touch her, beads of sweat glittered on her brow.

With seductive slowness, again he slid his fingers to her swollen folds. "Now, to touch you." He slid the length of his finger into her wetness and began to move in slow strokes.

Her body arched and shuddered.

"Just feel," he urged as he slid a second finger within and increased his pace, in awe of her passion, of how her innocence made him want her more. With each stroke her hesitation fell away, until she arched to meet him. "Now to taste you." His body on fire, wanting her with his every breath, needing to taste her, he swirled his tongue with excruciating slowness within her delicate folds.

Her body began to convulse.

Wanting to give her everything, to take her higher, he flicked his tongue faster.

Her body arched with an explosive shudder. "Trálin!"

"Let go," he urged, "feel."

"I—"

As she cried out with her release, he moved, then drew her body against him and savored her each shudder, too aware this special moment, this night, would end all too soon.

Hours later in his chamber, Trálin held Catarine's body against his, her soft breaths even in a deep, restful sleep. He could look at her forever. Through the rough pane of glass, he caught wisps of moonlight struggling into the chamber, their sheen as if a wish tossed into the night. With the thoughts invading his mind about her, of a life together, they were wishes indeed.

He edged back a swath of hair that'd tumbled against her cheek, then pressed a kiss against her brow. "What am I to do with you lass?" The sadness of his words echoed within the room. "Naught. We each have our own life path, which does nae includes the other."

She shifted, and a frown worked across her full lips. Lips he'd tasted, touched as he'd watched her fall over the edge many times over these last few hours. Never would he tire of making love to her. But this night, as his dreams to be with her, would soon end.

On a soft groan, Catarine shifted against him, then her hand reached out to touch him.

His heart squeezed at how natural it felt for her to reach for him in her sleep, as if they were meant to be together. If only he could tell her that . . . God in heaven, he loved her. Reality shattered the flicker of joy, of dreams of her in his life. Nay, he could tell her naught of his feelings toward her.

"Trálin?"

At her sleep-roughened whisper, he glanced down to find her watching him. He forced a smile. "I thought you were asleep."

She hesitated, pushed up on her elbow. "Why do you look so sad?"

As if he could tell her the truth—that he wanted to damn responsibility and have her for always. He swallowed hard, stroked his thumb across her cheek. "I was wishing the night would never end."

Sadness trembled in her eyes as she glanced toward the window. Caught in the battle of night, the moon flickered through the break in the clouds. "'Tis passing too fast."

"'Tis," he replied.

She turned. "Will you nae try and sleep?"

"I have caught a bit," he lied, refusing to divulge that he was too on edge to contemplate such. Nor would he lose another precious moment left with her. "You should try and catch a bit more sleep. You will need it with the hard travel ahead this day."

Catarine shifted closer and gave him a slow smile, that of a woman sated. "Never did I think a man's touch would bring so much pleasure."

"And now?" he teased.

"I fear I am ruined."

His laugh faded away. Indeed, as him. Never would he find another woman who moved him like her.

"Trálin?"

At the hesitation in her voice, he took her hand, pressed a soft kiss on the palm. "Aye?"

Her gaze flickered to his mouth, and red swept her face.

"What is it?" She cleared her throat, and he understood. "You enjoyed my tasting you?"

The flush on her face deepened. "Aye, but you did nae find relief."

Touched she thought of him, he smiled. "But I did. Watching you, aware 'twas me who made you feel such pleasure, is its own gift."

"But—"

A hard rap sounded on the door.

Bloody hell! Trálin sat up. No one could find her here! He put his hands over his lips.

She nodded. The rumple of sheets spilled over as she sat by his side.

With quiet movements, he slipped from the bed, slid his sword from its sheath, and crept to the door.

Another rap sounded, this time louder.

"Who goes there?" he demanded.

"'Tis Sionn."

Fear tore through him. Something horrible had to have happened for the fey warrior to be here this late. "What is wrong?"

"'Tis Princess Catarine."

Trálin glanced toward where she sat upon his bed.

Her face paled.

Please God in heaven, let them nae suspect she was with him. "Is she ill?"

"Nay, Lord Grey, she is gone!"

Chapter Fourteen

Sionn's announcement that she was nae in her chamber rattled through Catarine's mind like an avalanche. With a gasp, she hurried from Trálin's bed to where he stood beside the door. "They canna find me in your chamber!" she whispered.

Lord Grey shook his head. "Nor will they."

"Why would anyone be in search of me?" she asked, her mind fighting for reasons.

"After the events of the last few days," Trálin replied, "Atair must have set up rounds with your warriors to ensure you were safe throughout the night. I should have considered such."

"Lord Grey?" the fey warrior outside his chamber door again called.

"A moment."

With quiet steps, Trálin hurried to the bed.

"What are you doing?" she whispered.

He grabbed her gown from the bed, then returned. "Here."

Heat swept up her cheeks. God in heaven, rattled by Sionn showing up outside Trálin's chamber, she'd overlooked that she was naked. Embarrassed, she took her garb, tugged it on.

Once she finished, Trálin turned to the door. "What do you mean she is gone?"

"My lord," Sionn replied from the other side. "I went to check on Princess Catarine. The door to her chamber is open, and she is gone."

Open? Unease spread through her.

Deep brows creased Trálin's brow as he glanced toward her. "Your door was nae left open, was it?" he mouthed.

She shook her head.

His frown deepened. "I will be out posthaste."

"The other warriors and I are gathering in the great room," Sionn said. "Meet us there." The firm tap of steps in the corridor faded.

Nerves thundered through her. "We have a greater problem than my being discovered. Why was someone in my chamber?"

"It has to be one of your fey warriors," Lord Grey said.

"Nay, the others would have known." An unnerving thought came to mind. Nay, please let her be wrong.

At her hesitation, Trálin frowned. "What is it?"

"What if whoever entered my chamber was someone sent by the one my warriors and I are searching for?"

"God's teeth. Whatever mayhem is about, there is one way to find out."

"Aye, but I canna be seen leaving your room. Where should I go? My chamber is out of the question, but it should be somewhere where I will be *found*."

He rubbed his chin, now shadowed with dark rust stubble. On a grimace he dropped his hand. "For now, remain here. After I have left, go to the wall walk."

She arched a brow. "As if my men will have nae looked there?"

"Tell whoever finds you first that unable to sleep, you left your chamber earlier and have been walking around since."

"And they will believe that?"

"What other choice do they have?" he replied. "Besides, they will be relieved you were nae in your chamber and are safe."

"I canna," she said. "I never lie to my warriors."

"Nor will I ask you to now. But weigh your answer with the question of what they will think if they learn that over the past few hours you have been with me."

Guilt trampled thoughts of the impossibly wonderful things he'd done to her. Shaken, she nodded.

Trálin dragged on his garb, then caught her mouth in a long kiss. "Never will I forget you, this night, or what you mean to me." Before she could reply, he released her and slipped from his chamber.

The errant crackle of the flames filled the silence as she stared at the entry. What she meant to him? Hope ignited. Did he love her as well?

Nay, 'twas her own knowledge that she loved him which invited such foolish thoughts.

Saddened this special night had come to an end, she turned the bed where they'd made love, their hours together filled with more pleasures than she'd ever imagine. Never would she forget Trálin. Except, their night was over. Before anyone found her here, she must go.

After plaiting her hair, Catarine hurried to the door, cracked it open, and peered out.

Across the corridor, Atair stood leaning against the wall, his arms crossed.

Shock rolled through her.

Her senior fey warrior straightened. "You can come out. There is much we need to address."

A sense of doom shrouded her as she shoved the door wider. 'Twould seem she and Trálin had kept no secret. She exited the chamber, pushed the door shut. "I—"

"Nae here. Follow me." Atair strode down the hall toward the turret.

Her mind a mess of nerves and guilt, she followed.

At the steps, he started up. At the top, Atair pushed the door open and gestured for her forward.

The whip of cold air hit her as she stepped outside. The wall walk. Her supposed destination. Fitting.

Her senior fey warrior strode past several crenellations. At the corner battlement, after a quick scan, he stepped deep into the shadows and halted.

A light blanket of snow crunched beneath her feet as she walked like a woman sentenced. As she passed a crenellation, she glanced out. The windswept water of the loch shimmered beneath the rays of the moon. What she wouldn't give to be out in a boat there.

"Do nae linger," Atair said.

A shiver of unease swept through her as she moved into the shield of blackness.

"What were you thinking?" Atair whispered.

"I have compromised naught." The truth, if you considered she'd done nothing to produce a child.

"Naught? Late in the night you are absent from your chamber, and as I suspected, you were with Lord Grey. Thankfully, might I add."

"There could have been many reasons why I was absent from my chamber."

A sigh of exasperation fell into the night. "You are nae a commoner whose actions ignite but scorn and whispers, but a princess, one whose marriage to Prince Zacheus will bring peace to our realms."

She stiffened. "I am well aware of my status and consequences of my actions."

"Aye, 'tis the consequences of your actions we speak of," he agree, empathy in his voice. "Nor would I choose a loveless marriage for you. But 'tis done. And your agreement to wed given." Silence fell between them, broken by the distant cry of an owl. "Do you think your betrothed would marry you if he knew of this night's excursion?"

Embarrassment swept her, the intimacies of the hours before with Trálin vivid in her mind. "Lord Grey was naught but a gentleman."

Shrewd eyes studied her. "You did nae answer my question, nor is it one I will raise again."

If he'd spoken in anger, she could have found a reply.

"Catarine, though you shield your feelings for the Scot, to me they are transparent."

She stiffened. "What are you saying?"

"You love him."

"Atair, I . . ." As if denying the truth would convince him? He knew her too well. "I shouldna."

"But you do."

Emotions stormed her, and tears blurred her gaze. Frustrated, she wiped the tears from her eyes. "Is it wrong that I wanted but a few hours with a man I can never have?"

"What answer do you want me to give you?" he asked. "That of a warrior who wishes to bring peace to his realm, or a friend? Or, mayhap the question is nae for me to answer, but for you?"

He was right, the answer was hers to make. Humbled, she shook her head. "Never did I mean anyone harm. For a little while I wanted to be with Trálin, to have, however brief, that which will never again be in my grasp."

"I—"

"Once we depart," she interrupted, needing to finish, "never will I allow myself to be in a situation where my loyalty to my betrothed is in question."

"A wise decision." Atair paused. "I swear to you, none will know where you spent this night."

Grateful, she nodded. "My thanks."

An owl cried out, this time closer.

"We have other worries," he said.

At his somber tone, a shiver swept her. She remembered Sionn's words outside Lord Grey's door. "You speak of finding my chamber door open?"

"Aye."

"I did nae leave it so."

"I suspected as much," he said, "which is why I wanted to speak to you before we meet with the others."

A ripple of fear whipped through her. "You suspected as much?"

"Indeed, the reason I alerted the castle guards to your absence."

Mortified, she gasped. "Why would you alert the castle guards that I was nae in my chamber?"

"If you had been abducted," he replied, "I wanted no delay in our giving chase."

"Abducted? But you waited for me outside Lord Grey's chamber once he left."

"I accompanied Sionn in hopes to find you there—safe. Once we reached Lord Grey's door, I caught the wisp of your voice."

She caught her lower lip between her teeth. "Do you think Sionn heard me as well?"

"He gave no indication he had." Which assured naught. Blast it. So caught up in her time with Trálin, she'd nae heard her men's approach. And, what had Atair heard of her discussion with Trálin? She glanced at him.

In the shadows, he shifted.

As if he would tell her? They had more pressing concerns. "Who do you think went to my chamber?"

"Whoever it was, they did more than open your door, but entered."

"Entered?" She stilled. "Who would dare breach my chamber?"

A soft breeze, thick with the chilling cold, swept past. "Again the reason I wished to speak with you first in private. When I searched your room to ensure you were indeed gone, I caught a faint sense of evil."

She stared at her senior fey warrior in disbelief. "'Twould seem whoever we are trailing discovered I am in Scotland and searching for them. How is this possible?"

"I do nae know," he said, anger clinging to his every word, "but we must use caution. You are no longer safe."

"The king and queen!"

"Nay," Atair said. "I checked for any sign of an intruder's presence near their chamber."

"Did any of the fey warriors report someone trying to enter their chamber as well?"

"Nay."

A sinking feeling settled in her stomach. "Which confirms that the intruder came for me. And with your sensing the presence of evil this has a connection with one of the fey."

"And proof," Atair said, "that whoever is behind this intends for more than your uncle's life."

"'Tis my entire family they want dead." The somber truth weighed heavy on her as she scanned the moonlight touched land across the loch. "Do you think whoever entered my room is still within the castle walls?"

"My concern as well," Atair replied. "Before we were to meet, I sent the remainder of the fey warriors to search for any sign of the intruder, though I doubt they will find anyone. Whoever dared to enter Loch Leven Castle would nae be fool enough to linger and risk being caught."

Worry gave way to anger. "If they think to scare me away, they are wrong."

"Let nae your upset guide you," Atair cautioned. "Whoever is behind this is someone of great cunning. Do you have any idea who holds such high aspirations?"

"Nay," Catarine replied. "We worried the tracks from before would be covered. Now the point is moot. We will follow the intruder's trail."

"Lady Catarine?" a man called in the distance.

"'Tis one of the castle guards," Atair said. "Come. 'Tis best if they believe one of the fey warriors located you; fewer questions will be asked. We can continue our discussion once we are alone with our warriors."

"I agree." She stepped from the shadows, Atair at her side.

Chapter Fifteen

Trálin followed the castle guard as he exited the turret, thankful when he called out Catarine's name. Several paces behind, Sionn and the other fey warriors exited onto the wall walk in his wake.

In the moonlight, Sionn paused. "You found her?"

"Aye," Atair replied. "Unable to sleep, she was out taking a walk."

"Thank God you are safe." Sionn faced the castle guard. "Pass word to the others in search of Lady Catarine that she is safe."

The guard nodded.

As the guard hurried off, Trálin walked over with her fey warriors.

"I regret the upset my departure from my chamber has caused," Catarine said.

"'Tis relieved we are to find you unharmed," Trálin replied, giving the expected reply. In the sheen of the moon's silvery rays, he caught Atair's cool look. So, the senior fey warrior knew of her being in his chamber this night. The last thing he wanted was trouble between them, but 'twould seem 'twas too late to avoid that.

"Lord Grey," Atair said, his voice grave. "Lady Catarine and I have spoken of the situation."

"The situation?" With a frown, Drax glanced from Atair to Catarine. "We were told you were missing."

"Someone was in my chamber," Catarine stated. "Thankfully, unable to sleep, I had left to go for a walk."

"Do you know who it is?" Trálin asked.

"We are unsure," Atair replied, "but we believe their appearance is connected with the knights we chased into Scotland." His expression grim, he glanced toward his men. "Did anyone notice anything odd?"

"Nay," Sionn replied.

The remainder of the fey warriors shook their heads.

"If anything," Magnus said, "'twas as if an air of peace filled the night."

Catarine gasped. "A spell."

"A spell?" Trálin asked. The ramifications left him shaken. A warrior he could fight. One of the fey with their unearthly abilities was another matter. "Aye," Atair said with a nod. "It makes sense, and I should have figured it out before. Whoever murdered her uncle holds powerful magic, proven by their ability to bring humans into the Otherworld. And, having sent troops to follow us, once they were in close enough proximity, they used their power to infuse an air of peace over us. With our guards lowered and feeling safe within Loch Leven Castle, their man slipped inside."

"Proximity?" Trálin asked.

"Aye," Catarine replied. "For magic to work, whoever wields it must be within a league."

With a grimace, Trálin scoured the winding shores across the waves. "So whoever is behind this, they are near."

"Or was," Atair said.

"Blast it," Trálin said. And what if she had nae been with him? In her chamber and with whomever is behind this holding powerful magic, they would have taken her or . . . "What do you think the intruder wanted?" Catarine stiffened.

"At best, to abduct her," Atair replied, his voice grave.

Furious, Trálin met Catarine's gaze; she angled her jaw in defiance, but he saw the fear she tried to hide. "God in heaven, you believe they wanted you dead."

"Atair and I both agree 'twas an attempt on my life," Catarine replied, a quiver in her voice. "And confirms our fears that my uncle's murderer wishes to kill my entire family and seize the crown."

Trálin understood her concern for those she loved, but the thought of her dead left an emptiness inside.

His face taut, Atair crossed his arms. "We must stop whoever is behind this from returning to the Otherworld."

"Aye," Trálin agreed. "But how? With the ability of magic, will whoever guides their minions be able to shield them from our view as well?"

Her face illuminated by the broken moonlight on the wall walk, Catarine shook her head. "However powerful, one of the fey canna shield a human from view. But their attempt on my life will serve us well."

Lord Grey rubbed the growing stubble on his chin. "How so?"

"If we find whoever tried to kill me this night," she explained, "I believe he will lead us to the person we seek."

The fey warriors around him nodded, but Trálin caught the hard looks at him shot by Atair. A fact he couldna change after this night. However shameful, he didna regret the few hours he and Catarine had shared this night.

"One more concern," Catarine continued, nerves edging her voice. "My family should be hidden. Except, as king, my father will nae hide and wait for the next attack. With his brother murdered, he will seek justice. But in trying to locate who was behind the murder of his brother, without knowing whom he seeks is using magic, I fear he will place himself in grave danger. We must depart posthaste and see if we can pick up the intruder's trail."

Atair nodded. "By the time we gather food to travel and ensure King Alexander's knights are readied, the sun will be up enough to guide us."

Surprised by his claim, Trálin glanced toward the east. Indeed, against the sheen of moonlight, a wash of purple shimmered in the sky weak with stars announcing the arrival of the new day. To the west, an angry roil of clouds banked the sky. "Another storm is moving in. We must pick up the trail before it hits or any chance of tracking the intruder will be lost."

Dark clouds smeared with streaks of black convulsed overhead, the angry roil battering the majestic mountains around them with violent disregard. On edge, Catarine peered between two snow-covered boulders. Being wedged in the hillside, shielded by the clusters of stones, offered them excellent protection against the harsh elements, but any who passed below were also hidden.

In the distance, the narrowed rock walls fell away. Cradled in the rough roll of hills beyond, the stone ring stood defiant against the brutal elements.

Majestic.

How could anyone think otherwise?

Thoughts of the person who'd entered her room at Lock Leven Castle erased musings of the stone circle's grandeur. Again she scanned the narrowed passage with a critical eye. "I see no sign of the English knights."

"Nor I," Trálin said at her side.

"If the men are headed toward the stone circle as their tracks indicate," she said, "I would have thought we would have seen them by now."

"Mayhap they have already passed?" Atair said at her other side, voicing her worst fear.

"Nay," Trálin said. "The shortcut I led us through is known to very few. When we searched the break through the mountains below, neither did we see any sign of recent passage."

"With the frozen ground, we might have missed something," Catarine said, worry edging her voice.

Trálin shook his head. "With our numbers, I doubt such. With the storm closing in and the men a distance ahead, 'twas best that we moved ahead of them."

Mayhap, but a part of her wondered if once they'd found the tracks, they should have tried to catch up to the men regardless of the risk. Scraping her teeth against her lower lip, Catarine mulled the fact that when they'd searched for the intruder's tracks outside of Loch Leven Castle, she and her fey warriors had found naught. Except, as she'd suspected, Trálin had found signs of the men's passing.

Again she scanned the weather-smoothed walls of the narrow canyon, and prayed they'd missed naught. "We will wait here a while more."

An icy burst of wind buffeted the boulders, and errant flakes of snow holding the promise of the incoming storm whipped past.

"I think we should hold out the rest of the day," Atair said. "I worry that more knights have joined their ranks. If so, this is the best place for us to confront the English knights."

Catarine worried her finger across the sheath of her dagger. "We will soon find out. If indeed they have reinforced their ranks and we are greatly outnumbered, we will trail them and take them out one at a time. Once our numbers are close, then we attack."

Lord Grey's mouth tightened. "'Tis a dangerous backup plan."

As if she liked it? At least they had twenty of King Alexander's knights to bolster their ranks. Anxious, Catarine scanned the rough roll of land, then focused on the circle of stones that offered entrance to the otherworld. The grey, timeworn boulders stood proud against the murky day as if in subtle guard. How she wished this confrontation was over, the threat eradicated. Tension would remain within their realms until she and Prince Zacheus wed.

Shadows of movement flickered at the entrance to the pass.

"Someone is coming," she warned.

A moment later, through the narrowed entrance, a stocky man with long obsidian hair tied behind his back ran into view.

Catarine exhaled. "'Tis Ranulf returning."

"Let us hope he comes with news that those we follow are en route," Atair said.

She nodded.

In a half run, Ranulf hurried along the winding valley, then up the steep embankment toward where they hid. With one last glance toward the entry, the fey warrior slipped behind the aged stone and paused beside Catarine as the other warriors gathered around.

"Are they coming?" she asked.

"Aye, I counted seventeen English knights," Ranulf replied. "They are about half a league out."

"Whoever was in my chamber indeed joined with others," Catarine said.

"Still, I am surprised that their numbers are so small."

"So they can travel for speed," Lord Grey said, "'Tis what I would do if I wanted to make good time."

"Regardless, their small rank works to our advantage," Catarine said. "We should be able to capture them with minimal risk."

"After they dared enter your chamber in Loch Leven Castle," Lord Grey said, "I assure you, I have no problem interrogating them as to who is behind these attacks."

"Nor I," Atair growled.

Catarine frowned as her other warriors nodded in agreement. "The knights will remain unharmed unless they resist."

A muscle worked in Trálin's jaw.

Atair's eyes narrowed.

Her other fey warrior's expressions darkened, but they remained quiet.

"There they come," Ranulf said.

Catarine turned.

Between several large boulders at the entrance to the valley, English knights marching at a quick stride came into view, all well armed. Every so often, they glanced around.

"Do you think they suspect our presence?" Catarine whispered.

"Mayhap, they seem worried," Atair replied, "but if they tried to flee now, 'tis too late."

Across the pass, from behind the thick of stones lining the wind-swept angled rocks, she caught a brief wave; the Scottish knights hidden on the opposite side were ready for her signal.

Catarine clasped her sword and waited for the English knights to move below them.

Closer.

A few steps more.

She raised her fingers to her lips, blew. Her piercing whistle echoed through the valley as she and her men jumped from their hidden positions from either side of the steep incline.

"We are under attack!" the Englishman leading the knights yelled. With regimented precision, the slide of steel echoed as he and his men withdrew their swords and moved back to form a defensive stance.

"Robbery is futile," the lead English knight warned.

Catarine stepped to a lower stone, the nerves on the Englishman's face easy to read. "We are nae here for coin, but answers."

A distance below, the knight glanced at the other in disbelief. "Who are you?"

"Princess Catarine MacLaren."

An English knight stepped from the line, put his hands on his hips. "A lie."

Her anger built. "He didna deny knowing who I am," she said to those around her.

"Indeed," Trálin agreed, his voice hard. "To recognize your name, they are in league with whoever you seek."

"Who do you serve?" Catarine called.

Silence.

As if the knights would tell her outright? "Why do they want me and my family dead?"

A distant curse. "'Tis true, she is the princess," the lead English knight stated.

Murmurs rose from the men.

"Kill her!" the lead English knight ordered.

Fierce yells rose from the men as they charged up the incline.

"Remember, if possible we must save who we can so they can answer our questions," Catarine said as she raised her weapon.

Trálin's hard gaze met hers. "I will try, but I will nae allow any to threaten your life." He joined her warriors as they charged the oncoming men.

Blades clashed, curses rang out, and blood-lashed snow stained the fall-chilled earth.

An aggressor charged Lord Grey.

Steel screamed as Trálin's sword met the Englishman's. Muscles quivering from the impact, he tossed the enemy's weapon aside, moved his weapon to the man's neck. "Who do you serve?"

The Englishman reached for his dagger.

Trálin delivered a mortal thrust. Screams filled the air around him broken by errant curses.

"Behind you!" Atair called.

His blade readied, Trálin whirled.

"Bastard!" The English knight charged.

The shudder of steel met each swing, but Trálin held. He deflected the next blow and rounded to swing again, then hesitated. "Bedamned."

"What is wrong?" Catarine called from nearby.

"Look at their eyes!" Trálin replied.

She pushed back an aggressor, then gasped. "They are under a spell."

Trálin had suspected so, after seeing the glazed look of the knight raising his sword for another attack. As much as he wished to kill him, 'twould nae serve their need.

The knight screamed, charged.

Trálin allowed his fury for Catarine's life to drive his blade.

Sweat beaded the man's brow, but he held his own.

"Who do you work for?" Trálin demanded.

Fear flashed in the man's eyes, then they grew blank. "Why do you protect the fairy?"

"Why would a human care what happens in the Otherworld?" Lord Grey pressed as he delivered another blow.

The man's eyes darkened. His mouth fell open and his face contorted with pain. He stumbled back. Gritting his teeth, steadying himself, he again rushed toward him.

Trálin sidestepped the attack, barely.

Like a man possessed, the knight attacked.

Blades clashed over and again. However much Trálin wanted to take this man alive, 'twould seem whoever had put the spell on this warrior would nae allow him to be captured.

The aggressor lifted his blade.

Trálin shoved his blade deep into the knight's exposed armpit.

Shock, then pain seared the man's eyes. He collapsed.

"Stay back," Catarine warned from behind him.

Lord Grey whirled toward her.

Several paces away, two English knights closed in on where they'd cornered Catarine. To her right, Atair fought a man a foot taller than himself. The other fey warriors and Scottish knights were engaged with the remaining English knights.

Curse it! Trálin bolted toward her, taking the first aggressor down with one swing.

Breaths coming fast, her eyes widened. "Behind you!"

Trálin rounded, slashed his blade across the charging man's neck. He spun on his heel and joined the nearby Scottish knight wielding his sword who'd moved to protect her. "Catarine, get behind me."

She hesitated. "I—"

"Now!" Trálin yelled.

With a cool look, she complied.

Trálin focused on the aggressor, thankful to hear the silence of blades around them, praying their men's casualties were low if none.

Steps echoed.

Trálin glanced over.

Atair ran to his side.

A moment later, Drax and Kuircc joined them.

Encircled by the fey warriors, the English knight's eyes widened. Trálin held his gaze. "You are outnumbered, lower your sword."

His blade held high, a dazed look shielded the knight's eyes as he searched for a way to escape.

Bedamned, they needed answers. Trálin jumped toward the knight. Before the man could react, he laid his sword against his neck.

"I did not want to kill her," the knight rasped.

Catarine stepped forward. "Who wants me dead?"

The Englishman began to tremble with fear. "If I tell you I will die."

Anger stormed Trálin. "And if you do nae, I will deliver the same."

"Have m-mercy," the Englishman begged, "you do not understand."

"We know whoever you serve is a fairy," Catarine stated.

The Englishman's eyes widened with incredibility. "How?"

"It matters nae," she stated. "Their name."

Trálin hardened the pressure of his blade against the man's neck. "Tell us now or . . ."

The knight swallowed hard. "El-Elspeth."

Shock rolled through Catarine, then fury. "Where is she?"

At the knight's hesitation, Trálin pressed the sword harder. Blood trickled out, slid down his blade, then dropped onto the frozen ground. "Tell her."

"She is——" The knight's face paled. His face turned a mottled shade of red, then purple. Froth oozed from his mouth. On a gasp, he grabbed for his neck as he collapsed and writhed on the ground as if a man tortured.

Trálin knelt, tried to hold the man down.

The knight's body jerked. On a garbled breath, he stiffened, gave a desperate, bloodcurdling scream.

"Help me hold him," Lord Grey yelled.

Atair and Kuirc rushed over. As they knelt, the Englishman's body slumped to the ground.

A long second passed. Then another.

The man didn't move. His eyes remained fixed.

Lord Grey pressed his fingers against the man's neck, met Catarine's worried gaze. "Dead."

"Elspeth killed him," she whispered, her voice a raw emptiness laden with heartbreak.

Unsure what was bloody going on, Trálin stood. With the emotions rolling in her voice, how her body trembled, something of great magnitude had occurred—beyond the fact the betrayer was a woman.

"Who is Elspeth?" Trálin asked.

"A woman I believed my friend," Catarine replied. "A woman who is now my enemy."

"You know her well then?" Trálin asked.

A shuddering breath fell from Catarine. "Aye, she is my aunt."

Chapter Sixteen

The cold truth echoed through Catarine's mind like a blade of betrayal—her aunt was behind her own brother's death, and was plotting to kill her entire family. Hot tears rolled down her face, violent with the need for justice.

"Catarine?"

At the worry in Trálin's voice she looked up. "I . . ." Her body began to tremble.

"Bloody hell," he breathed. Trálin started to move toward her.

Frustrated at her show of emotion, Catarine wiped the tears from her cheeks, stepped back. Never did she wish to show weakness before her men.

Understanding flickered in Trálin's eyes and he stilled. He glanced at the others standing nearby, and then toward her.

The fey warriors remained silent; anger carved each man's face.

Trálin scanned the surrounding rough terrain, faced her. "How did she kill the man?"

With disgust she knelt beside the dead English knight, reached beneath his tunic. Careful nae to touch the gemstone, she jerked the pendant around his neck free. Bitterness rolled through her as she stood, lifted the glowing sphere twisting at the end of the chain for all to see. "Princess Elspeth uses gemstones to control the men. 'Tis a known method of directing a person's mind with magic."

His mouth slamming to a frown, Atair crossed his arms. "At least now we know who is behind the attacks."

"We do," she agreed. A part of her struggled to believe her aunt, a woman who'd taught her to shoot an arrow and to tend wounds to prevent infection, would have turned against her family. Or had ordered her own brother murdered. Except, the final tortured admission of the dead Englishman sprawled before her was devastating proof. "I had nae thought she delved in black magic. With her ability to control from afar, she must have practiced the craft for many years."

"Aye," Atair agreed, "she is indeed powerful to nae be within sight and wield her will through the man."

"Do you think she is near?" Trálin asked as he again scoured the narrowed valley.

"If so, and if she witnessed her knights' devastation," Catarine replied, "she is long gone."

Lord Grey cursed. "And without knowing her whereabouts, she could be headed anywhere."

"Except the stone circle," Catarine stated. "The open field around it prevents her from trying to cross with us in view." With a frustrated sigh, she laid the gemstone and chain on the dead man's chest. "My family must be warned."

"Aye," Atair agreed. "Blast her traitorous heart. I will kill her with my own two hands."

"Nay," Catarine stated, her voice slow, even, concealing the unbound fury burning to her core. "The blade that takes my aunt's traitorous life shall be mine." She took a deep breath, fighting for calm. To make a decision founded in anger could put their lives at risk. If any died, 'twould be Princess Elspeth. "We must split up. Several warriors will return to——"

Stones clattered nearby.

Her hand clasping her sword, she glanced toward the sound. 'Twas the Scottish knights King Alexander had sent with them coming up the steep incline. Catarine cast a warning look to her fey warriors to say nae more.

Her warriors gave a subtle nod.

The lead Scot heading the party stopped before them, and the remaining knights halted nearby.

Lord Grey nodded to the men. "We were discussing how to proceed."

"Aye, my lord," the head Scottish knight replied. "We await your command."

Thankful for his intervention, Catarine stepped forward. "We have learned that 'tis my aunt who is behind the treachery. Several of my warriors will return to my home and relay the news. The rest of us will remain together and track her down."

Atair's eyes narrowed. "'Tis dangerous to allow you to remain *here* without your full warrior guard."

"But necessary," she replied, her voice cool. "And, do nae forget that our number has been reinforced."

"Men who are unfamiliar with our ways," Atair said with intent, "and do nae hold their full protection for you in case of inescapable danger."

She stiffened. Atair spoke of the gemstones her warriors wore around their necks and the power sent out to protect her when joined. Regardless of the risk, her family must be warned.

At the tense silence, expression grim, the lead Scottish knight stepped forward. "I regret to report that we lost several of my men."

She damned her aunt's senseless greed. Yet more unforgivable atrocities.

"Lord Grey," she said. "Upon the completion of this mission, when you return to King Alexander with his warriors, please share my deepest regrets."

Deep lines deepened in Trálin's brow. "Aye."

"Atair, Magnus, and Ranulf," Catarine called, her voice betraying none of her angst. "Travel to my family's hidden locations. Inform them of all we have learned. They must move to a safer hideaway."

"With Princess Elspeth's knowledge of the royal family's hideouts," Atair said, his voice tight, "as well as her powerful friends, is there truly anywhere they will be safe?"

Nausea swept Catarine at the impact of his question. She considered the places her family could retreat to in times of danger—all safe havens known by her aunt.

"I do nae know," she replied. "Regardless, my family must be warned. My father will be out with his men; after you tell those hidden, find him."

The three fey warriors nodded. Sadness swept her for her father. Once he learned of Princess Elspeth's treachery, he would suffer the emotional cost of her betrayal and blame himself for missing signs of his sister's intent. As if any within the family had held suspicions of her nefarious aspirations? 'Twould see that whatever love her aunt had once held had rotted to vicious, selfish greed.

She shoved aside anxious thoughts. "Atair, once you reach my father, the three of you will remain with him."

Her senior fey warrior nodded. "As you request."

Catarine glanced to Sionn, Drax, and Kuircc. "The rest of you will stay with me. If Elspeth is foolish enough to remain nearby, we will find her."

"Take care," Atair said, then waved Magnus and Ranulf forward. The three fey warriors worked their way down the steep slope.

How she wished she could join them, see her family, and explain everything, but she must confront her aunt.

At the bottom, the fey warriors headed toward where the English knights had entered the valley. A necessity. Once she and the others had departed, her warriors would double back and enter the stone circle.

"There are many places Princess Elspeth might hide," Sionn said.

Catarine grimaced as she scanned the stark mountains carved against the beauty of the rugged land. "We will follow the men's tracks to where the others joined them."

Trálin rubbed his chin, paused. "What if the knights did nae come from her hideout?"

Frustration rolled through her. "A valid point."

"I am bothered by the fact that the English knights know their way about Scotland with such expertise," Trálin said.

"Given instructions I presume," Sionn said, "'tis a logical answer."

"Or"—Lord Grey scanned the bodies of the English knights strewn about—"mayhap they were following a map."

Hope ignited inside her. "A map. Of course, which the lead knight should have on him. Or another of his guard. We must search them."

A short while later, fatigue and grief weighed heavy on Catarine as she picked through the last pouch of the dead English knight before her. Blast it. Nothing.

"Here!"

At Drax's excited cry, she shoved to her feet and hurried over.

Parchment scraped as the fey warrior unfurled the map. Analytical eyes scanned the prepared skin, his mouth tightening at the edge.

Catarine halted a pace away. "Where does it lead?"

Brows drawn, Drax handed it to her. "See for yourself."

Uneasy, she took the map, scanned it as Trálin, Sionn, and Kuircc moved to her side.

"Bedamned," Trálin rasped, "they came up from England."

"How long will it take us to reach where the map ends?" she asked, her frustration matching his.

"'Tis rough terrain," Lord Grey replied. "Three days by foot at best."

Three days at best? Time they didn't have.

One of the Scottish knights who stood farthest away, who she was introduced to as Sir Rogier, was kneeling beside the Englishman who'd died after he'd admitted her aunt's name. At her gaze, Sir Rogier froze. Guilt flickered in his eyes, then he hurried to stand.

Unease slid through her. "Sir Rogier, did you find something else?"

He shook his head.

Gaze narrowed, Trálin glanced at the Scottish knight, then back to her. "Is something wrong?"

She studied the Scottish knight a moment more. It appeared that Sir Rogier was upset. "If it is of significance, I must know."

Sir Rogier cleared his throat. "My lady, I apologize for upsetting you. 'Twas nae my intent. Neither is anything wrong."

Trálin frowned at the knight as if unconvinced. "You are sure?"

"Aye, my lord," Sir Rogier replied.

"I am on edge," Catarine said. With everything to consider, how could she nae be? She focused on the map. "Lord Grey, are you familiar with the territory?"

Trálin watched the Scot a moment longer, then glanced toward her and nodded. "Aye, I will lead us there."

Once they'd finished discussing the last few details of the upcoming journey, Lord Grey started south with the rest following close behind.

As they picked their way through the sweep of land, at the bottom of the valley, Catarine glanced down to avoid a jutting rock. She frowned. "Odd, I would have thought we would see footsteps of the English knights."

Several paces away Sionn studied the rough terrain. "As I."

"What do you mean?" Trálin asked.

Stunned, she stared at him. "You see tracks?"

"Aye," Lord Grey replied. "They are clear enough."

She turned to Drax and Kuircc. "Do you see them?"

"Nay," they replied in unison.

Catarine looked at Scottish knights. "Do you?"

Confusion on their faces, the Scots nodded.

Stunned, she met Sionn's grim expression. "'Tis the same as before." Confirmation magic had indeed erased the trail, but only to the fey. What other unwelcome surprises lay in store?

Frozen ground cracked beneath his boots as in the fading sunlight, Trálin shoved up the steep incline, the whirl of snow rushing past. His legs ached from the hours they'd moved at a grueling pace. With a deep breath, he pushed on.

The earlier revelation that only he and the Scots were able to see the footsteps haunted his mind. How did one deal with magic, or exactly what it entailed? Another brutal gust battered him. He tugged the hood of his cape lower over his face, continued up.

"Can you see the top?" Catarine called from behind him.

He glanced back, frowned at the shards of ice misting her brows, and those clinging to the strands of hair that'd broken free from her braid during over the hours of hard travel. "We are almost there." At her nod, he found another foothold, moved on. Several steps later, he reached the pinnacle. Through the blowing snow, he scanned the weathered land, scoured the brutal gouges carved by rain and time. In the distance, he caught the distant roll of waves upon the shore.

"I can see the ocean," Catarine said, her breaths coming fast as she halted at his side.

Trálin savored the faint tang of salt in the air, a fresh scent he always enjoyed. "I wanted us to reach the ocean before it grew dark." The reason he'd pushed them so hard.

She scrutinized the churning sky, her eyes heavy with exhaustion. The snowstorm had been growing worse throughout the day. "We canna push on much longer."

Trálin pointed toward where remnants of haphazard stone near the shore struggled toward the sky. "See the outline in the distance beyond the next ridge?"

She nodded.

"'Tis an abandoned castle," he explained. "Parts of the internal walls have collapsed, but 'twill offer an excellent shelter. Though the storm will help shield us, we can nae build a fire. Other Englishmen who serve Princess Elspeth might be nearby."

Catarine surveyed the land in a slow sweep. "We canna be too cautious."

"A break from the wind will be welcome enough," Sionn stated as he paused beside Catarine.

"With the fierce storms known about Scotland," Trálin said, "my worry is that 'twill nae only slow us, but force us to remain here for days."

Her mouth tightened. "Then we must continue on."

With her uncle murdered, several of the Scottish knights dead, and her aunt behind the mayhem, Trálin understood her frustration. Neither would he allow her to make a dangerous choice. "We are all tired. 'Twill soon be night. In the morning, after a good night's sleep, if indeed the storm makes our travel treacherous, then we will reconsider our plans."

With a cool glance, she opened her mouth to speak.

"Nay arguments," Lord Grey said, "you are exhausted and all but ready to fall down." Before she could reply, he started down the next decline.

"Stubborn you are," she called from behind him.

He shot her a smile. "That I am."

As they reached the top of the next gouge of land, in the haze of the oncoming night, a rugged path worn by years of travel came into view. Hewn steps of stone led to the decaying walls of a once grand castle.

Breaths rolling out in a mist of white, Catarine halted beside him. "We made it."

"With the snow falling harder," Trálin said, "we arrived just in time."

The echo of waves slamming against the sheer rock beyond the walls grew louder as Catarine walked beneath the gatehouse. With each step the smell of the sea and decaying grass grew stronger, the cold biting her lungs.

Fatigue rolling through her, she halted at the bailey's entrance. Amidst the flakes of snow, somber greys of smothered light illuminated the muddle of stones long since toppled from the walls. Half-standing buildings stood helpless against the whip of wind while fragments of stone, wood, and abandoned household items from prior residents littered the ground.

"If the door to the gatehouse still is intact, we must secure it," Catarine said. Thankfully, after prying the rusted gate loose, they moved beneath the gatehouse, then secured it.

"This way," Trálin directed as he strode toward the keep. The door to the central portion of the fortress lay open in tatters. Perhaps destroyed during a skirmish? Little else explained such desecration, but with the exterior walls intact, the haphazard remnants would indeed provide welcome shelter.

Inside the remaining walls of the keep, a large hearth stood empty, the charred walls and remnants of wood proof that once life had flourished here.

Wind howled overhead. A burst of snow swirled above and the spray of flakes tumbled down around them.

"We can bed down here," Trálin said as he reached the far wall. "Once we eat, we will set up guards to keep watch throughout the night."

"Sionn and I will take the first shift," Catarine stated. However much she wished to be with Trálin, the last thing she wanted was to inadvertently expose her men to any hint of how close they'd become.

Trálin nodded. "One of the Scottish knights and I will take over at matins." The other men volunteered for the remaining hours.

Though her body ached and she wanted only to sleep, Catarine worked alongside the men to set the wine, bread, and dried meats out for everyone to eat. After she finished her meal, she wiped her hands, frustrated it had grown dark so fast.

"Are you ready?" Sionn asked.

She nodded and stood.

With shards of moonlight spilling between the breaks in clouds, they headed toward the decaying turret. The soft tap of their boots upon eroded stone echoed up the spiral walls as they started up. As they reached the wall walk, Catarine halted beside her friend, the broken landscape to the west, the rush of waves slamming against the sheer cliffs to the east making her catch her breath.

"'Tis amazing," Sionn said, "one that reminds me of the cliffs of my youth."

"Aye." Though wind screamed past, the blasts of snow like shards of ice, neither could detract from the magnificence before her. "'Tis easy to see why this land was chosen to build a fortress. With the rocks jutting from the water along the coast, no enemy could slip in from the ocean, nor any contingent reach the gates to the west without being seen." She exhaled. "'Twould take years to see every sight around us, then I doubt one person would see it all."

Surprise flickered in her friend's eyes. "You like it here then?"

"I do," she replied, her voice rough with wishes of things that never could be. "Never will I forget the time spent here."

"You mean your time with Lord Grey?"

With a quiet inhale, she met Sionn's searching gaze. So, as Atair, he'd heard her speaking to Trálin in his chamber.

"How can I forget a man who saved my life?" she asked. "A man who like this rugged land moves me as no other."

"Catar—"

"I know my duty to wed Prince Zacheus," she interrupted with soft regard. "And as I assured Atair, regardless of my feelings for Lord Grey, I will see it through."

In the errant wisps of moonlight, sad lines touched his brow. "Never did I question that you would do what was right. Know this, I have met many a man, but the earl is one of the finest. He is a warrior to admire, and a man of his word. With how deeply you care for him, I wish you could follow your heart."

Her chest squeezed at his words. "We canna always have what we wish for, can we?"

"Your wishes," Sionn said, his words somber, "I would like to see granted."

Her throat tight with emotion, she scanned the rock and turf and snow-covered land. Caught within the wind, wisps of salty spray reached her. Catarine savored the rich taste, that of freedom and the rugged land below. With ease she could see herself remaining in Scotland.

"I know 'tis difficult," Sionn said. "But with the way I catch Lord Grey looking at you when he thinks none are watching, neither will he forget you."

"Why does it seem we meet the person we were meant to be with at the most ill-opportune time?"

He shrugged. "Who knows why life offers the challenges it does?"

"Challenges?"

"Aye," Sionn replied. "Problems perplex us, challenges we can overcome."

A smile tugged at her mouth. "You are a philosopher now?"

Humor twinkled in his eyes. "When the time calls for it."

A thick flake twirled past, then another. A rumble of thunder echoed in the distance.

She straightened, searched the rough sweep of land. "Thunder when it is snowing?"

"Odd indeed." Sionn pointed toward the west, where a flicker of lightning illuminated the sky. A moment later, another echo of thunder sounded. He grimaced. "I willna miss the unusual weather outside of the Otherworld."

"Nay," she replied, sadness slipping into her voice, "that I willna miss. Once I wed, will you continue to guard me at my new home?"

"Will Prince Zacheus allow that?"

At his question, Catarine paused. "He will accept that I will keep my personal guard." But she wasna sure. Before, having accepted her fate to wed to bring peace between their lands, she'd nae given much thought of her life after she'd wed. She'd assumed if they chose, her fey warriors would stay with her and protect her in her new home.

What other details had she nae considered? As if she wanted to think about being another man's wife. The thought of the prince touching her with any intimacy made her cringe. Trálin had made her feel special, a woman cherished, their time together making her yearn to be with him forever.

How could she allow another man to join with her in the night?

But the prince would require that she give him an heir. If she gave birth to a princess, with him an only child, Prince Zacheus would insist on his marital rights until she provided him with a son.

Numb, she scanned the rugged land, the churn of dark clouds casting large flakes of snow. Indeed she wished for a child, one with Trálin's green eyes, a child born from their love.

Breaks in the clouds overhead flooded the land with moonlight. A blur of movement flickered on a nearby hilltop.

A moment later, another shadowed figure followed.

"Sionn," she said, her words tumbling out, "men are creeping up on the hill to the south."

Boots grated on stone as she leaned closer to the shambles remaining of the wall walk. "'Tis the English! How could they have bloody found us?"

"I am unsure," she replied. "We must warn the others we are—"

A man halted at the top of the hill, waved his arms forward. "Attack the castle!"

Chapter Seventeen

Yells echoed from outside the castle walls as Catarine bolted toward the decaying steps of the turret.

In the fractured play of moonlight and shadows, an arrow hissed past.

She ducked, reached the turret, then hurried down. "We are under attack!" she yelled as she ran into the great room.

Illuminated by the wisps of moonlight streaming through the holes in the ceiling, the men scrambled to their feet.

"How many are there?" Trálin asked as he and the others withdrew their swords.

"I am unsure," Catarine replied to the gathering men. "Sionn is holding off those trying to scale the walls to the west, but he needs help."

A boom echoed at the gatehouse.

Wood shuddered, groaned.

"They are smashing through the entry!" she gasped.

"I will aid Sionn on the wall walk." Drax ran toward the turret.

"Sir William," Trálin ordered, "take three men to close the entry and protect the gatehouse. Catarine, Sir Rogier and I will defend the southern portion of the castle walls. Everyone else, stay in pairs and fend off anyone who tries to enter elsewhere."

"Aye, my lord," Sir William and the other knights replied in unison. The Scots hurried toward their destinations.

"Come!" Trálin bolted toward the southern portion of the steps to the wall walk.

Yells and shouts rang from outside as Catarine raced beside him,

Sir Rogier in their wake. "With the blowing snow filling in our tracks as we traveled, how could they have found us?"

"They should nae have been able to," Trálin replied, and wove around a large chunk of fallen stone.

The slap of their footsteps echoed as they ran up the steps, fell away where the stone walls had crumbled to expose the snow-laden fields beyond. A moment later, the crenellations topping the wall of the southern exposure came into view.

At a break in the crumbling structure, in the fragments of moonlight, as she glanced over the edge and made out several men. "They are near the top of the collapsed portion of the walls!"

"Grab rocks," Trálin called. "We must hold them off."

Her muscles screamed as she lifted nearby stones toppled from a battle long ago and tossed them over the edge.

At her side, Trálin and Sir Rogier followed suit, half-rolling, half-shoving large rocks to the crenellations, then pushing them over.

The clatter of stone and screams from below melded with the whip of wind.

Lifting another rock, she turned, shoved it to the edge. As she reached to grab another stone, she caught the shadow of a man moving up the exterior wall on her left. Angling her body, she shoved the stone toward him.

The man's scream rent the air.

Solid booms echoed from the gatehouse.

"Blast it," Trálin spat as he threw another rock, "From the sounds of it, they are close to destroying the entry!"

"Once we are finished here"—she lifted another large stone over the side—"we will join them." She shoved.

A gut-wrenching scream pierced the night as the attacker plummeted to the rubble far below.

"I see no one else coming up," Trálin said as he surveyed fragments of moonlight scraping the wall.

"Mayhap they have given up trying to scale the wall," Catarine replied, "and are joining forces outside the gatehouse to break through."

"Aye," Lord Grey agreed. "Come, we must help—"

"Agh!" Sir Rogier screamed.

Catarine whirled, stilled. "Mother of God!"

At the shock in her voice, Trálin spun on his heel.

His face carved in pain, the Scottish knight grabbed at his throat.

Bedamned, he thought they'd stopped all the men scaling the castle wall. "Are you hit?" Trálin asked as he strode toward Sir Rogier, searching for an arrow, finding naught.

"Look around his neck!" Catarine gasped.

Trálin halted, glanced lower. "Something is glowing."

"A gemstone," she replied, her words filled with dread. "Remember after the battle with the English knights, how Sir Rogier acted apprehensive when I caught him kneeling beside the dead man?"

"Aye," Trálin replied.

"He must have seen me leave the gemstone on the dead English knight," she explained. "Believing it held worth, he removed it. Once we started our journey, he must have held the chain and slipped it over his head. And, it was the reason the men found us."

"Which makes bloody sense," Trálin agreed.

"We must take it off before it kills him," Catarine warned.

As it had the other man who'd died a tortured death. Bedamned! Trálin reached for the chain.

Eyes wide, the Scottish knight jerked back, shoved to his feet, and drew his blade.

"What in bloody hell?" Trálin demanded.

"Watch out!" Catarine screamed.

Sword held high, Sir Rogier charged Lord Grey.

Trálin deflected his blade, keeping his body between the knight and Catarine. "Put your weapon down," he ordered the Scot.

"He can nae hear you," Catarine yelled.

In the whisper of moonlight, Trálin understood. The knight's dull eyes stared at him, glazed with pain and confusion, the gemstone glowing with a fierce light at his neck.

"My aunt controls him."

With a yell, the knight raised his sword, again charged.

Sparks streaked into the murky night as their blades scraped over and again. Using his full strength, Trálin blocked his swing, then shoved the Scottish knight back.

Catarine moved to his side.

"Stay behind me!"

She readied her blade. "'Twill take both of us. We must hold him down and cut the necklace off, or he will continue to attack until we are both dead."

Bloody damn.

The Scottish knight regained his balance. Wild eyed, he raised his sword, charged.

Trálin deflected his blade, blocked the middle of his sword with his own. Hand trembling with effort, he pushed.

Sir Rogier lost his balance, stumbled back.

Before the knight regained his balance, Trálin dove atop him.

Arms guided by evil magic clasped around his neck, rolled him over.

In the fragments of moonlight, he caught the blur of Catarine jumping on the Scottish knight's back.

Trálin struggled to throw the knight off, failed.

The knight's body twisted as he released his neck with one hand and reached toward Catarine.

Nay! Trálin fought to break free of the man's inhuman hold as he struggled to breathe.

The knight's hand around Trálin's neck tightened.

Sir Rogier's face dimmed before him.

Catarine's blade flashed in the moonlight.

The glowing stone tied to the leather strap around Sir Rogier's neck slipped to the ground. In the waver of eerie light, confusion filled the Scottish knight's eyes, then he collapsed.

Catarine grabbed the strap of the gemstone, flung it over the wall.

Coughing, gasping for breath, Trálin sat up. He rubbed his neck. "You shouldna have jumped atop of him."

"A fine thank-you indeed."

Humbled, Trálin accepted Catarine's hand and stood. "My thanks. Still, you shouldna have risked your life."

"And let him kill you?" She released his hand, stepped back. "Admit it," she demanded, her voice a blend of anger and fear. "You are only upset because you didna protect me."

The Scottish knight groaned.

"He is coming to." Catarine knelt by his side.

Sir Rogier rubbed the back of his neck and stared up confused. "What happened?"

"You attacked Lord Grey," she stated.

Disbelief widened the knight's eyes as he sat. "Please, tell me 'tis a lie?"

"'Tis truth," Trálin's said, indeed irritated that he'd nae protected Catarine.

"My lord, my deepest apologies," he rasped. "I dinna know why I would do such a traitorous act."

"You took a pendant from one of the English knights, did you nae?" she asked.

The knight hesitated, then looked down. "Aye."

Trálin strode to the man. "Why?"

"I d-didna intend to." His face filled with regret, Sir Rogier glanced at each of them, then shook his head. "My fingers bumped against the strap holding the gemstone. I canna explain except to say that at that moment, I had to have it." He paused. "I know it sounds as if a lie crafted, but I swear to you both, 'tis truth."

Catarine hissed, met Trálin's hard gaze. A spell, she mouthed.

Lord Grey gave a curt nod.

"My lady," the knight pleaded, "please forgive me. Never have I done such before or can believe I have. 'Tis shame on my family I bring."

Yells and the clash of blades echoed below.

Trálin glanced toward the gatehouse. "'Tis done. We must join the others before the English break inside."

"Indeed." The Scot shoved to his feet, wavered a bit, then hurried down the steps.

"'Twas a spell," Catarine explained to Trálin. "Once Sir Rogier's fingers brushed against the stone, 'twas the connection my aunt needed to link with his mind."

"Why would she want me dead?" Trálin shook his head. "I have more questions, but first we must help the others." He bolted for the turret and prayed they would indeed overcome the attackers this night.

Purple streaks haunted the morning sky as Catarine completed one last check of her mount's saddle, the shambles of the castle sprawled in her wake. Without the reinforcements of the Scottish knights, too easily it could have been them lying dead. Overwhelmed by the emotions from the last few hours of battle, of how her aunt's treachery had left many more men dead, she laid her head on her steed's withers.

"Are you ready to depart?" Trálin asked as he walked up to his mount secured nearby.

At the exhaustion in his voice, guilt swept her, and she glanced toward him. "I am."

Trálin checked his steed's cinch, then glanced over. "'Tis a boon the English knights rode in to attack us. With their horses, 'twill cut down the time of our travel."

"Indeed."

Shrewd eyes studied her. "What is wrong?"

She took a steadying breath, rubbed her mount's withers. "So many lives have been lost because of my aunt's greed."

"Her choice," Trálin stated, anger brisk in his voice.

"'Tis, but I canna understand how she could make such a decision. Even the loss of one life outweighs whatever her goals of wealth or power could offer."

He grunted. "Sadly, for many, greed smothers any care for the atrocities committed against others."

A horse whinnied from the far end of the dilapidated stable.

For a moment she took in fey warriors working along with the Scottish knights as they finished preparing their mounts for the ride ahead.

"Catarine?" Trálin asked.

She met his gaze, his weariness a trait they all shared. "Aye?"

"A question haunts me. If your aunt controls the person wearing the gemstone, why would she direct the Scottish knight to ensure that I am dead?"

With all of the mayhem of the past few hours, she'd nae pondered his earlier question. Except now, with the English knights dead and a token of calm rumbling around them, his reminder sent shivers of dread through her.

"You are right. Beneath my aunt's influence, the Scottish knight should have tried to kill me. It makes nay sense that your life would be at risk. 'Tis nae as if my aunt knows you, or that you and I . . ." Fear crawled through her like acid, destroying her every shard of calm with painful intent.

And she knew.

Understood with shuddering clarity.

Green eyes narrowed. "What is it?"

Her body trembled as she held Trálin's gaze, wanting to be wrong, but 'twas the only answer. "My aunt is aware of my feelings for you." Her whisper clattered against the silence as if crystals shattering upon rock.

"How would she?" he asked. "We are nae from the same world."

"'Tis because of the stone," she explained. "'Twould seem, when the gemstone is worn around a person's neck, she can see what the wearer sees and somehow sense what others around the person are feeling."

Skepticism darkened his gaze. "It sounds incredible."

"Aye," she agreed, shaken by this unforeseen threat. "I have heard of this before, but only in those who have immense power. 'Tis so rare, I thought the ability a myth of fables. But, 'twould seem 'tis true."

"And you never suspected?" Trálin asked.

"Nay." She stroked her mount's neck, her fingers shaking. "All my life I thought my aunt was a bit different, her travels without proper chaperone earning many a censure from my grandparents. Except, I doubt even they, or any in my family, knew that she had immersed herself in the art of black magic."

He gave a rough sigh. "I understand nae wanting to see a darker side to those we love. Though, it sounds as if your aunt kept her studies secret."

She nodded. "A wise choice, as she would have been cast out of the Otherworld if my family had learned the truth."

"As if the news will nae earn her the same now?"

"It will"—Catarine's hand stilled—"if my family lives."

Snorts of horses broke the tense silence.

Trálin cleared his throat, then glanced around the dilapidated stable. "The men are almost ready to go."

'Twas only moments until they departed. She must tell him.

"Trálin," she said, her mind weighted with guilt, "when I first asked you to aid us, never did I mean to endanger your life."

Tenderness touched his face as he laid his hand over hers and gave a gentle squeeze. "More than once you have risked your life for me as well, a fact I deeply regret."

She withdrew her hand, fisted it at her side. "But I lived. With Princess Elspeth aware of your importance to me, the more I weigh the circumstance, the more I fear 'tis a fact she will use."

Shrewd eyes studied her. "How so?"

She hesitated, the enormity of her thoughts terrifying. "Before this day, I believed her intent was to destroy the remainder of the royal family within our realm, to ensure she has no opposition when she claims the crown. But her attempt to kill you proves if that was indeed her original intent, she now wants more."

"More?"

Catarine drew a deep breath. "If my aunt exposes my feelings for you to Prince Zacheus, it might infuriate him to the point where the war our marriage is supposed to avoid becomes real. And, in her twisted way, in a show of supposed concern, she can offer herself in my stead to bring peace between our kingdoms."

Infuriated understanding smothered the confusion in his eyes. "And in the end," Trálin said, his voice cold, "she would lay claim to not just one kingdom, but two."

Shaken, Catarine nodded. "I must inform my father." A meeting she dreaded. He would be far from pleased to learn she'd fallen in love with Trálin, but to save her realm a truth she would admit. Nor would it change her father's expectations that she wed Prince Zacheus.

Her destiny remained sealed.

"Now what do we do?" Trálin asked.

"Thankfully, with her men about, 'twould seem she has nae left for the Otherworld. We must stop her before she does." Responsibility weighed atop her guilt. "I pray my warriors have reached my father by now. Still, I need to send another of my warriors to update him of this latest threat."

Trálin slowly crossed his arms. "Do you nae think it should be you who explains?"

"I do, but the luxury of time for me to reach him does nae exist."

"You could go," Trálin pressed. "I will continue on with your warriors in search of Princess Elspeth."

Anger flared as she understood. "You want me safe, protected, but I am nae leaving."

"You are being stubborn."

"Nay," she replied, "if indeed she is still here, 'tis possible that she will speak with only me."

His mouth settled into a grim line. "And if you are wrong and she has already returned to the Otherworld?"

Fear cut through her. "Then God help us all."

"Then I will pray we find her here."

As would she. "I do have a concern."

"What is that?"

"Though we have a map, it ends in England without indicating a specific location of anything of significance. With my aunt's immense power, I fear if she doesna wish to be seen, we willna see her."

Expression hard, he unfurled his arms, dropped them to his sides. "Blast it, she has to have a weakness."

"If so," Catarine replied, "'tis none that I am aware of."

With a frustrated sigh, Lord Grey withdrew the map and tapped the location where the line ended. "For the most, the land holds naught of importance. But, we shall search here. For the sake of your family and realm, let us pray that she still remains in England."

"I must talk with Sionn. He is the best choice to send to explain everything to my father."

Trálin nodded.

Angst swirling inside her, Catarine headed across the stable.

At her approach, Sionn shot her a questioning look. "Is there a problem?"

"I must speak with you all in private."

His hard gaze glanced toward Trálin, then back to her. "This involves Lord Grey?"

"Aye." Rocks crunched beneath their feet as she headed toward a break in the castle walls, the rush of wind through the opening perfect to conceal their discussion from the others. Near the heap of scattered stones, she faced her friend. "I need you to return to the Otherworld and find my father."

Lines of confusion wedged in his brow. "You have already sent warriors to inform the king of your aunt's treachery."

"I have, but now there is another issue of great importance." In brief she explained her concerns about her aunt learning of her feelings for Trálin, her possible intent to use them to marry the prince and gain more power.

Sionn's mouth tightened. "The king will be furious."

"My father will be," she agreed. "'Twould be best if I spoke with him, but if we find Princess Elspeth, 'tis I who needs to confront her as I doubt she will speak to anyone but royalty."

"'Twill leave you with but Drax and Kuirce," Sionn said, his voice grim.

Apprehension slid through her. "I know."

"Blast it." Her friend rubbed the back of his neck, shot her a cool look. "I will do as you bid, but I do nae like it."

"My thanks."

"Do nae thank me," Sionn said. "When you eventually meet with your father, 'twill be far from pleasant."

An understatement. Her father would be outraged.

Large flakes of snow whipped past as Trálin followed the rider they'd come across earlier in the day after they'd crossed into England. After catching several glints of the rider's gemstone around his neck, he was sure the man he now trailed was under the control of Catarine's aunt.

As he topped the ridge and rode deeper on English soil, his concern grew. At least she and the others were safe, hidden in the shield of trees a distance behind. She'd nae liked his following the horseman, but could nae argue that 'twas easier for one person to follow the man to avoid being seen.

A horse snorted in the distance.

Reining his steed to a halt, Trálin dismounted and tethered him in a copse of trees. With care he worked his way through the thick swath of pines. Near a break, he lay on his stomach, inched forward, and peered through the brush.

A distance below, the lone rider cantered along a heavily used path toward two large buildings. At his approach, another man walked into view. The rider dismounted, handed his steed over to the man, then strode toward the larger building of the two.

An inn? Was the rider en route to meet with others before they departed for the Otherworld? There was only one way to find out.

Scrambling to his mount, Trálin rode to where Catarine and the others rested.

A short while later, he approached, and Catarine hurried to meet him.

"Where did the rider go?" she asked.

"To what looks to be an inn," Trálin replied.

Concern darkened her gaze. "Did you see other English knights there?"

"Nay, but I believe he is meeting someone there, which is why I returned." He laid the reins in his palm. "Remain here with our men at camp. Once night has fallen, I will enter disguised as a traveler and see what information I can learn."

Anger reddened her cheeks. "I am going with you."

Blast it. "I will nae risk you going in. 'Tis too——"

"Dangerous?" she interrupted.

His arguments fell away. She'd overcome a blizzard, fought the English knights at the broken-down castle, and had held her own in both. "I do nae like the thought of your putting your life at risk."

Her face grew tender. "I know."

Hours later blackness coated the earth as Trálin rode toward the two buildings, keeping his steed's gait easy. Catarine's soft breath on his neck as she sat behind him far from put him at ease. Aye, she had a right to be here, but how could he nae worry for her safety?

A break in the clouds sent moonbeams spilling to the earth, illuminating the clearing between him and the buildings.

She leaned close to his ear. "'Tis the inn."

"There is still time for you to dismount, and for me to go in alone."

"Trálin, well I know the dangers we face, but I appreciate your concern."

Concern? What the lass made him feel far exceeded the paltry word. Never had he met a woman who challenged him on every level, nor made him feel the depth of emotions she did. The thought of her leaving after this was over seemed impossible. As if he had a blasted choice?

From the shadows, a tall man, sword raised, stepped from the stable. "Halt, who goes there?"

"Here we go," Trálin whispered back to Catarine, and drew his mount to a halt.

Chapter Eighteen

Dropping his shoulders and allowing his body to slump, Trálin nodded to the tall man standing before the stable who held his sword raised. "We have traveled far and are weary. We seek naught but a room to rest this night."

Cast in torchlight, the lines on the Englishman's face narrowed in suspicion. "You are Scottish."

"Aye."

Catherine prayed he convince the man they were no threat or their entire plan to eavesdrop on the English knights working for her aunt would fail.

"We traveled south from the border," Trálin explained. "My wife has been ill, and we are on our way to procure herbs to help her."

His wife!

The man's eyes narrowed on Catarine, and he stepped back. "Is she contagious?"

"With child." Trálin replied without glancing toward her.

To her chagrin, after a long look at Catarine, the Englishman lowered his sword.

"There are several rooms available," the mans said, "but 'twill cost you."

After the man quoted a figure, Trálin dismounted and handed over the requested coin.

The Englishman lifted the fare to the light. With a satisfied grunt, he shoved the money within a hidden pocket. "Tell Godefray you have a room on the second floor for the night," the man said. "And a hot meal."

Relief swept Trálin. "My thanks."

"If you are ready to go in," the man said, "I will be stabling your horse."

"We are." Lord Grey turned and lifted Catarine to the ground. An arched brow in her direction assured her he knew that she was far from pleased with the story he'd concocted. "Are you well enough to walk?"

"Indeed," she said, her voice crisp.

Trálin handed the reins to the Englishman, took her elbow, and escorted her to the inn.

Hooves upon the bare ground echoed in their wake as their horse was led to the stable.

Once out of earshot, Catarine sent Trálin a withering look. "Pregnant?" she whispered.

Against the flicker of flames as they approached the weathered building, he had the grace to blush. "With the guard picking up my burr, I needed a topic that would throw him off guard and nae encourage questions."

"Off guard?" she asked exasperated. "There were many reasons you might have given him."

"And one would be?"

"That I was headed for a convent," she blustered out.

Frozen grass crunched beneath their feet. "Headed for a convent? And what reason could I give him of why I, a Scot, was in deep in the southeastern part of England?"

"To fetch me."

His brow arched as if far from convinced. "And you think he would be believing that?"

"Why would he nae?" she asked as he led her beneath a sturdy oak. "'Tis a good a reason as you gave. Nay, 'tis better."

A smile tugged at his mouth as he stopped and looked at her. "Do you think the man would be giving me a room with a lass who is about to swear her vows to God?"

Heat touched her cheeks. "He might have," she replied without conviction. So caught up in her shock at his claiming she was his wife, her wits had abandoned her.

He stroked his thumb across her lips. "With your bonny looks, I doubt he would trust me in a room alone with you for the night." Before she could reply, he wrapped his arms around her and drew her into a soft kiss.

A gust of wind kicked up, and bony branches scraped overhead. Catarine ignored the sound and sank into his kiss, wishing indeed they were wed. If so, this night, locked in their chamber, images of how he would touch her flickered through her mind, and her body grew hot.

He broke away, his breathing unsteady, and pushed back a loose lock of her hair behind her ear. "I have vowed to nae touch you again."

"You have." Her heart aching, she ran her fingers over his strong jaw rough with new growth, lingered on the firm line of his mouth.

"Lass, 'tis dangerous ground we tread."

She gave a slow exhale. "I know, but I can nae help how you make me feel."

On a groan, he leaned in, gave her another long kiss, and then broke free. "As if your answer makes anything blasted easier?" He took her hand. "Let us go inside before we both freeze to death.

"I am nae cold."

He grunted, tugged her forward.

Satisfaction filled her as she walked by his side, then she grew somber. Before, being innocent of a man's touch, she'd accepted the sensations he'd inspired with newfound awe, cherished each one, aware that they must last her a lifetime. Except now, understanding what he could make her feel, she found herself wondering what sensations their joining would bring. And what of him? Regardless of what he'd said that night in Loch Leven Castle, how could he have found pleasure merely watching or touching her? However wrong, she found herself convinced that if they spent the hours alone, 'twould take little to encourage him to make love to her in every way, regardless the cost.

Foolish thoughts indeed. Their time here was but a guise to eavesdrop on the English knight in league with her aunt.

The scrape of wood had her glancing up.

The hewn entry shoved open. In the spill of lantern light, a rough-looking man with unkempt hair straggling over his shoulders stepped out. Surprise widened his eyes as he glanced at her.

Trálin moved before her as Catarine's hand curled around her hidden dagger.

With a grunt, the stranger stumbled toward the stable.

Thankful, Catarine released her blade.

Trálin turned. "Are you okay?"

"Naught happened except we surprised a man who drank a wee bit too much."

"With the travelers within and their minds skewed by ale," Trálin cautioned, "with your beauty, 'twill be more than one man eyeing you with dark thoughts."

At the seriousness of his voice she sighed. "Trálin, well I know how to handle myself."

"Mayhap, but while you are with me, I will protect you."

His words moved her. Though her fey warriors kept her safe and were like brothers to her, Trálin's vow was driven by caring, that of a man who desired and respected a woman. A man whom, if circumstance allowed, would become more.

He stepped to the door. "Normally, I would hold the door for you to enter first. As we do nae know what awaits us inside, I will go first."

She nodded.

With a quick glance around them, her potent taste still on his mouth, Trálin opened the door to the inn, then stepped inside. The stench of unwashed bodies collided with rancid ale. The men gathered at the rough-hewn tables wore tattered garb. Several looked familiar, none for good reasons. Bedamned, this was the last place he would ever want Catarine. 'Twas nae fit for a pig, and he held doubts he'd bring the wee animal inside as well.

A shimmer of light glinted from the neck of a man seated near the back.

The man he'd followed earlier.

"What do you see?" Catarine whispered from behind.

"The man we seek. Do nae look at him or any of the others as we enter, but follow me," he whispered. "I assure you, the crowd within is an untrustworthy lot. It may be different in your world, but here, for our safety, let me speak."

She nodded. "I will."

Near the back of the large smoke-filled chamber, two tables away from where the man he'd followed here, sat two battered chairs and an empty table that look as if it'd seen many a fight. Good. They could feign eating while they kept watch of the man and mayhap catch a glimpse of who he'd come to meet. Trálin took Catarine's hand and led her inside.

A woman dressed in serviceable garb approached them, her eyes suspicious, her face weathered with age. She shot Catarine a dismissive glance, and her smile warmed as it settled on him.

"Would you be wanting to eat or," the woman purred with a saucy wink, "do you desire other services to satisfy your appetite, my lord?"

He ignored her crude advance. Too many times he'd dealt with women like her, women who believed him a man of worth, a man whom they could glean coin or other items of wealth or status. Nor would he ask her how she knew he was nobility. With the slovenly lot within, 'twould nae be hard to discern he was at the very least, a man of authority.

"I am seeking a man named Godefray," Lord Grey stated.

Disappointment flashed on her face, and she gestured to a red-haired man talking with another man at the other side of the room.

"My thanks." Trálin pointed to the empty table near the back. "Once I am finished talking with him, we will be seated there. We paid the stable hand for a meal. Bring it there."

The woman's mouth tightened into a hard frown. "Very well, my lord."

He ignored her dry tone. "Come." Catarine's hand tightened in his, but he caught the flash of anger in her eyes. Keeping her close to his side, he walked toward the man the woman had indicated. As they neared, the red-haired man continued talking to the man seated nearby, but by the way his shoulders tensed, he'd seen them.

"And that is the way it ended," the red-haired man spat. "Serves 'em right for going against the king. Bloody dead as they should be."

Although nae directed at him, Trálin heard the man's underlying warning that he would nae tolerate any interference. If Catarine was nae with him, the man would learn that threats, however subtly cast, could end with his death. This time, the man was fortunate.

The red-haired man lifted his mug of ale, took a long drink, then set it on the table with a heavy thud. "You are Godefray?" Trálin asked.

The rough-looking man glanced toward him, then shifted to Catarine. His eyes darkened with desire.

The bastard. "This is my wife," Trálin said in cold warning.

Godefray's hard gaze met his. "And what would the two of you be wanting?"

"We paid the man at the stable for a room this night," Trálin replied, his voice ice, "and a hot meal. He said when we came in, to ask for you."

With a grunt, the red-haired man glanced toward the woman Trálin had spoken with moments before. "I saw you talked with Mildryth when you entered."

"Aye," Lord Grey replied. "To order our meal."

"Once you finish your fare," the red-haired man stated, "Mildryth will tell you which room above is yours."

With a curt nod, Trálin led Catarine toward the empty table in the back.

Curious gazes eyed them as they passed, most resting on Catarine with undisguised interest.

Trálin glared at each man who dared eye Catarine until they looked away. Thank God. With the caliber of men crowded within this chamber, any show of weakness could invite a lethal confrontation.

A sticky substance squished beneath his boot as he stepped past a battered table. He glanced down. The meager torchlight aided him naught in deducting what smeared the aged wooden floor. With the dangerous lot that frequented this hovel, little telling what had spilled, ale, or blood. As if he expected different? For a secret meeting, 'twould be a fine setting.

At the table, Trálin shifted the chairs so the back of both his and Catarine's were against the wall.

She raised her brow.

"To ensure no one can sneak up on us from behind."

Her face paled a degree as she took a seat. "Wise. I pray the food will be more appealing than the inhabitants."

"We will soon find out," he replied as he settled in the chair beside her.

A while later, the woman the red-haired man had called Mildryth ambled toward their table. A loaf of bread sat on a trencher, and she carried two bowls of soup in the crook of her arm. Her lips pinched, she shoved the fare upon the rough wood with a clatter. Soup sloshed in the bowls, and several drops spilled over the edge. Shooting him a cool look, Mildryth whirled and strode off.

"How did she know you were a noble?" Catarine asked.

"A woman used to seeing scum, I doubt she has any problem deducting a man of higher stature." He leaned closer. "My only concern is that if she so easily figured out that I am a noble, how many others have noted the same?"

She stiffened, gave a covert glance around.

Bedamned, he'd nae meant to worry her. As if being in this blasted place invited calm? "'Tis too late to worry about it now. Once we learn what we can from whomever the English knight is meeting," he said in a low voice, "we will head to our chamber. Once we are out of sight, we will slip away."

Part of him regretted that they could nae delay their departure. As if that was wise? With him wanting her with his every breath, knowing she wanted him as well, naught good would come from their being alone in a chamber this night.

Naught good? Understatement. With a few uninterrupted hours alone, with the feelings she inspired, she would nae leave an innocent.

Catarine took a taste of her bread soaked with broth on the trencher, and her face twisted with revulsion. She returned it. "'Tis awful."

At her words, he pulled himself from his erotic thoughts. Trálin tore off a piece of bread, dipped it in the broth, and tasted. With a grimace, he swallowed. "Nor have we seen our chamber." He covertly scanned the aged interior, noted the cobwebs thick upon the ceiling, and the caked dirt on the floor. "From what we have seen so far, I doubt our room would be noteworthy." He cast a subtle glance to his side. "See that man sitting two tables away?" he whispered to Catarine as he made a show of dipping his bread in his soup.

"Aye," she whispered, keeping her eyes on her food as she hesitantly picked up her chunk of bread.

"'Tis the man I followed here. This close, I am hoping we can catch at least a wee bit of his conversation with whomever he came to meet."

She nodded as she tore off a small bit of bread, chewed, and swallowed it.

"After a few moments, look again. When you do, he is wearing a pendant, the same as the other English knights wore that you tossed over the castle wall."

Catarine took a sip of her wine, winced with disgust, then reached for another piece of bread. As she picked up her goblet, she slid a glance toward the Englishman, then away. "He tries to pretend he is nae waiting for someone, but he keeps peering toward the entry."

Tension rolled through Trálin. "Whoever he awaits must be arriving soon."

"Is it just me," she asked, "or is this the worst soup you have ever tasted in your life?"

A smile tugged at his mouth. "'Tis awful."

"It should be on the floor."

He gave a soft chuckle. "Mayhap it was."

With a grimace, she shoved aside her bowl. "Though a jest," she said as she wiped her mouth, "I am nae taking any chances."

"I agree. It may be safer to finish only the bread."

The rumble of voices filled the room, some low and secretive, others booming with their latest conquest. A man with unkempt hair scraggled around his shoulders leaned with menace toward another man.

At another table, a man grabbed a goblet of mead and upended the cup, sending the golden brew dripping from each corner of his mouth.

Trálin shifted to better protect Catarine. Braggarts, the lot of them. He would be pleased when they could depart this ill-gotten place.

With a yell of outrage, a man at a nearby table stood and drove his fist in the face of the man sitting across from him.

"Bloody hell," Trálin hissed. He stood, shoved Catarine behind him as he withdrew his sword. "Stay."

The man nearest them cursed, then dove over the table toward the aggressor.

The other man's head snapped back with a loud crack as the fist connected.

The first man swung.

Both table and chair went over as they crashed to the floor.

Curses spewed around them, some in outrage, others cheering the men on. Several shouted bets whether both men lived or died, or who would be the victor.

A glint flashed in the hand of the man on top.

"He has a knife!" Catarine gasped.

With a grunt, the man holding the blade slashed the other's neck.

Wild eyed, the man sprawled on the floor screamed as blood spilled down his filthy garb. His face grew to a mottled purple. Then, his entire body began to shudder. A moment later, he stilled.

As the man's lifeblood continued to seep out, a scraggly looking man nearby cursed, then handed over coin to his companion. Laughter echoed from across the chamber. Several occupants grunted with indifference and returned to their tables, talking and drinking their ale.

Amidst the flow of ribald conversation, two burly men lumbered over, hauled the body up, and dragged him toward the door.

Trálin glanced toward Catarine.

Shock widened her eyes as she watched.

Bedamned. He put his arm around her and turned her to face him. However strong she proclaimed herself, and though in battle—in self-defense—she'd claimed a life, what she'd seen this day should nae be witnessed by a woman.

A tremor rippled over her body. "'Tw-Twould seem this is a common occurrence."

Lord Grey's mouth tightened. "We will leave soon."

Pale eyes met his, their determination clear. "We will, but only when we learn what we came to."

His admiration for her grew. Many a woman would have retched at the grisly scene of moments before. And, it answered the question of what muck he had stepped in earlier, and what was the underlying stench in the room that neither food nor ale could nae smother. Bloody hell, the filth inhabiting this inn should all be hauled out and hanged.

One of the men holding the body shoved open the door. Together, they dragged the dead man out.

As the door started to close, a small, cloaked figure slipped inside and shut the door behind them with a soft thud.

Trálin stilled. The person they awaited?

Without hesitation, the figure headed toward the man they'd followed.

A thought flashed through Trálin's mind that he'd nae considered before. If this was one of the fey, would they recognize Catarine? God's teeth, would they nae sense her magic? Worried he'd placed her in danger, to shield her, he brushed kisses across her cheek. "Lass," he whispered, "if one of the fey, they will sense your magic, even if they dinna see you!"

Her body tensed.

"Do nae try and look," he said, "focus on me."

"Is the robed person headed toward the man we followed?" she asked as he brushed his mouth over hers.

"Aye." With a slow, subtle move, Trálin eyed the slender figure who, without hesitation, walked past the grim characters filling the inn.

"Nae worry, I brought along my bejeweled belt hidden beneath my garb for such a purpose. As long as I touch the stones upon it," she explained, "none of the fey will be able to sense me, but 'twill nae keep me hidden from their view. Each within the royal family is given such."

Trálin recalled catching sight of the belt when they'd first met. After everything he'd learned, he should have suspected it held magic. "What is happening now?" she whispered, her mouth against his, her hand remaining under the table and against the stones on the bejeweled belt.

"'Tis odd, none of the men within are paying the stranger any attention. Nae even a glance. 'Tis as if the person wasna here."

"Or they have a spell upon them so they canna be seen," she whispered.

"That doesna make sense," he replied against her soft mouth.

"Why?"

"How can I see them?"

She shivered. "Because you are linked with me."

"Linked to you?" He drew back, watched her eyes. "You meant by kissing you?"

A blush touched her cheeks. "Nae, because to a degree, we have been intimate."

Confusion shifted to concern. "If indeed 'tis an accomplice from the Otherworld, will they be able to detect our . . . link?"

Uneasy eyes held his. "I am nae sure."

The last thing he wished to do was to put her in harm's way. As if he hadn't been doing a bloody fine job since they'd met. He nuzzled her hair.

"What does the person look like?" she whispered, her voice trembling.

"Whoever it is, as if taking every precaution, he or she is still cloaked and wearing a hood pulled low to shield the face," he replied.

"Build?"

"Slender."

"How tall?" she asked.

"About your height. The person walks with almost an uncanny grace. If asked anywhere else, I would say 'tis a woman."

"A woman?" she whispered, dread filling her voice. "Oh God, 'tis Princess Elspeth!"

Chapter Nineteen

Fear tore through Catarine as she fought for calm within the smoke-filled inn. "Though she keeps her hood up as a precaution, I canna believe my aunt would dare risk exposing herself."

"'Tis brazen." Trálin whispered, his body continuing to block hers from the woman's view.

"Indeed." The savage deeds her aunt had initiated proved how strong she'd become. And her suspicions of her needing to join with the Comyns or to be in league in the abduction of King Alexander fell away.

A shard of hope filtered through her, a hope nurtured by the years past. "Trálin, mayhap 'tis nae her? If I saw her, regardless of her cover, I would know."

"If 'tis Princess Elspeth," he cautioned, "'tis dangerous to risk her catching a glimpse of you."

She swallowed hard. "The stakes are too high. We must be sure."

Trálin hesitated a moment, then with a muttered curse, he shifted a degree.

The slender figure walked with a steady gait toward the man who sat two tables away, but the thick robe shielded any other discerning features. From the way the person moved, 'twas indeed a woman, but was it her aunt? The height was correct, but without seeing at least a glimpse of her face, Catarine could nae be sure. And as her hand was hidden within the cloak, if indeed it was Elspeth, Catarine would nae be able to detect such.

As the mysterious woman sat, the flowing robe settled around her in a shielding heap. Naught but the tip of a boot lay exposed.

Trálin shifted closer and kissed her. "Do you recognize her?"

"I canna see her face," Catarine replied. "Mayhap if I heard her voice."

The mysterious person leaned forward.

Catarine focused, listened with her extra sensitive fey hearing.

The man nodded once. A moment later, he shook his head.

"Anything?" Trálin whispered.

Frustration built as she tried to catch a wisp, an inflection of the tone. "'Tis too noisy for me to hear either of them."

"Blast it," he whispered. "The reason I suspect she chose this inn as a meeting place. Still, given your fey sensitivities, I would have thought you would have heard something."

"I as well."

Frustration carved his brow as Trálin moved and shielded her from the woman's view. "Should we confront them?"

"Without the fey guard to back us up, and with her power," she replied, "'twould be too dangerous."

He paused a long moment. "You do believe we will be able to stop her?"

Nausea churned in her gut. "I do nae know." She shifted again to catch a glimpse of the woman. "But there is——"

The robed figure stiffened, turned toward them.

Catarine stilled.

"What is it?" Trálin asked.

"Whatever it is, it has turned our way!" she whispered.

Bedamned! He put his arm around her, drew her face against his neck, but allowed a wedge of space so she could continue to see. "Is the figure still looking at us?"

Her body trembled. "Aye."

"Can you see who it is?"

A long second passed, broken by crude laughter a table away.

"Nae . . . Oh no!" she whispered. "The person is standing."

Trálin clasped the hilt of his dagger.

"Wait," she cautioned in a low voice. "It is turning toward the front entry."

On a rough breath he dropped his hand. "Once they leave, then we will follow."

On an unsteady breath, she nodded.

Through the crowd of men, a faint scrape of the door sounded. Trálin shot a covert glance toward the entry. A wisp of the robed figure exited into the night, then the lone stranger departed in their wake.

He caught Catarine's hand. "Come. We will keep our pace easy to nae alert anyone."

Her fingers trembling in his hand, after several steps, she tugged him to a halt. "You are heading for the stairs."

"Aye," he whispered. "We canna use the front door. No doubt whoever is behind this has someone inside this chamber watching for anything suspicious, or if anyone tries to follow."

"We do nae know the room we are supposed to stay in."

"Indeed." Trálin took Catarine's hand. "Mildryth is carrying food to a back table. We will ask her."

Moments later, with the location of the room supplied, he led her toward the steps, keeping their pace slow.

The soft thud of wood echoed below them as they headed up to the next floor.

Out of sight, he dropped her hand. "Hurry." He sprinted toward an open door facing the front of the building. After Catarine entered, he shut the door, then crossed to the window. Through the smear of filth, Trálin scanned the area below.

"What do you see?"

"The man at the stable is bringing out their horses," he replied. "Once we know what direction they are riding, we will alert the others and follow."

"With them on horseback, how are we ever going to pick up their trail once we rejoin with our men?"

Trálin scanned the sky. "Clouds are shielding the moon, so odds are, with the rough lay of land, wherever they are traveling, 'tis nae far."

Catarine crossed to the window. In silence she watched as the two figures mounted, then guided their steeds into the night. "They are headed southwest."

"Aye." A soft scrape broke the silence as Trálin lifted the window. "Follow me." He paused, turned to give her a quick, hard kiss, then slipped out the window to a nearby tree.

With a glimpse at the unused bed, on a sigh, Catarine followed in his wake.

Several hours later, thankful to have rejoined with their men and for the clearing skies that'd allowed them to pick up the trail, Catarine guided her mount across the uneven ground.

"We have nae seen tracks for a while," she said as she glanced toward Drax. "With the many places to hide, I doubt we will find the pair unless we stumble upon them."

"Aye," Drax agreed.

On edge, she navigated her steed down a steep incline, the hard clip of hooves upon the frozen ground. Were the riders close enough to hear them? And what of her fey guard she'd sent to the Otherworld to warn her family? Had Sionn reached her father as well?

Riding at her side, Trálin reined in his steed. "I see a light ahead. Everyone hold!"

Along with the others, she drew her horse to a halt. A bundle of nerves, Catarine peered through the clusters of rock and errant brush. In the distance beyond a snow-dusted ledge, she caught a faint glow. "'Tis a campfire, but I see only one person."

"As do I," Kuircc said.

Drax shifted in his saddle. "Whoever was with the man should be nearby."

"Or, they have left to meet with others," Catarine said.

"Aye," Lord Grey agreed. "If so, why leave the man there, unless his presence is meant to lure us in?"

Uneasy, Catarine glanced over, the scent of cold earth and the night filling her every breath. "Do you think the robed woman suspected that we would follow her?"

Trálin shrugged. "I do nae know. We caught signs of their passing since we picked up their trail, but we canna be sure that she is nearby or has continued on."

"There is only one way to find out," Drax said. "We go in."

Frustration slammed her. "We canna risk riding much closer. With the lack of cover, if 'tis indeed a trap, 'twill be too easy to be seen."

Trálin cursed. "We must wait for sunrise."

Thankful the clouds had cleared throughout the night, she scanned the hue-laden heavens. "With faint hints of the dawn streaking the sky, 'twill nae be long." Logic suggested that the man's campfire and supposed lack of concern of being seen was a ploy to catch them, but a part of her held doubt. "Mayhap the mysterious person has continued on. I agree with Lord Grey, 'tis best if we wait here."

Leather creaked as Drax dismounted. "Never have I seen the likes of our surroundings. The blasted land is a maze of cliffs and flat sweeps of land."

"I have heard of this odd lay of land before," Trálin said as he swung off his mount, then walked his steed to a nearby boulder, "but I have nae been this far Southwest in England and seen it or the myth it holds."

Unease swept through her as she jumped to the ground. "Myth it holds?"

"Aye," Trálin replied. "If you continue southwest, 'tis said to be a maze of caves crafted by an underground river over the years."

Her disquiet grew. "You know someone who dared enter the caves?"

"Aye," Trálin replied, "or so he said. I know the man and he is given to tell a tale or two, so I dismissed his stories as naught but a bard's tale."

"What did he tell?" Kuirec asked, his voice tense.

Lord Grey hesitated. "You believe the caves are important?"

"I do," Kuirec replied.

"Did the trail on the map end near here?" Catarine asked.

"Blast it," Trálin said. "I should have mentioned them before. With the area so barren and disbelieving the stories, I dismissed the caves as a possibility."

"'Tis no time for regrets," Catarine said as she led her steed to where the others secured theirs. "Tell us what you were told."

Lord Grey nodded. "Inside, the man spoke of rock formations as thin as your finger in clusters hanging from the ceiling, and of underground waterfalls. He also mentioned odd faces crafted by the water." He paused. "And, the man said when he exited the cave, 'twas as if voices chased him out. At the time I thought his words were a bunch of rot."

Her entire body stilled. "What type of rock are the caves made from?"

"Limestone," Lord Grey replied.

Catarine shivered. God help them. "I was afraid of that."

Drax cursed. "Are you thinking what I am?"

"Unfortunately," Catarine agreed.

Trálin glanced from one to the other. "What does it matter?"

She swallowed hard, then glanced toward the Scottish knights in accompaniment, thankful they rested far enough away so they could hear naught. "To bathe in a pool of water filled in a limestone is how a fairy goes into deep meditation."

"Meditation?" Trálin asked.

"Aye," she replied. "It is how the fey recover if they receive a serious wound. Or, if they are involved with magic, 'tis how they become more powerful."

Lord Grey's breath left him with a hiss. "You are saying the stories the man told me are nae only true, but you believe Princess Elspeth is using the caves to build her powers?"

"Along with the strength of her army," Catarine added.

"'Twould explain why no one else searched the caves further after the man's stories," Trálin said. "Or, if they indeed found the entry, dared to go inside."

"Dared to go inside?" she asked. "Why?"

"Remember how I told you the man railed of how he had heard voices as he was leaving?"

What else would he reveal? On edge, she nodded.

"When the man told others of what he'd seen and heard," Trálin explained, "like wildfire word spread that the caves are haunted. And with each telling, the fable grew to include ghosts, and outrageous tales of evil that if witnessed, 'twould turn a man into stone."

"That explains why the caves remain left alone," Drax grumbled.

Realization dawned. "'Twas planned," Catarine whispered. "The caves are difficult to find, are they nae?"

Lord Grey nodded. "Very much so, the entry is all but hidden."

"And if any came across what they suspected the entrance, with the whispers of evil haunting the caverns," she explained, "none would dare go inside."

"Blast it," Trálin said. "It makes sense."

The curl of wind slid past, casting loose snow and leaves past. As she stared at the flicker of distant flames, trepidation filled her. "Princess Elspeth used fear and humans' belief that the caves were haunted to ensure no one dared to venture near."

"How long ago was it that the man told you about the caves?" Drax asked.

"Before I was knighted," Trálin replied. "'Twould be more than eight summers ago. Even then, the man told me his experience had happened many years prior."

"From the few things we have seen," Catarine said, "Princess Elspeth has been there a long time and used her time well. She has grown strong in her magic and is extremely dangerous. Regardless of the risk, we must search the caves. She and her men may still be within."

God in heaven knew what they would find inside the twist of stone. How many weapons had her aunt ordered crafted? No doubt all spell-tipped to allow the English knights to kill the fey? And with the years passed, how many well-trained knights stood readied to destroy her home? However many men they faced, somehow, they must figure out a way to stop them.

"First," Catarine said, refusing to allow her fears to guide her, "if the man ahead is alone, we must find out what he knows."

"If 'tis possible," Trálin stated. "Like the other two men, she might kill him before he reveals anything."

"I pray this time is different." But she held doubts.

Muscles aching, she stretched her shoulders, then caught herself before she yawned. "With the hard miles we have traveled, however brief, we all can use the rest. Kuirce, pass word to the men we are taking a short break." Without waiting for a reply, she walked toward the outcrop of rocks near the edge of a stone-shielded cliff.

His mouth tight, Trálin watched her leave. However worn out she was, and regardless of her brave words, she grieved her aunt's transition to evil, a woman she loved and respected—an important person in her life whom she could no longer trust. Mayhap he could say something to help ease the emotional burden she carried? He started after her.

Drax stepped before him. "Lord Grey, she wishes to be alone."

He met her fey warrior's cool stare. "A warning?"

The fey warrior crossed his arms over his chest. "A caution."

As if he'd bloody stay away. Catarine was struggling, and however much he could, he would be there for her. His heart aching at all she struggled with, Trálin moved past the warrior and walked to the flat slab of rock she sat upon, her knees up, her head resting against her legs.

"It doesna look like a comfortable position," he said.

Her body stiffened, but she didn't look up. "I am nae trying to sleep."

Far from put off by her sharp tone, he sat next to her, winced as his exhausted body settled against cold stone, tugged up his cape against the cool gust of wind, and stared out over the land. "You ponder your aunt's betrayal and worry about what we will discover in the caves."

"Go away."

Somber, he looked over.

Wind tugged at her braid, and she kept her head down.

How he wished she would open up to him, but however frustrating, the choice must be hers. "Do you truly want me to leave you alone?"

A tumble of wind-laden snow rushed past.

"Catarine?"

"Nay," she replied, frustration lacing her voice. Lifting her head, she glanced over. "What do you want from me?"

"I want you to know that if you need to speak with someone, I am here."

In the wisps of newborn light, a sad smile touched her mouth. "I know you are there for me now, but 'tis too easy to turn to you. A fact of late I find myself doing without thinking." She paused. "A much as I wish otherwise, Trálin, 'tis dangerous to allow myself to weaken when it comes to you. The reason I came here to think."

Anger brewed within, grew. "Turning to me is nae a weakness."

"Is it nae? I am a princess, a person who others seek for protection and guidance."

"Turning to me is a sign of trust, natural between friends."

She gave a rough laugh. "Friends, is it? A fool, I thought after what we shared, 'twas more."

"You know what I mean."

She gave a heavy sigh. "I do indeed. Sorry I am that our choices can nae be different."

"As am I."

Silence fell between them, thick with the passage of time, time that offered naught but loneliness ahead. However wrong, with each passing moment, he wanted her more.

Wanted her forever.

Shaken by the emotions she inspired, he stared east, toward where the sky held hints of dark purple, evidence of the coming dawn. With the dangerous confrontation that lay ahead, it was a fact he needed to focus on.

"There is something I must tell you that only those within the royal family know," Catarine said, her words trembling.

"What is it?" he asked.

"If during our confrontation, something were to happen to me—"

He stiffened. "It willna."

"Willna?" she repeated with a shake of her head. "Neither of us can say when it is our time."

Bedamned. The thought of anything happening to her tore him apart.

"Listen to me," she urged, "'tis important that you know."

Unsettled by the graveness of her voice, Trálin remained silent.

She took a deep breath, exhaled. "During my youth, as he did with each of my siblings, my father hand-selected each of the fey warriors to protect me. Before each man began his service, he swore an oath to keep me safe, even at the risk of his life."

"A common enough request," Trálin said, unsure where this was leading.

"Aye, except once each swore their oath, my father gave each warrior one of five different gemstones, which they wear around their neck."

"Why?"

Warmth of the memories of that special moment as she'd watched each of her fey warriors receive their pendant filled her. "Each gemstone holds a strength to aid the wearer. There is only one moss agate, which holds the ability to make warriors powerful and shield them from those who would bring them harm. This my father bestowed to Atair."

"Which makes sense as he is the senior fey warrior."

"Aye," she agreed. "The other gemstones are the azurite, which helps to control over your emotions and reactions, and to give the wearer greater insight. This he presented to Drax. The magnesite, to guide one's emotional fate, is held by Ranulf. The malachite, which promotes inner peace, was given to both Magnus and Kuircc. And the sapphire, known for its powers of prophecy and wisdom, was granted to Sionn. The sapphire is also called the stone of destiny, because of its ability to aid the wearer in clarity of mind for those who seek the truth."

"The stone of destiny?" he asked.

"You do nae believe in the power of the stones?"

"The Scots believe in many things which from other cultures draw skepticism."

Catarine hesitated. "You mean things which they deem witch-craft?"

"Aye."

"As your belief in the fey?"

In the first rays of morning light peeked over the land, a smile tugged at his mouth. "Indeed."

Warmth tumbled through her. She would miss her time with Trálin. "As for the stones," she said, turning the discussion back to where she started, to where it needed to be. "The power each gemstone holds bolsters an inherent weakness of whoever wears it."

Trálin's brows raised with surprise.

"Except, the stones have one more purpose," she continued, how-ever hard to contemplate, needing to explain. "If ever I am attacked and my fey warriors find they canna protect me, they have one last responsibility."

Worried eyes searched hers. "What is that?"

Emotions stormed her, and she struggled to speak the words.

"Catarine, tell me."

A shiver swept through her. "If I am in danger, the fey warriors will remove their gemstones and place them together. When the stones touch, their power merges. In a trice they explode and release a surge of focused energy directed on the threat."

"God in heaven," Trálin hissed, then stilled. "With three of the warriors away, if needed, you do nae have the full impact of their power to protect you!"

"I know, but each gemstone alone is very lethal. And each one added increases the power of the energy. But . . ."

"But?"

"To save me," she rasped, aching at the thought, "each fey warrior who adds their gemstone to the group offers the ultimate sacrifice—his life."

Chapter Twenty

Stunned, Trálin stared at Catarine as she sat beside him as the soft light of dawn caressed her face. "Each fey warrior who places his stone with the others to protect you dies?"

She gave a shaky nod.

In the fragile rays sweeping the land, Trálin caught the fear in her eyes. Now he understood her abrupt departure from where the men had gathered moments before. "You wished to be alone, because you are afraid for your warriors' lives."

"Aye."

"God, lass." Wind spun around them, tossed loose snow past in a whispered hush as he lay his hand over hers. However much he wished to draw her near, with her men in sight, he'd nae dishonor her. "I pray 'tis unnecessary for your warriors to merge their gemstones."

Tortured eyes met his. "My thanks."

He removed his hand, frustrated he could offer her nay more than words. Neither would he assure her that her men would survive. Well a warrior knew the risks made to defend those they served.

Still, how could she nae struggle with the possible loss of men who she looked upon as brothers? In the short time he'd spent with her fey warriors, he'd gained immense respect for each man.

"Catarine, if the warriors are forced to combine their gemstones, with how powerful you believe your aunt has become, do you think 'twill be enough to stop her?"

"I must have faith 'tis possible."

But he heard what she didna dare say. Even if her men sacrificed their lives, it guaranteed naught. "And if we do nae stop her, how would you reach your father?"

Her breath fell out in a rough wobble. "If you are dead, I—I will find a way to return to the Otherworld."

Aye she would, alone, upset, and exhausted. Unsure what to say, he glanced toward the sky.

Streaks of dawn crept brighter across the sky. The purple rays held a hint of gold, like a promise.

And he hoped 'twas a positive omen.

Catarine stiffened. "Trálin, the English knight is preparing to leave."

Irritated at becoming caught up in his thoughts and nae on their mission, he peered through the breaks in the rocks.

In the distance, the man they'd followed from the inn knelt, then began to roll his blanket.

"I see no sign of anyone else hidden nearby," she said.

He scanned the area. "I see naught as well, but the remaining shadows and the rough lay of land along with errant shrubs provides an excellent place for men to hide."

"They do," she agreed. "As much as I wish to wait for the sun to fully rise, if we linger, he will be gone. We must catch him now."

"Aye." Trálin kept low as he headed back to camp.

A short while later, with the men informed and everyone having moved to their planned location, Trálin peered through the rocks above the ledge.

With stiff movements, the English knight secured the saddle roll on his horse.

Thank God Princess Elspeth's man hadn't heard their approach, nor seemed to be in a hurry. Trálin stood as he motioned for his men to surround the English knight. Stones clattered as he and the other warriors stepped into the clearing.

One hand reaching for his mount's halter, the English knight whirled. The horse snorted, stepped sideways as the man withdrew his blade and faced Lord Grey. "What do you want?"

"Information." Sword drawn, Trálin walked closer as Catarine and the others encircled the knight, their blades readied.

His eyes wary, the Englishman backed closer to his mount. "Who are you?"

"Who did you meet at the inn?" Trálin demanded.

Shock, then fear rolled through the man's expression.

"'Tis a woman of great magic, is it nae?" Catarine asked as she stepped to Trálin's side. "One nae from this world."

The Englishman's face blanched. "The woman you met and left with at the inn is Princess Elspeth," she stated.

Eyes darting from her to the surrounding warriors, the Englishman began to tremble. "I can reveal naught."

Trálin raised his sword. "You will."

"The gemstone at his neck!" Catarine warned, "'Tis beginning to glow!"

On a cry of pain, the Englishman's face turned a ruddy shade of red. He gasped for air as he clutched the stone, tugged. His sword fell the ground with a clatter.

Blast it! Trálin ran to the Englishman, reached for the gemstone.

"Do nae touch the stone while it is glowing!" Catarine yelled.

He ignored her warning. They could nae lose this man before they had information! Trálin reached for the gemstone caught between the man's fingers as he worked to tear it free. Lord Grey's fingers brushed against the smoothed glowing gem. Waves of energy built around him, doubled. Shattered.

Wind rushed around Trálin as he was thrown back, slammed against the earth. His vision blurry, and with his muscles aching, he looked up.

The slap of footsteps increased, halted. Worried eyes studied him as Catarine knelt beside him. "Are you hurt?"

Trálin touched his head as he fought to focus. "It feels as if a mace was driven through my skull, but otherwise, I am fine." He sat, then on shaky legs, pushed himself to his feet as she stood with him. "What bloody happened?"

"Nay time to explain." Catarine turned to their men. "Everyone back! I am going to try to intercept the connection."

At her command, Drax and Kuircc released the Englishman as he fought to tear the gemstone free. They along with the Scottish knights ran for cover.

Head pounding, unsure what in Hades was going on, Trálin stepped toward her.

Anger swept Catarine's face. "Trálin, get back, now!"

"Lord Grey, move!" Drax yelled.

Furious that in some way she was endangering her life, he hesitated. However much he wanted to protect her, he must trust she knew what she was doing. Cursing the entire situation, Trálin sprinted around a nearby rock, peered above.

Eyes focused, Catarine reached toward the sky, started to sway back and forth in a lyrical dance.

A keening cry filled the air.

Wind swirled around her and the man. Leaves and snow were swept up in the fierce spiral, tossed away as fast. Her hair flowing in the torrent, wild as if a gypsy, she reached for the Englishman's gemstone.

As her hand clasped it, her eyes widened in stunned surprise, then pain. The veins on her face throbbed. Smoke, thick and grey belched around her and the knight. A roar filled the air, and the haze began to thicken around them both, erasing them from view.

Bedamned. He'd nae let her die. They'd find her aunt without the English knight's bloody help! Trálin stood.

"Get back!" Drax yelled.

Like bloody Hades! Trálin ran.

An explosion rattled the air.

Reverberations slammed him to the ground. A grey-black haze churned before him as he shoved to his feet. The stench of flesh burned his nostrils as he staggered through the putrid swirl.

"Catarine!" he yelled, fear for her life tearing through him. "Catarine!"

Her cough echoed several paces away. "Here."

Thank God! Two more steps through the rancorous muck and he caught her outline and the image of the dead knight nearby. "What were you thinking?" he demanded as he knelt beside her, caught her shoulders to help her sit, wanting to shake her for taking such a risk.

"That we n-needed answers."

The morning light cutting through the murky grey exposed the ash smudging her face and the fear in her eyes.

Trálin's anger fell away. By God, he'd come so close to losing her. "We needed answers, aye, but nae at the risk of your life."

Pain-filled eyes narrowed. "And would you nae have risked the same if given the situation?"

His mouth tightened.

"Aye, you would have," she said before he could speak. "'Tis no different.

However much he wished to argue, she was right. "You never mentioned how dangerous it is to touch the gemstone."

"There was no need before," she replied.

Memories flickered in his mind and he understood. "And the reason you tossed the gemstone over the wall as well as placed it on the English knight's neck using the tie?"

"Aye."

Footsteps echoed behind him as he stood, reached down to help her.

She gave him a weak smile, then set her hand in his. "My thanks, Lord Grey."

He helped her up, pushed her wild, soot-laced locks from her face. "Thank God you are okay."

"Catarine?" Drax called from within the blur of smoke.

"Here," she replied as she moved away from Trálin.

Her fey warriors stepped into view. Panicked eyes scoured her, then relaxed to concern.

"What did you learn?" Drax asked.

"When I touched the stone," she replied, "for a moment I sensed Princess Elspeth's power, caught a glimpse of her."

Kuirec's face grew taut. "Did she see you?"

Catarine hesitated, then nodded.

"Blast it," Drax muttered. "Is there anything else we need to know?"

"As we suspected, she is still in the cave. With our connection but a trice, thankfully, she has no idea exactly where I am, except she believes I am closing in on her location."

Trálin crossed his arms over his chest. "We still have the element of surprise. But, we have a day, two at most, to find her. After that, she will be expecting us. But, to slip inside the caves will be dangerous."

Worry darkened Catarine's eyes. "Now, she will have the entrance and throughout the cave well-guarded. But she has nae left. I will be thankful for that."

"We will stop her," Kuircc said.

Or die trying, Trálin silently agreed. He took in the dead English knight and grimaced. The man's face was frozen in pain, hard lines dredged in terror, a gruesome expression like the two men before who'd died a cruel death.

In the wisps of smoke sifting through the early morning light, sadness touched her face. "Like the others who wore the gemstone, he was innocent of treachery, naught but a pawn in Princess Elspeth's twisted game."

A gust of wind whipped past, delivering a welcome breath of fresh air. A glint from the English knight's dagger lying on the ground nearby caught Trálin's attention. He picked it up, stilled.

"What is wrong?" Catarine asked.

Intrigued, Trálin studied the blade. "Whoever made this weapon has a fine hand. And, 'tis crafted of silver." He turned the dagger in his hand, frowned. "There is an inscription carved on the side, but 'tis in a language I have never seen."

A concerned look passed between Catarine and Drax. "Let me look at it."

Lord Grey laid it in her palm.

As Catarine read the inscription emblazoned in the blade, lifted her gaze to his. "'Tis written in fey."

"What does it say?" Kuircc asked.

"Knight of The Silver Dagger." The blade trembled in her hand. "'Twould seem Princess Elspeth has done more than gather men, but has created an elite force to assassinate the royal family."

Kuircc cursed.

"Nor would I dare touch the tip," she continued. "I suspect like the blade used to kill my uncle, 'tis spell-tipped." With care, she handed it back to Trálin.

Lord Grey sheathed the weapon on his garb. "Do you think she has sent the elite knights ahead?"

"I suspect so," she replied. "With the information provided by Atair, Sionn, and the others, no doubt my father will be out with troops to destroy any threat."

"Except," Trálin said, understanding the cause of the nerves in her voice, "your father and the others are defenseless to the spell-tipped arrows."

"They are," she admitted in a rough whisper, "which is why we must reach my aunt first. Her death will break the spell over the Knights of The Silver Daggers. Regardless of where they are, what vicious task they are en route to, with her death, they will remember naught."

Wind tumbled snow blew past as Drax rubbed his jaw. "How long before we reach the caves?"

"The entrance to the caves is less than a day away," Trálin replied.

Sadness swept Catarine's face as she took in the dead Englishman.

Trálin grimaced. The explosion of energy had left his body scarred, his gruesome expression a testament to the agony he'd suffered. "We will bury him before we depart."

Shimmers of fading sunlight slipped through the break in the thickening clouds overhead, and danced upon the sweep of land with wilting intensity as Catarine stared at the odd-leveled mound at the base of rock that built into a formidable ben.

Trálin pointed toward the center. "The entrance to the cave is near the bottom."

Searching for a blackened indent, she scoured the slid of land. "I see it, barely. With the sun setting and the erratic formations of rock, 'tis hard to make out the entry amongst the shadows."

"Even in the full light of day," Trálin said, "'tis difficult. Unless you stumble upon the opening, one must know what they are looking for."

Drax glanced over. "The area around the entrance is too exposed to approach during the day, and with the irregular countryside, treacherous by night."

"Another reason Princess Elspeth selected this cavern." Catarine took in the sky thick with clouds, the swirls of grey smothering the errant flickers of sunlight. An omen? A shiver rippled through her. "We are all exhausted and will remain here this night. At dawn we go in."

Trálin, Drax, and Kuircc nodded.

She glanced to where the Scottish knights waited a short distance away. "Lord Grey, did you explain to them the circumstance of the English knight's death?"

"I did," Trálin replied, "but as we discussed earlier, nae until they took an oath of silence."

"My thanks. I am sure after the Englishman's death this day, they had many questions. Neither do they need any surprises when we face the remainder of my aunt's warriors."

"They do nae," Drax agreed. "I hope after Sionn gave your father an update of the situation that he has sent warriors to aid us."

With a hard swallow, she studied the near-hidden entry. "However much we wish it so, we canna count on anyone but ourselves." She glanced at Kuircc. "Pass to the Scottish knights our plans to leave at first light."

With a nod, her fey warrior started to walk away, then turned back, his brow deepened by worry. "Do nae stay up this night; you need sleep as well." Kuircc turned on his heel, strode toward the men.

Surprised by his request, she watched him walk away, unsure if she should be grateful for or upset by his protectiveness.

"He worries for you," Trálin said. "A concern I share."

Her frustration toward her warrior fell away. "And he is right. I do need sleep, as do we all."

"Aye." Trálin took a deep breath. "Catarine, I want you to know I will never forget you."

Emotions rolled through her, her love for him so strong, she wondered how she'd live without him once the time came to part. Her heart heavy, she touched his cheek. "Nor I you."

Meager hints of moonlight spilled through the angry churn of clouds, reflecting a wee bit of light on the sleek blanket of the snow-covered ground. After a check of their surroundings to ensure nay imminent threat existed, Trálin made his way toward the wedge of rocks. As he rounded a boulder, through the falling snow, he made out Catarine's outline. Seems he was nae the only one who couldna sleep. As if wondering if you would live through the next day invited calm?

With each battle he faced, nerves played a part. Except never before had his worries included a woman, one who made him feel, want more than any other woman in his life.

The steady breeze increased, and Catarine tugged her cape closer. "With the blanket of clouds, it looks as if it will snow throughout the day."

Startled, he halted. "How did you know I was there?"

"I saw you when you left your pallet."

So she'd been watching him as well. Satisfaction filled him as he walked over. "The snow will help shield our approach."

A hint of a smile tugged at her mouth. "Always the optimist."

"Nay," he said, sitting a hand's width from her on the flat rock, "a man who takes what he is given and makes the best of it."

A gust of wind swirled past. "'Tis nae always simple to do."

"But in life, 'tis often necessary."

The moonlight slipping through the falling snow illuminated her slender figure with alluring grace. "I canna help but worry for my family. I pray they are safe."

"Whatever happens after the morrow," Trálin said, his words somber, "you are a strong woman and will move forward."

"Like marry a man I do nae want?"

Silence fell between them.

Catarine cleared her throat. "I should nae have said that."

"You said only what is true."

She sighed. "Still . . ."

"'Tis done," Trálin stated. "We both understand our duties."

"We do. Nor would it be wise to remain here together." She stood. "With only a few hours left, we must try to rest."

Fatigue rolled through him, and with the reality of the morrow, he found himself tired of secrets. The too real possibility existed that after the battle, either of them might be dead. Or both.

Trálin stood, caught her arm. He may be damned for his words, but if he died, 'twould be with her knowing. "Catarine, I——"

She tensed.

Bloody hell, mayhap he should say naught. He was a fool to even contemplate sharing his feelings where if they both lived, 'twould only make their situation worse.

"What is it, Trálin?"

The hope in her words gave him courage. "Catarine, if something should happen to me, know that I love you."

Chapter Twenty-one

Stunned, overwhelmed, Catarine stared at Trálin, exuberant tears burning her eyes. "You love me?" She'd dreamed of this moment, for his feelings to match hers, and for their lives to be one, forever. "Trálin, I—"

In the brim of moonlight, he pressed a soft kiss upon her lips. "Say naught. I struggled with if 'twas wise to tell you. Even now, I wonder if I was wrong."

"How can you feel wrong about telling me when it fills my heart with joy?"

"How can it nae feel otherwise? Once the battle is over, if we both live, my love for you changes naught."

Angst tore through her happiness at the devastating truth. So caught up in his declaration of love, she'd forgotten reality. Hurt, trying to find some level of acceptance, she pulled away. "Then why tell me now?"

"Because on the morrow," he replied, his voice rough, "if I didna live, I wanted you to know."

The humble finality of his words gave her pause. He'd given no apology. Considering the challenge they faced and his lack of any magical power, in his mind, his demise was a logical deduction. More sobering, a warrior, a man used to fighting battles, he'd nae asked to fall in love. Caught in the turmoil of his emotions, he'd reached out the only way he knew how.

With honesty.

"I may die as well," she whispered, her voice unsteady. "But 'tis nae what worries me. 'Tis the thought of losing you. And, I fear for the lives of my men, and for the knights sent with us from King Alexander."

"I know," he said, "I fear for them as well."

The soft hush of wind swept past.

For a long moment she stood, savoring this moment alone with him. In but hours they would depart. And her life would have been poorer if Trálin had nae spoken.

"Though you wish me to say naught, since the moment I saw you, I felt a connection. I love you, Trálin. To know you feel the same for me is both humbling and amazing. Never did I expect to feel this way, but I do. You need to know that no matter what happens, I will cherish this moment, and your love, forever."

Trálin touched her face, his heart aching in a way he'd never dreamed possible. "I love you so much." He claimed her lips lightly, then stepped back. "However much I want you, I canna allow anyone to see us together."

A fresh round of tears burned Catarine's throat for what never could be. "'Tis best." Frustrated, exhausted at the emotional battle she waged within her, she struggled to focus on what for her must be most important—the battle on the morrow. "I love you." Before he could speak, she turned and hurried toward camp. As she approached where the fey warriors slept, Drax stirred awake.

He glanced toward Trálin following a distance away, then back to her.

"Lord Grey worries for me," she said, before he made a comment.

Drax grunted. "Have you made your decision about what to do with Lord Grey and his men?"

Their earlier discussion, and the options given, came to mind. "Until moments ago, I was unsure."

"And now?"

She nodded. "We will go ahead with what we discussed."

"I know the decision was nae easy," Drax said, his words somber, "but 'tis for the best."

"I have to believe so."

"Go to sleep, there is nae much time before dawn."

She would try. With her mind raw with emotions, Catarine crawled inside her bedroll, and covered up in the cocoon of warmth.

And with the slide of wind and flakes of snow tickling her nose, thoughts of Trálin's vow of love sifted through her mind.

And she cried.

Tension pounded through Trálin as he pressed himself flat against the wedge of rocks and peered toward the entry to the cave a stone's throw away.

Two guards stood outside.

He glanced toward Drax flattened behind him. In the first flickers of daylight, he held up two fingers.

Drax nodded, passed the information to the others.

Lord Grey scanned their surroundings. The heavy snow that'd make the trek to this position a challenge had also shielded them as they'd moved across the open field as well as covered their tracks.

Since the sun had risen, he'd caught no sign of the guards making rounds. With the way they ignored their surroundings and talked to each other, 'twas obvious neither expected any threat. Princess Elspeth was either convinced Catarine was a distance away, or the fairy princess had grown so powerful she believed her niece was nae a threat.

He struggled with the reality of his looming death. If he didna live past this day, his brother, Faolan, would inherit the title of earl and take care of Lochshire Castle. A brother he would greatly miss. But his greatest concern was that Catarine's life be spared.

Boots crunched in the snow as Catarine, Drax, and the others crept closer.

"Any change in the guard?" Catarine asked as she reached him.

Trálin shook his head. "'Tis been the same two men by the entry since we arrived."

"The men I sent to search our surroundings reported back no sign of anyone behind us as well," Drax said. "We will go ahead with our plans. With them both nae on alert, I will become invisible and take them out."

With a grimace, Trálin wondered if he'd ever become used to the fey's ability to become invisible.

Drax started to move past, then hesitated. "Before our venture begins, know this, Lord Trálin MacGruder. You are a man I greatly respect."

Humbled by the warrior's somber claim, Trálin nodded. "A feeling toward you I share."

"I am honored." With one last glance toward Catarine, Drax moved around the brush, then vanished.

Several moments passed.

A guard cried out a second before the other. Both men collapsed.

Drax became visible, waved them forward.

"Princess Elspeth wants us to come inside," Catarine stated as she moved beside Trálin.

Trálin glanced over. "Why do you say that?"

"'Twas too easy to take out her guards."

At her matter-of-fact tone, unease swept through him. Where was her surprise? Her upset? Blast it! "You knew all along that your aunt was aware we were close and awaited our arrival?"

Turquoise eyes filled with regret. "Nae for sure."

"Nae for sure?" he repeated, his anger growing with each breath. "You had a sliver of doubt mayhap, but you were fairly positive she knew of our approach. Except you kept it from me?"

Silence.

Trálin's anger built. "We could have discussed it."

At his hard tone, her face paled. "You are right, we could have. I chose otherwise."

"You chose otherwise?" Bloody unbelievable! "'Tis nae as if we are armed with an equal force to conquer Princess Elspeth. We have but a handful of men, and we need to work together."

"We have the stones," she stated, her voice cool, distant.

"Only two," Trálin said.

Her face hardened. "Along with the stones on my belt that will allow us to move close enough to her before she senses us, they will be enough."

"Are your warriors aware of this decision?"

At the bite in his words, for a long moment she remained quiet. Finally, she nodded. "Aye."

Trálin cursed. "And when were you going to let me in on the fact that you were going to allow your blasted self and your men killed?"

Silence.

"You were nae going to tell me, were you?"

"You would nae have followed us," she replied, no emotion in her voice.

The pieces came together in furious understanding. "You had this planned."

Turquoise eyes held his. "Since last night."

Lord Grey stepped to within a hand's breath from her face. "You will nae——"

The soft thud of Trálin falling into the snow made her heart break. A moment later, the echo of the other Scottish knights succumbing to the fey pressure against their necks to make them pass out sounded behind her.

Drax arched a brow as he stepped beside her. "I had hoped we would get inside the cave and find a place to hide them before they discovered our intent."

"Lord Grey began asking questions," Catarine explained, guilt edging her words.

Drax shook his head. "Have no regret for your decision. If Lord Grey and the Scots were with us once we confronted Princess Elspeth, they would die."

"I know." Angst filled her as she took in Trálin sprawled on the snow. However angry he would be when he came to, at least he would be alive. She met her warrior's gaze. "You are confident the spell we put on them will keep my aunt ignorant of their presence?"

Drax nodded. "Aye, as long as they remain asleep, they are safe. Even if Princess Elspeth was aware of their presence, with them nae being fey and without powers, I doubt she would find them any threat."

In silence Catarine knelt beside him and took in his strong features one last time. Her hand trembling, she withdrew her dagger, secured it beneath Lord Grey's garb. "Give this to my father," she whispered, pushed the thought into his mind.

The crunch of snow sounded as Kuircc joined them.

Standing, she took in each of her fey warriors, humbled by their loyalty, aching that after this day, their bravery would cost them the ultimate price. "Let us go." Catarine headed toward the entrance of the cave, and she prayed the two stones set together would indeed be strong enough to stop her aunt.

In the growing light ahead, long spears of white jutted from the arched stone ceiling like macabre daggers.

"The cave is opening up," Drax whispered.

"Thank goodness," Catarine replied, smothering the candle she'd used. The haunting blackness they'd woven through left her unsettled.

The murmur of soft, methodic voices echoed ahead.

She halted, kept her left hand atop the gemstone on her belt.

"It sounds as if a chant," Kuirce said.

"Aye, a dark one." Uneasy, she crept forward. The waver of light grew, exposing the sharp angles of grey, the glitters of the spears of stone above appearing even more grotesque. 'Twas as if a macabre shrine to evil.

Near the edge, she lay down, crawled to the end of the ledge, and peered over.

Illuminated by a magical glow of light, in the cavern below, hundreds of armored men surrounded a fortress of stone. High upon a sweep of crude steps stood Princess Elspeth. She raised her scepter, a grotesque creation topped with a golden snake spiraling up to embrace a globe.

Silence fell within the cavern.

"This day we march north to Scotland and enter the stone circle to the Otherworld," she said, her clear voice echoing with a smooth, lyrical ring. "*None* will stop us."

Her men lifted their swords and cheers thundered through the cavern.

"Once the MacLarens have been destroyed," she continued, "I will be the new queen, I will rule their lands, and when we are through, I will control every realm in the Otherworld."

Another round of cheers echoed.

She lowered her scepter.

Her men quieted.

"Except," she said, her words ending in a hiss, "there are those from the MacLarens who know of my plans and seek to stop us, which I will nae allow." Head held high, Princess Elspeth scanned the cave. Her gaze halted on where they were hidden.

Chapter Twenty-two

Coldness prickled Catarine as Princess Elspeth's eyes remained on where they were hidden. Oh God, she knew they were there! Nay, she couldn't. She'd kept hold of the gemstone on the bejeweled belt since they'd entered.

A moment later, her aunt's gaze continued to sweep the immense cavern, then she focused back on her men. "But, they are close."

Shaken, Catarine returned to her men's side.

In the dim flicker of light, Drax's worried gaze met hers. "I saw her look this way. Do you think she saw us?"

"If she had," Catarine replied, "she would have ordered her men to attack. Regardless of her power gained, the belt protected us. More disturbing, she has gathered more men than I had anticipated. We canna allow them to leave the cavern." Her warriors nodded. Long heart-wrenching moments passed. 'Twas time for her to give the order, one necessary, and one she damned.

"Catarine," Kuirce said, his voice grave, "we knew a possibility for this moment would come, and have planned for such. We give our lives for you, for our kingdom, with honor."

Tears burned her throat. She took a ragged breath, wishing with all of her heart that she had another choice. Except, none to save her realm existed. "I could have no finer friends."

"Here." Drax's hand trembled slightly as he lifted his azurite from around his neck and placed it on her palm.

Kuirce lay his malachite beside Drax's. "We are ready when you are, Princess Catarine."

His formal words brought tears to her eyes. Her heart heavy, she curled her hand, the weight of their gemstones heavy upon her palm. This moment, they offered more than their loyalty, but their lives. As much as she wished to hand the gemstones back and leave, she would nae shame her warriors with the actions of a coward.

Her family depended on her.

Her realm's safety lay in her hands.

And indeed, that moment had come.

"My thanks to each of you," she whispered to her men as her gaze rested with reverence on each. Memories of the years with both, of the challenges and laughter they'd shared together slid through her mind. She savored each and every one, then focused on her next step.

Blood pounding, keeping her hand upon the gemstone belt, she edged toward the rim of the cavern.

A dull throbbing pulsed through Trálin's head as he opened his eyes. In the distance he caught a glow of light at the mouth of the cave. He was inside a cave? What bloody happened? He was talking with Catarine as they prepared to enter the . . .

Catarine!

Her confirmation that she'd never intended for him and the Scottish knights to go with her and her warriors to confront Princess Elspeth rolled through his mind. Then he'd passed out. Passed out? Nay. He rubbed his neck where strong fingers had pressed just before he'd lost consciousness.

Drax. He must have turned invisible, returned and knocked him out while he spoke with her. A muscle worked in his jaw as he scanned the surrounding chamber. Unconscious, the other Scots lay sprawled nearby.

They all had been duped!

He made to push up, and his hand brushed something tucked within his garb. With a frown, he reached beneath the folds. His fingers touched the cool hilt of a dagger. What in Hades? In the faint light, he lifted the weapon.

In his palm, Catarine's blade shimmered in the soft light.

Give this to my father.

Her request echoed through his mind. Why would she ask such? As if he could travel to the Otherworld? Or, did she expect her father to arrive with reinforcements too late?

As if his questions bloody mattered? She and her men were in danger, and by God, he'd nae give up on her. There must be something he could do to save them.

If they still lived.

Blast it, they did. He refused to believe otherwise.

With haste, Trálin shook each of the Scottish knights awake. After he quickly explained his intent to catch up to the other warriors and help, he withdrew a candle he'd stowed for their foray into the caves. Using his knife and a flint, he lit the taper. Lifting the candle before him, Lord Grey waved his men forward.

Twists and turns of rock littered their pathway, the damp smell inside ripe with the scent of limestone and hints of other odors he didna wish to identify. As they traveled deeper, the cavern walls flattened and at times, they had to squeeze between the narrowed rocks.

The soft gurgle of water sounded from ahead.

"We are nearing a stream," Lord Grey passed to the others. As he started forward, a dim glow came into view. After several steps, he paused. Over the slide of water, another sound was barely audible. "Voices." Trálin frowned. "Nay, 'tis in cadence."

"I believe 'tis chanting, my lord," the knight closest to him whispered.

"Chanting?" Lord Grey strained to make out the words. "If so, the voices are coming from an enormous contingent." They'd found Princess Elspeth, except 'twould seem she'd recruited more men than he or Catarine had ever considered. He scanned the area. Where had she and her warriors gone? Blast it, they must find her. Dagger clasped in his hand, he guided his men forward.

The dim shimmer of light grew.

As they made their way around the next boulder, Trálin halted, then held up his hand.

In the weak outline ahead, Catarine was crouched near her warriors several paces from the ledge.

Thank God she was safe! He glanced toward the Scottish knights. "Keep low and follow me."

Before he could move, Catarine began crawling toward the ledge.

At her next movement, a glint of light flickered from the palm of her hand.

Her warriors' gemstones! Fear sliced him. She was about to use them as she confronted her aunt! Lord Grey bolted toward her.

As Catarine began to inch closer, the soft pad of boots on dirt echoed in her wake.

They'd been discovered! Her pulse racing, she clasped her blade as she whirled to face the assailants.

In the muted light, Trálin came into view. Determination carved his face, his knights on his heel.

Her body's trembles of fear shifted to outrage. The gemstones clutched in her hand, she scooted back, confronted him as he moved through the thin alley of rock. "What in blazes do you think you are doing?" she hissed. "You are *supposed* to be asleep!"

With a frustrated hiss, Trálin held up her dagger. "You forgot this."

Guilt rolled through her, and as quick, her angst returned. "I do nae want you here. Leave. Now."

A muscle worked in Lord Grey's jaw. "We are staying."

The stubborn man!

"You woke up?" Drax said dryly as he moved to stand beside her.

Lord Grey's eyes narrowed on her warrior. "A fact you should thank me for. From the thunder of chants coming from the cavern below, 'twould seem each extra man is needed."

"We had a plan," Catarine stated.

"Aye," Trálin growled as he shot a hard look toward where she held her warrior's gemstones, "I saw exactly what you planned. Regardless, we are here."

His bravery left her humbled. As if she'd expected less of him? "Lord Grey, the situation is dire. You must take your knights and go."

"And allow you and your men to sacrifice yourselves?" Lord Grey demanded. "There must be another way to stop Princess Elspeth."

Grief balled in her chest. She shook her head, prayed enough time remained for Trálin and his men to escape. "I and the warriors have considered every angle. There is none. Now, go. Please."

Trálin's body tensed. "If Princess Elspeth didna have a force, could she be stopped?"

She hesitated. "I am unsure."

"Why?" Lord Grey asked, "because of the strength of her magic?"

"In part," she replied.

Hope flickered in Trálin's eyes. "In part? Why else would you believe her unstoppable? Wait. You sent Atair back to inform your father of your aunt's treachery, so you believe there is a way to stop her. And if I am right, 'tis more than by sheer force."

"You have no idea of what we are up against," she warned.

"Catarine," Trálin said, his voice hard, "we are at war and must use any of her weaknesses against her."

She swallowed hard. "My dagger."

With a frown, he stared at her blade. "You asked me to give it to your father. Why?"

"Because though a chance exists," she replied, "I canna be sure the power of the two gemstones together will stop my aunt."

"And the dagger will?" Trálin asked.

She nodded. "The reason I asked you to give it to my father." Catarine paused, steadied herself. "The dagger was given to me at birth, passed down throughout the centuries. 'Tis more than a simple weapon that offers protection, but one blessed by the high priests, one able to kill another of the fey holding magic. With the enormity of his forces, I believe in battle my father could fight his way close enough to her to use it."

Trálin glanced toward Drax and Kuircc. "And your fey warriors knew of your dagger's potential."

She nodded.

His eyes narrowed. "Why did you say naught before?"

"Did you nae hear me explain that with the sheer mass of her forces, for me and my men, 'tis impossible?" she replied, frustrated.

"I say we try. However slight," Trálin said before she could speak, "we have a chance. I say we use it."

Catarine glanced toward her fey warriors, then back to him. "How?"

"Wait here," Trálin said.

In stunned disbelief, Catarine watched as he moved toward the ledge.

A moment later, Lord Grey paused, then moved back. A safe distance away, he crouched and hurried toward her.

Regret filled her as he halted before her. "Now you see what I——"

"I believe I can climb around the pillars of stone behind her," Trálin interrupted. "Once I get close to her, I need you and your men to create a diversion."

"I am nae sure it will work."

"We lose nothing to try," Trálin stated.

"Nay," she whispered, "We lose your life as well as the lives of your men."

Lord Grey's fierce eyes narrowed. "We swore to help you. Nothing has changed."

However she wished otherwise, he was right. Fearful for his life, Catarine nodded.

Sweat clung to Trálin's back as he reached up and wrapped his hand around the next jut of rock descending from the cavern's ceiling. Shoving his foot into an indent, he pulled and hauled himself up, the rich scent of limestone cloying. A chunk of stone broke loose beneath his boot. His body dropped. He reached for a nearby crevice, grabbed hold, and caught himself from falling.

Below, the fragment of rock bounced with a soft clatter as it descended.

Muscles aching, he glanced between the weave of slender, milky white columns to where Princess Elspeth was giving orders to her men below.

Amidst the faraway tumble of water, standing above the immense throng of her warriors on stone steps, Catarine's aunt continued to speak.

Thank God, she'd nae heard. Wiping the sweat from his brow, Trálin glanced toward the ledge where Catarine and the others hid readied to create a diversion. And if that failed, to combine the fey warrior's stones.

A tactic he was determined would nae happen.

Catarine's dagger weighed heavy in his sheath as he reached up and wrapped his hand around the next misshapen pillar. He shoved his foot in a crevice. At his next step up, water dripped onto his face, the smell of limestone strong. He pushed on.

"Ensure you have all of your weaponry," Princess Elspeth ordered, "and prepare to march."

The sea of warriors below her cheered.

Trálin moved closer.

Long black hair flowed free down her back, her body-fitting gown of purple clad with weaves of gold and pearls. A finely hammered crown upon her head, Princess Elspeth crafted a picture of seductive evil. As she raised her scepter, the clear globe atop, embraced by the snake, began to glow.

Streams of light began to swirl and dance around the orb, then pulsed.

Waves of energy washed over Trálin.

Magic. A force that built an invisible wall seemed to breathe its own life.

Bedamned, he had to reach Princess Elspeth before the power she was sending out became too strong for him to push past.

The inverted pillars of stone before him began to swell and spiral, weaving around him as if a cage.

He ducked and moved through the complex tangle at an even faster pace.

The cavern began to quake.

Jolted back, Trálin grabbed hold of a pillar.

The pulses of light around the scepter increased to a frantic pace. "I will now open our path to depart!" Princess Elspeth aimed the ornate staff toward the far wall of the cavern.

Trálin cursed. He was nae close enough to stop her!

"Halt!" Catarine's voice boomed.

Her aunt whirled, fury carving her face. The scepter's glow weakened, and Princess Elspeth lowered the staff. "So you have arrived," she stated with contempt. "But you are too late."

"Am I?" Catarine held the two gems in her palm toward Princes Elspeth.

Trálin silently cursed.

Princess Elspeth—ignorant of his presence—smiled with putrid glee. "Princess Catarine, your gemstones are nae strong enough to do me harm." Fierce eyes narrowed. "You know naught of how strong I have grown, but understand this, now, you and your men will die."

Nae if he could bloody help it! Trálin withdrew Catarine's dagger and slipped through the last of the stones.

Princess Elspeth raised the scepter. The globe began to glow. Light pulses again swirled around the orb. Eyes bright with malice, she angled the staff toward Catarine.

"Nay!" Trálin yelled as he lunged.

Shock widened Princess Elspeth's eyes, and she jumped back. Her scepter shifted. Focused energy burst from the globe, slammed into the cavern wall far away from where Catarine and her warriors stood.

As chunks of limestone and rock shattered, the power of the blast slammed Trálin against the rock, but he kept hold of the blade— barely. Against the rattle of stones falling through the cavern, he started to rise.

A cold laugh sounded.

Another burst of energy threw him against a pillar. Rough edges of the time-hewn limestone jammed against his back. Pain raking his body, he stared in dread as Princess Elspeth's gaze narrowed on him.

"You dare try and touch me, human?" she hissed.

For Catarine, he would dare anything. Ignoring the pain, aware 'twas his last chance before she would kill him, he stood and lifted the dagger.

"Think you a mere dagger is a threat?" the princess asked with disbelief.

Let her think his blade no threat. Trálin charged her.

Princess Elspeth aimed her scepter at him. "Be gone!"

White light flashed around him; Trálin was hurled against a large pillar of stone. Blackness threatened as he struggled to retain consciousness.

A shimmering of purple glowed around Princess Elspeth. "Now," she hissed, "you will die!" She raised her scepter, and rings of energy shimmered around the globe. Satisfaction gleamed in her eyes, and with cold intent she lowered the staff toward him.

"Nay!" Catarine started to raise the gemstones in the palm of her hand.

Without warning, an explosion sounded. Rocks splintered, slammed against the far wall.

Amidst the streams of light flooding the cavern, Trálin shoved to his feet. What in Hades was going on? Gasping for breath, he shielded his eyes.

A gaping hole lay in the side of the cavern, and an army of warriors began climbing through.

Outrage splashed Princess Elspeth's face. "Kill them!"

With a roar, her warriors raised their weapons, charged the incoming force.

A large grey-haired man brandished his sword with lethal precision as he headed the charge and quickly disposed of one of Princess Elspeth's warriors before cutting down the next with barely a breath.

Relief swept through Catarine. "Father! Princess Elspeth is up above you!" she yelled as she stood at the ledge.

King Leod's gaze quickly met hers. He nodded, then worked his way toward the chiseled steps.

Behind him, another man, hair black as coal, a fierce expression on his face, moved with a fierce stride, his each swing of his blade taking down one of Princess Elspeth's warriors.

Relief at seeing her father plummeted to shock. Prince Zacheus! Of course, as her betrothed, she should have expected he would come. Except in the mayhem, she'd nae given any consideration to his reaction when he learned of her being in danger.

What of Trálin? In the sheen of dust-smeared light pouring in from outside, she searched the rubble. Near a large boulder, he was climbing to his feet. Thank God he'd survived.

A movement from the stairway caught her attention.

Her face tight with outrage, Princess Elspeth raised her scepter. Orbs of light swirled around the globe as she aimed it at her father.

"Father, watch out!" Catarine yelled.

As the burst of energy shot from the scepter, Prince Zacheus charged up the steps and shielded her father.

"Prince Zacheus," the king yelled, "Do nae——"

Waves of brilliant light encircled Catarine's betrothed; Prince Zacheus evaporated, and his sword clattered to the ground.

Catarine covered her mouth in horror.

"Now, to eliminate you." With a sadistic smile, Princess Elspeth lifted the scepter. Once pulses of light swirled around the scepter, she aimed the globe at her brother, the king. Energy burst in a bright light toward Catarine's father.

Outrage splashed on King Leod's face. He jerked a gold medallion from around his neck, lifted it before him as if a shield. Light reflected off the polished metal and back to engulf her aunt.

Shock, then pain ripped across her aunt's face. Within the shimmering light, Princess Elspeth twisted, turned, wove together with the purple aura, then disappeared. Her scepter clattered to the limestone.

As the purple aura slowly faded, one by one, her men dropped their swords, turned to stare at where Princess Elspeth had once stood. Dazed disbelief, and then as they continued to stare, then relief swept their faces. The clang of swords filled the cavern as her aunt's warriors began to throw down their blades.

Realization hit Catarine as she watched. The men had been under her aunt's spell. Why had she not thought of this before? And, with the spell broken by her death, the warriors would nae fight.

Joy filled her as she hurried to her warriors to explain.

A short while later, as the warriors continued to file out of the cavern, Catarine hugged her father. "Th-Thank God you arrived when you did."

"Lady Catarine had doubts of me reaching you in time, Your Grace," Atair stated, his voice dry.

"I was unsure," she admitted, still trying to absorb all that had occurred. As she stepped back, she caught sight of Prince Zacheus's blade. Sadness filled her. However much she didna love him, he didna deserve to die. "I canna believe he is dead."

"He was a man of honor," her father said, his words choked out. "When he learned you were in danger, he refused to stay away."

"And for his bravery," she whispered, "he paid the ultimate price."

The king's face darkened. "I should have told him of my medallion, but never did I believe my sister had grown so strong."

"Father," she said, her voice rough with tears, "with Prince Zacheus's death, what of the peace between our realms?"

King Leod gave a heavy sigh. "I will speak with his father. It saddens me to bring him news of the tragedy of his son's death, but I have faith that we can work out an alliance that will serve us all."

And she prayed he was right. She took in where moments before her aunt had stood. "I still canna believe Princess Elspeth is dead."

Regret filled King Leod's eyes as he lifted the gold medallion, and grimaced at the slight mar across the front. "A fate she brought on by her own evil." He tucked it beneath his garb.

As Catarine started to speak, she caught sight of Trálin as he wove his way between the warriors toward them. Thank God he was nae harmed! She caught the angst on his face and understood. He hadna met her father and was uncertain of the reception he would receive.

Nerves rattling through her, Catarine met her father's eyes. "Father, I bid you to meet the Earl of Grey, Trálin MacGruder, a man who helped us to find Princess Elspeth."

Her father's gave a solemn nod. "Sir Atair explained the circumstance, including why you found it necessary to turn to a human." He nodded to Trálin. "Lord Grey, my deepest thanks to you and your men for helping my daughter."

"Your Grace," Trálin stated, "I owe Princess Catarine my deepest thanks. Without the aid of her and her warriors, King Alexander and his queen would be dead."

"Sir Atair passed along the adventures as of late," King Leod replied. "'Tis much to take in, details we will discuss later." With quiet steps, he walked to where Princess Elspeth's scepter lay and picked it up. For a long moment he studied the extraordinary work, then looked toward Catarine. "I will make sure this is never used for evil again." He nodded. "Come, 'tis time to go home."

Epilogue

Excitement filled Catarine as she remained still, her eyes closed tight, the lingering scents of lavender, rosemary, and chamomile filling her each breath and heightening her curiosity. For two months now, she'd watched masons and carpenters move up the steps to the new addition on the third floor of Lochshire Castle. And with every question, Trálin had refused to answer, except to reply that in time she would see.

"Can I open my eyes now?" she asked.

"My wife is anxious."

Trálin's soft chuckle warmed her heart. "Aye, my husband." Never would she tire of saying those words, or take for granted every day of the miracle of their lives together.

"Now, my love," he said, his deep burr tender, "open your eyes."

Unsure what she would see, she lifted her lids. A single arched window heralded a pure stream of sunlight that filled the entire room with its brilliance. Near the wall stood a bed, covered with an elegant, hand-stitched coverlet, the color of moon-kissed daisies. A small table sat nearby, adorned with a myriad of her personal items; intricately carved jewelry, a bone comb, and an ivory-framed mirror. On the far wall hung a beautifully crafted tapestry with images of fairies woven amidst the leaves.

Emotions stormed her. She'd anticipated many things about what the chamber would look like from her view in the courtyard, but nae this.

"The embroidery King Alexander gifted me," she whispered, moved beyond belief, "with images of my sisters woven within."

Love shone in her husband's eyes. "His thanks for your aid."

"'Twas unnecessary. King Alexander's support and allowing us the help of his knights in finding Princess Elspeth was payment enough." Grief swept her at thoughts of her aunt.

"You look upset."

She gave a shaky exhale. "Though over half a year has passed since her death, I canna believe the poor decisions my aunt made, nor that she is gone. I grieve for the lives she destroyed, and for the loss of Prince Johan and my uncle. Never will I forget them."

Sadness weighed on Trálin's face. "All because of Princess Elspeth's greed for power."

"Never will I understand my aunt's twisted decisions." Tears blurred her eyes, and she wiped them away. "Look at me, mulling what I canna change when you brought me here to surprise me with the gift of this chamber. 'Tis beautiful, Trálin. More than I ever imagined."

A warm smile touched his mouth. "I am glad you like it. I was hoping you would."

"As if with the magnificence inside, I would do anything else?" She paused. "What will we do with the claymore presented to you by King Alexander? I admit, I was surprised by the crafted fairy he had installed on the leather-bound hilt, but his explanation 'twas to represent our merged worlds touched me deeply."

Trálin lifted her hand, pressed a kiss upon her knuckles. "I have decided to have portraits made, one of each of your warriors holding their respective stone. Nearby, I will hang the claymore."

"'Twill be perfect."

He arched a playful brow. "There is another surprise."

"More?"

"Aye," he said. "Look up."

Up? What could possibly . . . "Ohhhh." Captured in various aspects of flight, hand-painted images of fairies adorned the ceiling. Overhead lay a raven-haired fairy in a moss-green gown, her silver-tipped wings caught in mid-flutter, hiding behind a lush, purple-tipped thistle.

Overwhelmed, she glanced toward the wall hanging, then back up. "The images of my sisters on the ceiling are an exact match to those in the tapestry!"

He chuckled. "They are indeed."

"Who did such a beautiful painting?"

Pride shone on his face. "Sionn."

"When could he have done this? How could he . . . It must have taken—"

"—a fortnight to be exact," Trálin finished. "'Twas his wedding gift to you."

Moved beyond belief, she shook her head. "I never expected anything so grand."

"'Twas nae planned," Trálin admitted. "When I explained that after you had sacrificed living in the Otherworld and given up your fey powers to wed me and live in Scotland, and that I was building you a special chamber to celebrate your homeland, Sionn asked if he could paint this for you." He gestured toward the bowl on the small table. "Look inside."

Humbled by the outpouring of love, the thoughtfulness in each detail, Catarine walked to the table. "Oh my . . ." She lifted her warriors' gemstones in her palm.

"Atair brought them," Trálin explained. "With you no longer living in their world, you had nay need of their service. And they, nay need for the gemstones. He thought you would want the stones to remember them."

"As if I could ever forget my fey warriors?" Fresh tears slid down her cheeks. "I will cherish them always." She hesitated. "Why are they halved?"

Trálin walked over to her side. "Each of the warriors kept half, to remember you."

She sniffed. "'Tis amazing." She gently set them back within the bowl. "I shall honor my warriors as well. I shall pass the halves on to our children."

"Our sons," he said, pride in his voice.

She laughed. "Or our daughters."

Trálin drew her to him, caught her mouth in a tender kiss, then slowly drew away. "I will love our children, regardless."

Memories of Trálin's brother shadowed her thoughts, and she looked away.

"Catarine?"

"I think of Faolan. I am sorry for the rift between you and your brother at my arrival to Lochshire Castle."

"Do nae apologize," Trálin replied, a touch of anger in his voice. "I could nae allow Faolan to remain when he confronted me and stated he'd fallen in love with you and planned to win you over."

Memories of that horrible day replayed in her mind of Trálin and Faolan's falling-out. "I was stunned by his claim, that he wanted me as his wife." She shook her head. "Never could I love anyone but you, neither would he believe me."

He lifted her hand to his mouth and placed a tender kiss on her knuckles. "I know, my love, but my brother could nae accept that fact. I have confidence that over time I could deter Faolan's belief that he could win you over. But when he drew his blade against me, he was fortunate to leave Lochshire Castle with but a broken sword arm."

Leave? Nay, cast out in a fierce fight. "What will come of Faolan?"

He released her. "I didna wish to worry you, but a month after my brother left, I found him living in a crofter's hut with a woman. In an attempt to make peace, I gave him our mother's lands."

Warmth filled her. "'Twas a wonderful gesture."

"Mayhap," Trálin said, "but he was still in love with you and angry from our fight, and my attempt to repair our family bond mattered little. I tried to reason with my brother, but he would have none of it. Before his woman and I, Faolan denounced the MacGruder name and claimed that of our mother, Brom."

Regret swept Catarine. "I am sorry. Mayhap with the years will come reason?"

"I pray so, but regardless of how close my brother and I were in the past, with his irrational anger, I doubt we will ever see him again."

Tense silence filled the chamber.

She exhaled. "'Tis sad."

He nodded.

Catarine offered a prayer that in time Faolan would find the strength to release his anger. She again gazed around the room, focusing on this special moment, and the man to whom she'd pledged her love.

"Thank you, Trálin, I am humbled by your gift. Whenever I am within this chamber, 'twill indeed bless me with memories of my homeland."

"'Tis worth anything to bring you happiness." A twinkle lit his eyes. "Do you think any in the future will wonder about the fairies in the tapestry or on the ceiling and of their origin, or the touch of magic your presence gives the chamber?"

"If they do, I shall explain that while I was in the woods gathering herbs, King Alexander was hunting with several men nearby. His mount stumbled and the king was injured. I witnessed the entire event and offered to care for him. In return he gifted me with the tapestry."

Trálin chuckled. "'Tis close to the truth."

She smiled. "Close enough."

"Aye." He swept her in his arms. "I love you, Catarine MacGruder, and I am blessed to have you as my wife."

"And," she said, her heart full, "I am blessed that you are my husband."

"I admit I held doubts your father would allow us to handfast," Trálin said. "But, in private he admitted that he knew you were unhappy with your betrothal, but proud of you for planning to adhere to your promise. Never did he wish you unhappiness. And, with you free to wed, he was thankful that you would marry for love, one I assured him I felt for you. And, that always would I protect you." He strode with her toward the bed.

"Protection you are about to offer, is it?"

He laughed. "I believe," Trálin said as he lay her atop the coverlet, "I am going to make love to my wife."

Her heart full, Catarine savored his every touch as he caught her mouth in a heated kiss. Aye, she was indeed blessed, for this day was but the first in their forever.

A retired Navy Chief, AGC(AW), DIANA COSBY is an international bestselling author of Scottish medieval romantic suspense. Diana has spoken at the Library of Congress, appeared at Lady Jane's Salon, in New York City, in *Woman's Day*, on *Texoma Living Magazine*, on *USA Today*'s romance blog, "Happily Ever After," and onMSN.com.

After retiring from the Navy, Diana dove into her passion—writing romance novels. With 34 moves behind her, she was anxious to create characters who reflected the amazing cultures and people she's met throughout the world. Diana is currently working on the sixth book in the award-winning MacGruder Brothers series, and in August 2013, released her story "Highland Vampire" in the anthology *Born to Bite*, with stories by Hannah Howell and Erica Ridley. Diana looks forward to the years of writing ahead and to meeting the amazing people who will share this journey.

Please visit her at www.dianacosby.com.

**Don't miss the other books
in the MacGruder series**

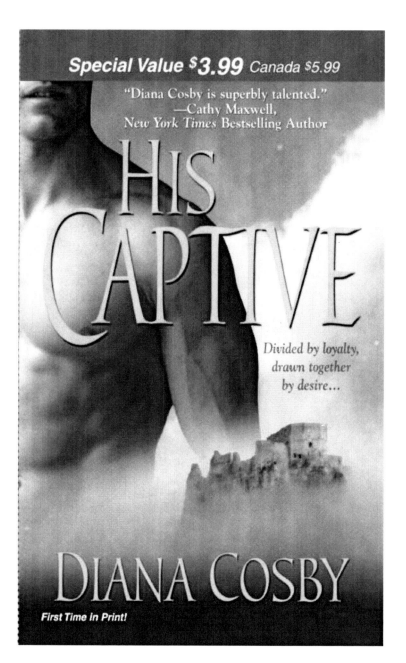

"Diana Cosby is superbly talented."
—Cathy Maxwell,
New York Times Bestselling Author

HIS CAPTIVE

*Divided by loyalty,
drawn together
by desire...*

DIANA COSBY

*When Alexander MacGruder kidnapped his enemy's daughter,
he never expected Lady Nichola Westcott to steal his heart.*

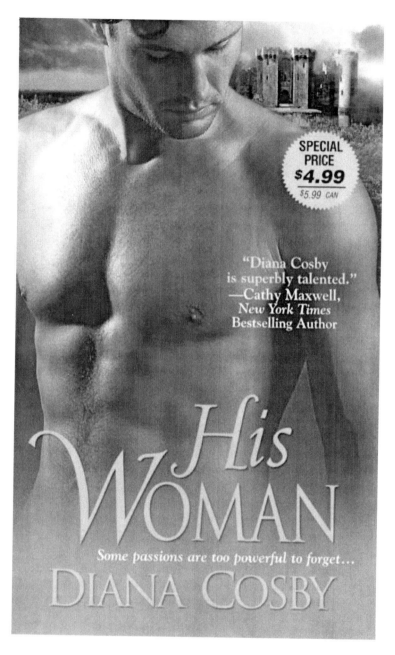

"Diana Cosby
is superbly talented."
—Cathy Maxwell,
New York Times
Bestselling Author

His
WOMAN

Some passions are too powerful to forget...

DIANA COSBY

*Forced to protect the woman who once broke his heart,
Duncan MacGruder soon realizes that Lady Isabel Adair
will always be the only one for him.*

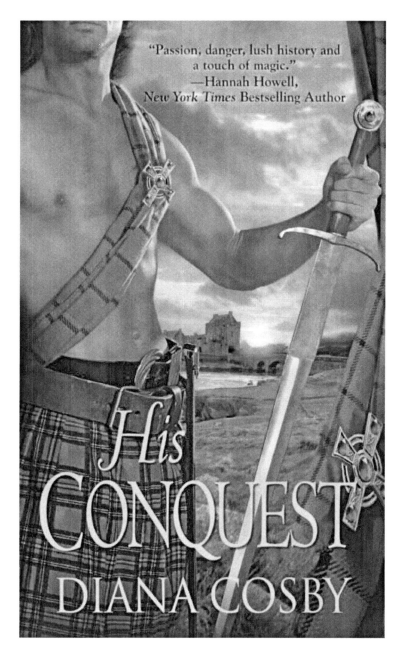

"Passion, danger, lush history and
a touch of magic."
—Hannah Howell,
New York Times Bestselling Author

His
CONQUEST
DIANA COSBY

*In exchange for his freedom, Seathan MacGruder
agrees to help Linet Dancort escape her treacherous family,
embarking on a journey more rewarding
than he could ever have hoped.*

DIANA
COSBY

His
DESTINY

"Medieval Scotland roars to life in this fabulous series."
—Pam Palmer, *New York Times* Bestselling Author

When Sir Patrik MacGruder rescues Emma Astyn
from a fate worse than death, he must choose:
between the duty that has always driven him
and a chance at a love that could conquer all.

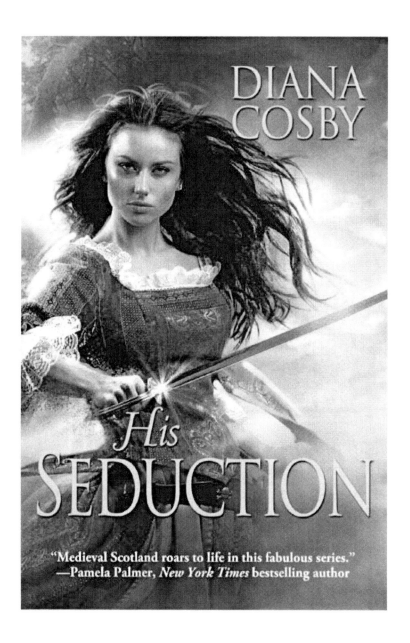

DIANA
COSBY

His
SEDUCTION

"Medieval Scotland roars to life in this fabulous series."
—Pamela Palmer, *New York Times* bestselling author

*When Rois Drummond questions the honor of Englishman
Griffin Westcott, Baron of Monceaux, she finds herself
with completely unwanted consequences—
hastily married to the enemy!*

CPSIA information can be obtained at www.ICGtesting.com
Printed in the USA
BVOW04s0231250614

357284BV00001B/17/P